LOST AND FOUND

LOST AND FOUND

A Logan McKenna Novel

VALERIE DAVISSON

To John, my rock in swirling waters.

PROLOGUE

JANUARY 13

2:00 A.M.

Mateo stood at the railing, feet planted firmly on the deck, staring into the dark. A few silver strands glinted in his thick, wavy hair. Other than the captain in the wheelhouse, everyone else was down below, sleeping or, more likely, playing cards. Taking the Guatemalan's money, no doubt.

The forty-six-foot boat sliced through the glossy, black sea. He welcomed the cold air pushing against his face, washing away his sins.

A three-quarter moon emerged from behind a ragged cloud, spilling pale light across the deck, unfurling on the water like a celestial blessing.

He ran his hand along the railing and frowned. It was rough and rusted in spots. The mooring rope was coiled sloppily, and he'd noticed mold spots on the canvas cushions below. If this were his boat, he would take much better care of her.

But it wasn't his boat, so it wasn't his problem. It just had to hold together until they got home. Tonight's job had been

1

successful. And that's all he was there for. They'd sent him and the Guatemalan in. All they had to do now was return to port. The captain promised to pay them as soon as they docked.

Mateo searched the sky and made out a few faint but familiar stars. He only knew their names in Spanish. It had been years since his father had taken him out on his little fishing boat and taught him how to find his way.

Mateo sighed. He didn't even know if his father was still alive. That world had been lost to all of them, long ago.

The boat he was on was officially a fishing vessel, larger than his father's and uncles' small *pangas* back home. Next week it would be out on the water with all the other commercial fishing boats in Newport when the season opened. Crabbing was good money, but the bulk of the season only lasted a few weeks for the big boats, then everyone moved on to the next fishery—sablefish, shrimp, and groundfish. He didn't know them all. It took a lot of work to pull a living from the sea.

The captain of the *Sea Gypsy* had discovered a much more lucrative and faster way to supplement his earnings. And unlike Mateo, he wasn't being forced to do it. He was just lazy. Mateo knew of no other Newport fishing vessels that smuggled drugs, but, of course, he hadn't known about this one until tonight.

It would be almost dawn before they got back. The captain said there would be another opportunity for him in a couple of months. He would be in touch. Like they were *compadres*. Mateo had muttered a non-committal response. The captain hadn't looked happy, but Mateo didn't care.

He had no plans to do another run. In fact, before they could threaten his family again, he would find a way to stop them. This man was just a small-time operator, not with the cartel. There must be a way. Until then, he would pretend to go along with them.

He thought back to the day when everything changed, the day after Christmas when these men dropped evil into his life.

LOST AND FOUND

He'd been working at one of the nicer seafood restaurants in Newport for the last two years. One night, after helping the owner close, two men he didn't know waited for him by the trash dumpsters. The owner had already driven home. Mateo walked. He didn't have a car.

The two strangers seemed to know all about him. They offered him a ride home and a job for one night that paid very well. He knew something was off. Before he could think of a way to refuse, they made sure he understood that if he didn't take the job, they knew where he lived. And that he had a lovely wife and a pretty daughter.

Not much of a choice. Mateo wanted absolutely nothing to do with these guys. He hated drugs. He and Gabriela had fled from their small village in Mexico because he refused to work for the cartel, and now here he was, helping bad people smuggle drugs anyway. From Canada, not Mexico, but that hardly made a difference. The irony did not escape him.

It was just the one time, he told himself. He wouldn't even keep the money, even though they needed it. When they docked and the captain returned his wallet to him—he'd kept their ID when they did the exchange—he would find a place to hide the cash at home until he figured things out.

What a mess.

He thought back on his decision to flee north to this country. In spite of the hardships, whenever he looked at his smart, beautiful daughter, he knew he and Gabriela had made the right choice. Vanessa was such a good student. She deserved to go to college, and it was only a year away.

No, he didn't need dirty drug money. Their family had made it this far; they just needed to keep working. It would all work out.

The thought made him feel somewhat better. His shoulders relaxed and the night seemed gentler, more hopeful. Maybe he could work some extra shifts at the restaurant, buy something nice, something beautiful for his *Corazón*, and get Vanessa that computer she needed for school.

Deep in his thoughts, Mateo didn't hear the soft steps coming up behind him.

1

Logan McKenna looked at the clock on her dashboard. Her pickup time at Fred Meyer wasn't until two o'clock. Plenty of time to enjoy the drive from Depoe Bay to Newport, every inch of which boasted breathtaking views of the Pacific Ocean.

Though sometimes smooth as glass, more often the Pacific exhibited her wild-child side, crashing up against the rocks, spray arching over the road, drenching cars and tourists alike. Other times, the whole tableau was more subdued, shore pines and cedars standing guard, cloaked in mist, or caressed by soft, steady rain.

Other than a few tourist shops and a gas station, Depoe Bay was just a wide spot on the 101. Its claim to fame was having the world's smallest harbor, whale watching tours, and charter fishing trips. Twice a year, the population tripled during whale watching weeks when Depoe Bay attracted tourists from Portland and all around the world to see migrating grays.

What Depoe Bay didn't have was a grocery store, hence the quick trip to Newport to get all the ingredients Ben needed for tonight's dinner. Their friends, Sam and Tim, were coming over and she was looking forward to the visit. Logan often volunteered to make these food runs, as long as Ben made a detailed list so she didn't get the wrong brand of Dijon mustard—who knew there was more than one?

5:15 P.M.

Crunching gravel announced the arrival of their guests. Logan turned down the music and went to get the door. It wasn't full-on dark yet, but the sun had set, so she flipped on the porch light for Sam. Sam definitely needed help to see where she was going. At seven-and-a-half months pregnant, she hadn't seen her feet in months.

Sam's five-foot frame barely had room for her internal organs, let alone a baby, but the doctor said mother and child were both doing well. She was on schedule to deliver a bouncing baby girl on February 14. Logan watched as her friend picked her way up the walk.

As always, Ben was in charge of the kitchen. Logan was more of an assembler than a cook and had no problem letting Ben take the lead in all things culinary. Tonight's featured dish was tomahawk steaks. Currently, the huge slabs of meat were resting on the kitchen counter—reaching room temperature. Ben never put a cold steak on a hot grill. He had told Logan why many times, but she just nodded and smiled whenever Ben tried to give her cooking pointers.

Sam came in and leaned in to give Logan a hug. Handing his host a bottle of wine, Tim did the same, but didn't look like he was in the best of moods. Understandable. A commercial fisherman, Tim would normally be out on his boat, but the opening of crab season had been delayed for over a month now. Crab was one of the most lucrative fisheries, so delays were not welcome.

Avoiding that topic, Logan simply thanked him for the wine and took their coats while Ben pushed a beer into Tim's hand and a mineral water into Sam's, herding them into the living room by the fire. He and Logan had already started on a good bottle of sturdy Cabernet. Logan deftly steered the conversation away from the delay of crab season toward the upcoming arrival of Sam and Tim's baby.

"Have you guys picked a name yet?" she asked.

They both blurted out answers at the same time.

"Miriam!"

"Magnolia!"

"Miriam was my mother's name," Tim said, crossing his arms.

Sam insisted Magnolia was a better name. "Miriam sounds like someone's grandmother."

Logan didn't point out the obvious that if Miriam were alive, she *would* be the child's grandmother. She knew when to keep her mouth shut.

Before long, the aroma of seared meat and sea salt baked potatoes wafted out from the kitchen to beckon them to the table. Logan refreshed everyone's beverages and by the time they were seated, Ben had dinner on the table, and everyone dug in.

After dinner, Tim, in a much better mood after his steak and a second beer, agreed with Logan that Ben had outdone himself. He toasted the chef with the bottle.

"As soon as we can get out on the water," he promised, "we'll have you over to our place for as much crab as you can eat!"

"They'd better let them out soon," Sam added, "I want this daddy to meet his daughter when she arrives, not be out on the ocean in a cold crab boat!"

2

Logan tucked the last of Ben's frozen packages into the cooler, then dumped a layer of ice on top. Crab season opened tomorrow, and Ben was making good on his offer to supply some pre-made meals for Tim and his crew, who were leaving first thing in the morning. Standing on her feet to chop and cook was tougher on Sam now that she was so far into her pregnancy, so she appreciated the help.

Since Logan was meeting Sam in town for lunch anyway, she volunteered to drop off the cooler for the *Sara Lynn* down at the docks. Ben helped her load it into the car, leaned down to give her a distracted kiss, then walked back to the house.

With broad shoulders and tousled white-blonde hair, Ben looked like a Viking, albeit one with a few extra pounds he was always trying to lose. Logan thought he was perfect the way he was. And she had a pretty good idea what was bothering her Viking this morning.

Ben missed Purgatory, the Greater Swiss Mountain dog he had raised from a puppy. The gentle dog had passed away last year. Ben had not talked about getting another dog, but maybe that would help cheer him up.

The very thought of getting a pet brought Logan a momentary stab of panic. Dogs were fine, but she had never had one. They were a lot of responsibility. Plus, she liked her life the way it was. Her daughter was grown, and she had plenty of time to compose her music and play Bella, her violin.

But Ben without a dog just wasn't Ben. Maybe if he did all the poop pickup, it would be okay. She shook her head as she backed out of the driveway.

She didn't have to decide anything today.

It was only a thirty-minute drive to the Historic Bayfront in Newport. She'd been instructed to meet Tim near Dock 5. Except for one woman walking a miniature collie, the boardwalk was empty, but almost every parking spot was taken. Logan cruised until she found one and pulled in just as Tim and another crew member walked out to meet her. Tim made the introductions.

"Hi, Logan. This is Francis Mickelson, my right-hand man on the *Sara Lynn*."

"Nice to meet you," Francis said, reaching out said hand to shake hers.

Logan lifted up the lid of the cooler and gave them a quick tour of the contents. Lifting one baggie up, she said, "This one's *coq au vin*—it is *so* good—lots of chicken and mushrooms and wine. That one's beef stew. There are pork chops with mashed potatoes and gravy, and lasagna, and I forget what the other ones are, but they're all good," she assured them, closing the lid, grinning from ear to ear. "I know because I was the official taste tester."

"Sounds like a good gig," Tim said. "Be sure and thank Ben for us, again. If we don't catch any crab, it won't be for lack of nourishment!"

Each man grabbed a handle and hoisted the laden cooler between them.

"What time do you leave tomorrow?" Logan asked.

"Nine o'clock," said Tim. "They let us drop pots a couple days ago, but we can't go see what's in them until tomorrow."

Logan wished them luck and texted Sam to let her know she was on her way. Sam was holding a table for them at Gino's, a local eatery Logan hadn't tried yet. She told Tim she'd come back for the empty cooler after lunch.

3

Even though the temperature was in the thirties, the Bayfront was bustling. Sam had snagged one of the picnic tables on the patio, waving Logan over to make sure she didn't miss the restaurant, but she needn't have worried. No one could miss the masses of colorful fishing buoys draped around the place, defining Gino's outdoor seating area.

As she sat down, Logan took off her gloves but left her jacket on. They had menus and water in front of them in seconds and the server was back to take their order soon after—fish and chips for Logan, a half-pound cheeseburger with fries for Sam.

"How's the tutoring going?" Sam asked, pushing her signature rhinestone-encrusted, hot pink, cat-eye glasses back up on her nose.

Since Logan's music was bringing in enough money to live on, she recently decided to do some volunteering at the local high school. Their server slipped two steaming plates of food in front of them, asked if they needed ketchup, vinegar, or tartar sauce, delivered the same, then hustled back inside.

Lifting her burger off the plate with both hands, Sam asked, "Have you started yet? How many kids did they give you?"

"I don't know yet," Logan said, shaking malt vinegar onto her fish and chips. "They said just a few to start with. I think they want to see how I do first. How about you? How'd your checkup go?"

The poor woman's belly couldn't possibly get any bigger.

"Doc says great," Sam said, between bites, "I had that spotting, but that's all gone now. No need for bed rest or anything."

"How long are you planning on working?" Logan asked.

As far as she knew, Sam was still putting in full-time hours as a reporter for the local paper.

"Well," Sam said, wiping the grease off her chin with her napkin, "the good news is that Oregon finally got around to offering paid maternity leave. The bad news is the new law doesn't kick in until September 3."

Logan groaned, "That sucks."

"The paper will give me unpaid leave, but I've kind of gotten used to eating, so I'll work as long as I can. It's a good thing the boys are back on the water tomorrow," she added, "bringing home the bacon—or in this case, the *crab*!"

The server brought the check and Logan made sure to grab it before Sam could object.

For dessert, they stopped at 2 Kids Candy for caramel apples. A plain one for Sam, a dark chocolate, sea salt for Ben, and one rolled in everything from Reese's Pieces to pretzel bits for Logan. With an extra—just in case she got hungry on the way home.

Never hurts to be prepared.

While they were savoring their treats, a shiny, green Range Rover sped by, splashing their legs with cold mud. Logan caught a glimpse of the driver as she sped away. Short, platinum-blonde hair. Black leather jacket, lots of silver zippers. The vanity plate read FASHN4.

"Roxy," Sam said—as if the name alone explained everything. Maybe it did.

"Who's Roxy?"

LOST AND FOUND

Sam pointed toward the docks. "See that boat over there? The big, white one with the blue stripe?"

Logan squinted, located a boat nearly twice the size of the *Sara Lynn*, and nodded.

"That's the *Freya*, Craig Peterson's boat. And that little piece of hell-on-wheels is his lovely wife, Roxy."

4

Once Logan and Sam were safely on the other side of the street, Sam continued her story.

"The Petersons are one of those fishing families that have been around here for years. They go way back. Craig's dad, Walt, fished with his dad, Lars Peterson, so three generations at least, maybe more."

Even though Sam hadn't been raised in Newport, being married to a local, she knew everybody's business.

Sam thoughtfully chewed another slice of her caramel apple then said, "Tim went to school with Craig."

"Is Craig as rude as his wife?" Logan asked.

"No, Craig's a great guy," she said. "Not sure why he married Roxy."

"What's her story?" asked Logan.

"Roxy was *not* born into a well-off fishing family. Her dad was a fisherman, but he was better known for his drinking. When he wasn't on a bender, and sometimes when he was, he crewed on other people's boats—never had his own.

"The mom had some kind of speech impediment and was usually sporting a bruise or two—stayed home mostly."

"A lot of people have rough childhoods," Logan said. "Not all of them become assholes."

Sam almost choked on her last bite of apple. When she could talk again without laughing, she said, "Yep. Roxy could have gone all Mother Teresa on everyone and joined a convent, but no such luck. Instead, she looked around and married into the family she wished she had been born into."

"What happened to her parents?"

"The dad's still around, although he's too old to fish anymore. Don't know what happened to the mom."

"Think Roxy was headed out to help her husband stock their boat? I assume he's going out first thing tomorrow, too," Logan said.

"Oh, hell no," Sam said. "If Roxy went to see Craig, it was to get something, not give anything. Roxy likes the money fishing brings in, but she has nothing to do with the boat. Craig set her up with her own shop in town and that's where she spends most of her time. That's probably where she's headed in such a hurry. It's in Newport, as far away from the docks as she could get."

"What kind of shop?" Logan asked, curious in spite of herself.

Sam shrugged, "It's called Fashion Forward. Clothes and shoes no one around here wears. You know, $200 t-shirts and thigh-high patent leather boots. She couldn't possibly turn a profit; I never see anyone in there. She may sell tourist stuff, too, to keep afloat; I don't know."

Eyebrows raised, she peered at Logan over the top of her glasses with her best Dame Maggie Smith look. "And I doubt I'll *ever* know. Fashion Forward is *not* a shop I care to frequent."

5

When they got to the harbor, Sam led the way down one of the finger docks, which was lined with fishing vessels. Most were filled with bustling crew, getting ready to leave in the morning. Three boats down from the *Sara Lynn*, Logan saw the white and blue boat Sam had pointed to.

Queen of the harbor, the *Freya* floated serenely in the water. Two men were working on deck. One, a redhead, was kneeling in front, working on some piece of equipment Logan couldn't identify. His chapped lips, peeling nose, and rough skin made Logan wonder why he chose to work in a job that kept him constantly exposed to the sun and wind. The other man, younger, with dark hair, stood in back, near the wheelhouse.

Sam stopped and called up to both men, "Hey, guys! How's it going?"

The redhead looked up, smiled, and gave Sam a short wave with his wrench, but after glancing at his boss, put his head down and returned to his work.

The dark-haired man came over to the rail. "We're getting there, Sam. Just waiting on Liv to bring the rest of the food. Checking everything twice. You know how it is. Better here than out there."

Sam started to introduce Logan, but Craig turned away before she could.

"Well, say hi to Liv for me," Sam said to his retreating back. Then, to no one in particular, since neither man was looking at her. "Good luck out there tomorrow!"

When they were a few feet past the *Freya*, Sam turned to Logan and made a face.

"Here's your hat, what's your hurry?" she whispered as she and Logan walked to the *Sara Lynn*.

"Who's Liv?" Logan asked.

"Craig's sister," Sam said. "She grew up crewing on the *Freya* just like he did. It's very much a family business."

When they were on board, Sam asked Tim, "What's up with Craig?"

"Roxy," Tim said.

"Oh, got it," said Sam.

Which seemed to be all anyone had to say on the subject.

"I saw Doyle on deck," Sam said. "Craig get Sean and Lonnie again this year?"

"Yeah," Tim said. "They already signed on."

Sam looked somewhat worried at this news.

"Don't worry, hon," Tim said. "I've got the half-share guy and the *Lucky Charm* might have over-hired. I'll pick up another hand if we need one, but Francis and I can catch crab by ourselves if we have to, right Francis?"

"With one hand behind our backs, boss!" Francis said, miming the action.

Her friends had a lot to do, so after retrieving the now-empty cooler and promising again to pass along their thanks for the gourmet meals to Ben, she said her goodbyes.

Being naturally nosy, Logan wondered what Roxy and Craig's fight had been about.

*****

LOST AND FOUND

Logan hesitated at the top of Bay Street, then turned left at the light. It would just take a minute to see if Roxy's shop was as tacky as Sam said it was. GPS said it was up here somewhere.

Fashion Forward was not hard to find. Located in an old brick building, bookended by a laundromat and a pawn shop, you could see the name of the shop a mile away. Bright red neon signage rose high above the roof, dwarfing the front door. Feeling a little silly for spying, Logan was about to make a U-turn and leave when the proprietor blasted out of the front door.

Striding onto the sidewalk on four-inch, stiletto-heeled black boots, Roxy made quite the picture. The slashes in her t-shirt made it look like she had been attacked by a stray tiger escaped from the zoo. The few remaining ropy shreds didn't cover much. And the leather jacket was for looks, not warmth.

Aiming her key fob at the back of the Range Rover like a Star Wars weapon, Roxy beeped it open, then reached in and yanked out a heavy gym bag. Hoisting it effortlessly onto her shoulder, stomped back inside.

Not a single wobble. Impressive. How does she walk in those things?

Logan shrugged as she made a U-turn at the light. To each his own, but she doubted she'd ever shop there. Logan liked her boots comfortable and her t-shirts unripped.

6

DOYLE

Around five o'clock, the captain called the *Freya* ready. This being Doyle's second year crewing for Craig, he knew the next few days and weeks would be long, hard ones, so he planned on taking advantage of the break to turn in early.

As he walked back to his apartment, he felt the fissure of excitement running through the Bayfront. Everyone felt it, it seemed, but Doyle. Craig once told him his spine actually tingled at the beginning of every crab derby. He said he could just *feel* all those big, heavy crabs out there waiting to be scooped up!

His excitement was almost contagious. Almost. But to Doyle, this was just a job. Even Craig didn't seem as enthusiastic about the whole thing this year, but maybe his fight with his wife this morning had put a damper on his mood.

Earlier, Liv Peterson, Craig's sister, had invited Doyle to join them at the Barge Inn for a burger before turning in early.

He didn't want to be rude, but Craig didn't look like he was in the mood for company, so after he stayed for one beer, Doyle politely made his excuses and headed for the door.

Technically, Liv was a deckhand like him. Being a Peterson, she could have lorded it over him and the other crew members, but never did. He liked working with Liv. She knew her way around a crab boat and didn't try to push off the stinky or dangerous jobs to others. She worked as long and hard as they did and could fix anything that broke, even in high seas.

The only difference between him and Liv was that Liv seemed to love everything about commercial fishing, and he only took the job because he had no other options. No one else would hire him. At least no businesses in town.

As Doyle was leaving the bar, Craig reminded him they were leaving first thing in the morning, which was unnecessary, but Doyle nodded without comment. He cut Craig some slack. That Roxy was a piece of work. She always seemed to know how to push her husband's buttons. His boss's fight with his wife had been a big one this time. They had gone down below, so he couldn't hear every word, but he could hear them yelling.

Outside the Barge Inn, Doyle turned the collar up on his jacket, shoved his hands into his pockets, and started walking home. When he'd arrived in Newport, he hadn't had a home to walk to. He found work at the docks quickly enough, but it did take a while to find a place to live within walking distance. And a landlord who didn't ask too many questions.

Finally, a ground floor, one-room at the Orchid Palace Apartments with a commanding view of the trash bins opened up. Mrs. McIntyre only required a small security deposit and first month's rent, not last. Since that used up most of what he had, he took it. He couldn't afford to be picky.

Twenty minutes later, stomach growling, Doyle let himself into his apartment. He hung up his jacket and opened up the small refrigerator. The contents hadn't changed since yesterday.

LOST AND FOUND

Mustard. Quart of milk. Half a loaf of stale bread and some bologna starting to curl around the edges. Hot dogs. Strawberry jam. He didn't have to look at what was in the cupboard. Peanut butter and Cheerios. He was sick of both.

Not exactly the extravagant meals he and Blain used to enjoy almost every night after work. Sushi, twenty-four ounce ribeye steaks, rack of lamb, that chocolate cake with the thin shaving of gold on top. He shook his head. Did he really think a kid right out of college would be given a corner office and that kind of expense account? The hotels, the travel! What an idiot he'd been. But that was then, and this was now. No sense dwelling on the past.

Opening the tiny freezer compartment, he sighed and took out a Hungry Man TV dinner. Meatloaf and mashed potatoes. There were two left. Good thing Liv stocked the *Freya*. At least he'd eat well on the boat—well, whenever they had time to eat . . . or sleep. The first few weeks on a crab boat were crazy.

He'd asked Liv once why it was called a derby. She explained that unlike other fisheries, crab fishing was a race. The fishing boats were like horses at the starting gate. Once the season opened, they all went out at once. It was a race to see who got the most crab, with hundreds of thousands of dollars on the line. It didn't happen much here in Newport, but he'd heard stories of some boats even wiring the competition's crab pot doors open so all the crab would escape. That'd piss you off.

Pressing the refrigerator door shut carefully, waiting a beat to make sure it didn't pop open again, he took the TV dinner out of the box, peeled back the corner, and placed it into the microwave.

When it was done, he carried the hot tray by the edges over to the scarred, wooden table.

As he ate, he thought of the upcoming season. He hoped he'd made the right decision by sticking with the *Freya*.

The *Freya* was a bigger boat, so it caught more crab and paid its crew more, but only after the owner got paid. Two years ago, when he crewed for Tim Pullman on the *Sara Lynn*, Tim made sure the deckhands were paid first, no matter how long the season start was delayed. This year, the season had been delayed over a month and a half. If he had stayed with the *Sara Lynn*, he would have been paid during that time and not had to dip into his savings.

Last year, that wasn't an issue. Crab season started right on time, December 1. Owners not only sold a lot of crab for Christmas and New Year but were getting top dollar for their product. Doyle made enough that season to pay his living expenses plus sock away $3000 into a savings account.

But this year, with the long delay, rent and food had whittled that down. He only had a couple of thousand left. Not nearly enough. He had it all mapped out. His goal was to open up a small accounting office. He'd done some research and surprisingly, there was no law against handling other people's money, even with an embezzlement felony on your record.

But plans weren't enough. It took money to lease a space and set up an office even for a modest business. And he would need enough to survive on while he built a client base. He wished he could wear a sign on his forehead that said how good he was! He could make breakfast with tax law! Since getting out of prison three years ago, he'd started to clean up his credit, and it was improving, but not fast enough. A $500 Visa card limit wasn't going to cut it. What he needed was a lot of cash.

Not even bothering to watch TV, Doyle got himself into what he wished was a long, hot shower—but the water only got up to lukewarm and in two minutes started coming out cold. Oh, how he missed long, hot showers with lots of water pressure in his old house. He dried off and dabbed some Vaseline on his chapped lips. He grimaced in the mirror. They'd be worse after this next week out.

LOST AND FOUND

Taking a last look around the apartment, he pulled on a sweatshirt and jeans and crawled into bed. Saved time dressing in the morning. His boots were by the door. Last thing he did was set the alarm on his phone and turn out the light.

At least he didn't have roommates, he consoled himself. It was a rat hole, but it was his rat hole. He'd had enough of roommates in prison.

7

Roxy jerked the door open and threw her gym bag behind the counter.

"Fuck you, Craig!" she sputtered through gritted teeth, "Just FUCK you!"

For emphasis with the second invective, she kicked the trash can, sending it skidding across the floor.

"One lousy load of stinkin' crab would pay for it!" she shouted. "We've got the biggest damn boat in the harbor and catch more crab than anybody. What's $40,000 to you? Nothing! Pocket change!" she fumed.

An hour later, pacing around the empty store, straightening already perfect stacks of $300 jeans, she ran out of things to do. She pulled out her phone.

10:00 A.M.

Too early for lunch, but what the hell? What was the point of owning your own shop if you couldn't close up for a few hours when you wanted to? A potential customer peered in the window but didn't come in.

Why did she bother? These people wouldn't know fashion if it bit them in the ass.

Roxy made a quick call, locked up, and headed south toward Yachats for a sympathetic ear and some stress release. Too many prying eyes in Newport.

Roxy arrived first, checked in, then parked her car in back. No sense advertising her presence. Walking back through the breezeway, key in hand, she came around the corner too quickly and plowed into the cleaning cart, almost knocking over the housekeeper, a middle-aged woman with an armful of towels.

Without apologizing, Roxy muttered something about stupid Mexicans and kept going. When she got to room 105, she used the low-tech key to let herself in. The housekeeper, muttering a few choice Spanish words of her own under her breath, shook her head and got back to work.

Fifteen minutes later, Roxy was pouring her second drink when a truck whose brake squeal she recognized pulled up out front. Søren didn't care who saw him.

The Hideaway Inn barely came with a bed and a bathroom, let alone a mini-bar, so Roxy always brought her own. Smirnoffs. She used to drink whiskey, but switched when she learned people couldn't smell vodka on your breath. It was nobody's business when and if she decided to have a drink. Besides, vodka had the fewest calories, and it didn't spike your blood sugar like wine.

Unlike her father, Roxy had her drinking, along with everything else in her life, under strict control. She'd learned that lesson well. From working out to diet, she made a plan, worked her plan, and kept working it until she achieved her goal. That's why she weighed 120 pounds and could bounce a quarter off her abs. That's why she drove a brand-new Range Rover and owned her own shop. Roxy made things happen.

Until now. Why did Craig have to be so selfish? It was her money, too! They were married—if not happily, at least legally.

LOST AND FOUND

A burning ball of resentment grew in her chest. She was so angry she couldn't think straight.

When Søren came in, he barely had time to kick the door shut before she grabbed him, shoved her tongue down his throat and pushed him onto the bed. Unphased, he reciprocated by unzipping her jeans and roughly flipping her over.

Their lovemaking had little to do with love, but momentarily quenched the fire. No mushy talk. She was fine with that. It was just sex.

Besides, what was she supposed to do? Craig hadn't touched her in months. Ever since she got rid of the baby.

And Craig was so vanilla. Ugh. Four years of lying there, pretending to enjoy his pathetic attempts, waiting until she had enough money to get the hell out of Dodge. She chuckled at the thought of Craig doing what this man had just done to her. Never in a million years. If only she could combine her current lover's dark, sexy intensity with Craig's money.

She snatched her clothes up off the floor and started getting dressed. Smoothing her t-shirt over her flat stomach, she remembered the knockdown, drag-out fight she and Craig had this summer when he found out she'd had an abortion.

Craig wanted a baby, an heir to the Peterson throne. She'd convinced him they just couldn't get pregnant, hinting it was maybe *his* fault. Without him knowing, she was on the pill, but even the pill wasn't foolproof. Apparently, she was very fertile.

When she missed her period, she wasn't too worried. She worked out so much that sometimes that happened anyway. Then she thought she had the flu, but no such luck. She was two months along when she discovered a Peterson had taken up residence in her uterus after all. Being careful as always, she found a clinic in Corvallis and made an appointment.

Unfortunately, some high school slut from Newport had gone out of town for the same reason. The girl's mother recognized

Roxy in the waiting room and wasted no time getting word back to Mama Peterson. They all hated her.

Obviously, she had to get rid of it. Getting pregnant was an accident! Definitely not part of her plan. There was no way she was going to wind up like every other woman in town, tied down by kids, family, and fishing. That's all any of them cared about! Hell, Craig's sister, Liv, even crewed on the *Freya*, which was a man's job, but then again, Liv kind of looked like a man, Roxy thought uncharitably, or dressed like one, anyway.

And Emma. Mama Peterson.

Roxy polished off her drink in one swallow to wash out the bitter taste the very thought of that woman left in her mouth. Craig's mom had never approved of her precious boy marrying the town drunk's daughter. Oh, the old bat was polite, never came right out and said it, but Roxy felt her disapproval. Every. Damn. Day.

No, she particularly didn't want to wind up like Emma, whose whole purpose in life seemed to be to cook, clean, and go to Newport Fishermen's Wives meetings. Roxy had no idea what they did at those meetings, but she prided herself on never having been to one.

She yanked on her second boot and pulled up the zipper.

There had to be a way to speed things up. She just hadn't thought of it yet.

8

SØREN

Thin afternoon light slanted across the floor as Søren Vestergaard slid onto a stool at the end of the bar and ordered a cheap whiskey. Other than the bartender who delivered his drink, the place was empty.

Stuffing his watch cap into his pocket, Søren raked long fingers through stringy, dark blonde hair and scrubbed his scalp. These all-night runs were taking a toll. He needed to find another line of work. But they paid well.

His Danish good looks were somewhat soured by a slightly curled lip, and in the right light, a hint of a sneer briefly flitted across his narrow face. Nothing you could put your finger on, but every now and again, something deeply disturbing rippled behind those blue eyes. It gave him a certain bad-boy look some women found attractive.

Just 5'8" when standing straight and tall, which he rarely did, Søren didn't draw attention to himself. Fading into the background was not a skill he had consciously cultivated, but it had served him well during his thirty-four years.

For one thing, he'd so far managed to avoid jail time. A couple of stints in juvie didn't count. In fact, they'd been instructional. He'd learned early to avoid the common mistakes that got his friends popped. He never bragged, never got in over his head, and never partook of any product he helped move.

His day jobs were a great cover for his less-than-legal ones. Born and raised in Newport, Søren had done every job there was to do in and around the docks, from hosing fish guts off the floor at Pacific to crewing on any and all kinds of fishing vessels that went out of the harbor. Crabbing made the most money the fastest, so that was his preference.

Working intermittently suited him. It wasn't that he wouldn't have liked to have more money, but he couldn't envision himself being one of the successful commercial fishing vessel captains he crewed for. They had houses and families and went on vacations, but Søren hadn't the faintest clue how to get those benefits without having to take on all those obligations. Just thinking about being tied down made him involuntarily shudder. Especially kids. That's why he was careful. He didn't need any rug rats.

He did need a new truck, though. And he wasn't getting any younger. Maybe it was time to think about a bigger score. Clean up. Move someplace sunny. Umbrellas in the drinks. He smiled at the thought.

Next to his left hand, his phone burred. In answer to the short text, he tapped a thumbs up, paid his tab, and left. A few minutes later, he slowly pulled his truck onto the 101 and headed south.

LOST AND FOUND

*****

Forty-five minutes later, he and Roxy were lying in bed, talking. Well, Roxy was talking, he was listening. Well, not exactly listening. He mostly tuned her out when she was complaining about her husband. All he had to do was catch enough of what she said to utter supportive grunts now and then.

"He put me on an allowance! Can you believe it?" she said. "I'm never going to have enough to get away from the rotten smell of stinking fish! I can't even get enough money to buy new inventory for the store!"

Reaching for another cigarette, he nodded as Roxy ranted and punched the pillow for emphasis. He almost felt sorry for her.

Finally, she ran out of steam. This was her usual routine.

He'd known Roxy since high school. In a small town like Newport, everyone knew pretty much everyone, but they'd never hooked up until earlier this year.

He took it for what it was—another unhappy wife screwing around on her husband—that was his specialty—but with Roxy there was something more. He sensed a kindred spirit. Roxy was a cold bitch. He didn't have to slather on the compliments or sweet talk her to get her into bed. She could have written the playbook on the "wham, bam, thank you ma'am," but she was the one doing the whamming and bamming. He had no objections. It was great.

He took a thoughtful drag of his cigarette and tapped the ashes into his empty glass. On the drive down, an idea had begun to form in his mind. He decided to test the waters.

"Then why don't you do something about it?" he said.

That stopped her in her tracks. Momentarily stunned by the interruption, she gave Søren a hard look. She was either going to take the bait or kick him out.

"I *have* tried, Søren," she said slowly and evenly. "But Craig's got all the *Freya* money locked up . . . there's a separate account for the business."

"You're his wife, don't you have access?"

Roxy clenched her jaw. "I'm sure I do, but he's in that account every day. He watches every dime."

"Why don't you just leave, then?" Søren said. "You're his wife, you'd get half at least, right?"

The silence in the room was deafening.

9

Later that night, Roxy threw her phone on the bed. She'd been home for hours, but still had no message from Craig. She was too proud to go down to the docks and check, but he was probably on the boat. After their fight, he might even sleep there tonight.

Restless, she got up and went into the front room, then for lack of anything better to do, wandered aimlessly around the house, pushing down an increasing sense of panic.

Maybe she'd pushed him too far this time.

The short hallway brought her back to the living room, which she hated. When they'd bought this house, she'd been so excited. It was much nicer than any place she'd ever lived.

Now, seven years later, she saw it for what it was. 1300 tiny square feet of boring, furnished in 'fisherman chic,' chunky furniture, upholstered in fake leather or nubby, plaid, stain-proof fabric. Hand-me-downs from Emma.

"Good for when your little ones come along!" she had said.

Another reason to hate it.

The Peterson house had hardwood floors, a huge kitchen, walk-in closets, and an awesome view. She and Craig lived in a tiny cracker box with only a view of another cracker box across the street. They couldn't even see the water.

She had begged Craig to sell this place and move, trade up—the real estate market was hot! Values had skyrocketed the last few years—but *nooo*, he wanted to live near his *mommy*, and, of course, every dime they earned went right back into the business. Engine, gear, whatever. Something on that boat always needed to be fixed or replaced.

She had to wheedle and beg for scraps! Scraps! Just so she could keep her store afloat. No one took *her* business seriously. If it didn't have fins, shells, or gills—to a Peterson, it was worthless. Besides, it wasn't her fault sales were down. No one in Newport understood the first thing about style. She swore they all shopped at Goodwill.

Roxy plopped down on one of the couches and began chewing her thumbnail. She'd had the nasty habit since she was a kid. She'd forced herself to overcome it but allowed herself the left side of her right thumb when she really needed to gnaw on something.

Whatever money Craig made should be *hers*! It was *their* business, right? I mean, when they got married, he said they'd share everything, but after she'd bounced a couple of checks, he'd opened a separate account just for the business. He paid her out of that. Now, she had to live on an allowance. Like a child!

Grabbing one of her red, satin lipstick pillows from the store, she pressed her face into it and kicked her heels on the awful carpet.

ARRRrrrggghhh!

She threw the pillow across the room.

Passing headlights raked across the window, providing no warmth. Roxy narrowed her eyes and sat in the dark. Thinking.

She knew exactly what she wanted. She could see it all very clearly in her mind's eye: her shop—the kind she deserved, the one she had the architect draw plans for, with plenty of inventory—her car, her life—living in a big city, eating out every night, laughing with cool, interesting friends.

Keeping that vision front and center, she let all the circumstances, all the factors free float until an idea began to form. She didn't have all the details worked out yet, but an outline of a plan began to take shape.

Søren was right. Why should she wait? Her rotten husband and his whole selfish family were never going to change. If anything was going to happen, it was up to her.

They'd pushed her into a corner, and everyone knew: 'Nobody puts Baby in a corner!'

Dirty Dancing had always been one of her favorite movies. Patrick Swayze was so hot. She always did like bad boys. What had she ever seen in Craig?

With a new sense of purpose and mission, she ran out to her car to make sure what she needed was still in the back seat. It was. Then, almost giggling, she reached for her phone.

She had three calls to make and one of them required a change of clothes.

10

ROXY

Three nights later, Roxy stood in front of her closet, hand on her hip, deciding what to wear. Tonight called for something special . . . something new . . . hmmmm . . . She pushed hangers around and considered her options.

Maybe the purple feather boa with matching thong . . . no, she wore that Friday. When Craig didn't come home that night, she knew he must be sleeping on the *Freya* to teach her a lesson. So she had surprised him with a virtual booty call.

It totally worked, as she knew it would.

After reassuring her husband all she wanted to do was have his babies and stay home and cook, it had taken her less than three minutes and a few fake moans to make him forget all about last summer's abortion and their argument that morning. A good strip tease usually worked. So easy to manipulate men . . .

Ahhh . . . this one would do nicely.

She hadn't worn this one yet. Black, lace-up bustier with see-through undies and the whole matching garter belt/seamed nylons getup. Very 1940s with a kick. She'd picked it up in Portland at a little shop called Down & Dirty.

She checked the time. Craig had called her earlier from the *Freya*. They'd only been out a day, but they had another great haul, and as soon as they unloaded, he was heading home to his wife for some more lovin', then back out again in the morning.

He offered to take her out to dinner after he cleaned up, but she told him just to pick up some pizza on the way home. She didn't want to waste time going out, she wanted him *bad!*

Oh, brother.

She fluffed the pillows and laid her outfit on the bed. Before she shut her underwear drawer, she pulled out a phone Craig didn't know she had and sent a short text.

2nite, stay ready.

Stuffing the phone back under a silk cami, she shut the drawer with her hip and went to take a shower. She'd make sure Craig took a good, hot one, too. There were only so many things she was willing to endure for the cause, and the reek of stinky fish wasn't one of them. She had her standards.

Later that night, husband satisfied and plan in place, Roxy rolled over and poked Craig in the shoulder.

"Honey? You awake? I really, really, *need* some ice cream," Roxy whined in her best flirty babytalk. Before he could object, she batted her fake eyelashes at him and pleaded, "Please? I can't help it, Craig, you wore me out!"

She didn't care that her husband had to be up early to meet the crew on the *Freya*. She just needed him out of the house for twenty minutes.

Giving his wife a kiss on the top of her head, Craig pulled on a sweatshirt and pants and grabbed his keys.

"What kind?" he said, yawning.

"Mmmmmmm . . . I want that Umpqua one, the one with all the caramel and peanuts in it," she said.

"They only have that one at Safeway," he complained. "You like cookie dough, how about cookie dough? I promise to get you the caramel one next time."

Roxy pouted. "Aww, please? I really want that one, Safeway's only a few more minutes away."

Craig capitulated and said he'd be right back, but he sounded grumpy. It was always better to ask a man for a favor *before* you had sex with him. But tonight, that wouldn't have suited her needs. Once the rumble of her husband's old truck faded, Roxy retrieved her phone and texted,

Now!

Then she sat on the edge of the bed, waiting impatiently for the next act of her little play.

Oh! She almost forgot. Quickly, she started the water in the shower, stepped in for a second to get wet, let the mirror steam up a little, then wrapped a towel around herself and opened the window blinds. It was pitch-black outside, but, as the weather site had promised, it wasn't raining.

A man's ghostly white face suddenly appeared at the window.

Instead of screaming, Roxy dropped her towel, wriggled, and gave him a thumbs up. The ghostly face grinned and made an obscene gesture. Then, as fast as he had appeared, the man disappeared.

Wrapping the towel back around her body, Roxy got her regular phone and dialed 911. Closing her eyes, she took a deep breath and got into character.

"911. What is your emergency?"

"Well," Roxy whispered. "I'm not sure it's an emergency—I think they left, but someone was looking in my window!"

11

The dispatcher tried to get a word in edgewise, but the caller just kept talking in a panicky, high-pitched voice.

". . . I think they left, but someone just tried to get in our house! I was getting ready for bed when I heard someone outside our bedroom window. I'd just gotten out of the shower, so I couldn't do anything, but I heard them trying to open the window! I yelled and said I had a gun, but I don't have one, of course. Then, I heard running, I think they ran away, but they were right here! Please, can you send someone? I need help!"

Finally, when she was able to break in, the dispatcher asked, "What is your address?"

"418 Seastar, Newport—just up from the harbor," the woman said. "Please hurry!"

"Is anyone there with you? Are you alone in the house?" asked the dispatcher.

"No, it's just me! My husband went to the store to get me some ice cream. No one's here!"

"Okay, you're doing fine," said the dispatcher, trying to calm the caller down. "This is what I want you to do. I want you to remain calm, stay inside. Make sure all the doors and windows are locked and stay on the line with me until help arrives. I'm right here."

"Okay," the woman said, her voice shaking. "I'm pulling on a robe, now, I can do that."

The dispatcher stayed on the line, hearing the woman moving around the house, making locking noises, shaking windows and doors to make sure they were completely closed and securely locked.

*****

When Craig Peterson pulled up in front of his house, a police car blocked the driveway. Leaving the ice cream on the passenger seat to melt into a pile of caramel and peanut goo he would discover in the morning, he jumped out of his car and raced inside.

"Roxy?!" he shouted.

A uniformed officer was seated with Roxy at the kitchen table, while another one was walking around outside the house with a flashlight.

"Craig!" Roxy yelled, running into her husband's arms.

"Are you okay? What happened?" he said, holding her at arm's length, checking her over.

Once he saw that she was all right, he helped his wife back to her chair.

The officer introduced himself.

"Mr. Peterson? Officer Rasmussen. 911 received a call from your wife at 10:55 p.m. and we were dispatched for assistance. We have checked the interior of your home and found no intruders. We also looked around outside, but whoever was here, if anyone was . . ."

Roxy gave the officer a dirty look.

". . . they're gone now." He leaned back in his chair but did not get up. He'd wait until the obvious effect this attractive woman was having on his very healthy libido was less evident. He wished he had more control over that thing. Felt like he was still in high school sometimes.

He looked her in the eye so as to avoid letting his gaze drift south where her robe had slipped, and her ample assets were on display. He hoped her husband didn't notice.

"This is a pretty safe neighborhood, ma'am, so it was probably a possum or a raccoon. I had one trapped under the porch last year, and believe me, they can make a lot of racket."

Seeing the look on Roxy's face, he added, "But to be thorough, my partner is checking the exterior of your home again right now. None of your neighbors have reported seeing or hearing anything suspicious, but we'll take a couple of extra passes by here tonight just to be sure whoever it was isn't still hanging around, or in case they decide to come back."

He turned to Craig. "Sir, do either you or your wife have anything of value a thief might be after? Do you keep a safe in the house or firearms?"

"No, nothing like that," Craig said, pointing out the window down to the docks. "All of my money is floating right down there in the harbor. I captain the *Freya*. We just got in with our first run today."

"Congratulations! My cousin crews for the *Golden Girl*. The *Freya's* a good boat."

"So," Officer Rasmussen said, getting back to his official duties, "What time did you get home tonight?"

Craig looked at Roxy. "I don't know exactly, it was dark. Probably seven, seven-thirty. We had to offload and prep the boat. We had a great first day. Filled up! We're going back out tomorrow, first thing." He turned to Roxy, "That is . . . that is if it's okay with you, hon?"

"Of course, honey," she said. "You men have to do what you have to do. I will be fine."

"Don't worry, Mr. Peterson," Rasmussen said, "You've got a deadbolt on the front door. You may want to add one on the back, but we didn't see any signs of an attempted break-in and like I said, my partner and I will keep an eye out at night."

Craig turned to his wife, "You can stay at mom's if you're worried, hon."

"My parents live just up the hill," he explained to the officer.

"No, I don't want to be a bother to anyone," Roxy said. "I'll be at work during the day, and I promise to lock up tight when I get home. I'll be fine."

Craig walked Rasmussen back outside, where his young partner was carefully inspecting the exterior bedroom window frame while studiously avoiding stepping on the ground directly beneath it, taking pictures of everything.

Officer Rasmussen rolled his eyes.

"*Rookie*," he whispered to Craig. "These young guys watch *way* too much TV. He'd fingerprint the squirrels if we'd let him."

"Fowler!" he shouted, "Let's go!"

The rookie slipped his phone back into his pocket and jogged back to the patrol car. As Rasmussen backed down the driveway, he radioed in—code four, letting the dispatcher know their unit was returning to service. Out of habit, he slowly scanned the homes and yards as they rolled by.

When they reached the end of the street, he peered up at the sky through the front windshield, appreciating the sprinkle of stars.

"Well, at least it stopped raining for five seconds," he said. "Looks like it's going to be a clear night. Keep your eyes peeled. If there was someone peeping in that lady's window—and I can't say as I blame him—he might still be out here."

12

NEWSTIMES
"BODY FOUND ON ROCKS AT DEPOE BAY"
JANUARY 17
SAMANTHA BADGER

Early Monday morning, January 16, while walking his dog, Tom Katz, a resident of the Depoe Bay community of Little Whale Cove, discovered the body of an unidentified man washed up onto the rocks near his home.

"Lexi and I were walking along the ocean path—Lexi's my ten-year-old Aussie. She started barking, which is unusual for her. She pulled me over to the edge onto the rocky area there, and when I looked over the edge, there it was, about forty feet down. Tide was going out. This little inlet here is very narrow. Things are always getting hung up on the sharp rocks in there—fishing buoys, pieces of driftwood. Never expected to see a body, though. Not something I ever want to see again."

The Lincoln County Sheriff's office, with the assistance of the fire department in Depoe Bay, were able to extract the body from its location before it washed back out to sea with the next tide. It was transported to Demeter's Mortuary in Newport.

There is currently no additional information regarding the identity of the deceased man, and the circumstances and cause of his death are yet to be determined. Anyone with information related to this incident should contact the Lincoln County Sheriff's office at 555-978-2350.

*****

NEWSTIMES
"MAN'S BODY FOUND ON ROCKS AT DEPOE BAY"
WEDNESDAY, JANUARY 18
SAMANTHA BADGER

The identity of the body discovered in a rocky inlet in Little Whale Cove, Depoe Bay, Monday, January 16 is still unknown. According to Lincoln County Medical Examiner, Dr. Jean Pullman, the body is of a middle aged male, 67" in height, approximately 155 pounds. It is estimated he had been in the water for several days. Due to the condition of the body, a more exact time of death cannot be determined.

Dr. Pullman indicated fingerprints and dental work could still be used to identify the man, if and when records could be found for comparison.

Lincoln County Sheriff's office has opened an investigation, but as of now, no missing persons have been reported and no accidents involving a male of

LOST AND FOUND

this description have occurred. Anyone with information related to this incident should contact the
Lincoln County Sheriff's office at 555-978-2350.

13

Logan and Sam were already halfway through their breakfast burritos when Jean arrived. Sam's sister-in-law always made an impressive entrance. A bold, white skunk stripe accentuated her dark chestnut hair, pulled up into an elegant French twist. Heads always turned when Jean entered the room.

While everyone else on the coast wore typical Oregon attire, rugged, warm, and waterproof, Jean wore nothing but dress slacks and cashmere sweaters. Her only nod to the frequent precipitation was a long, Burberry raincoat and matching umbrella, which rarely left her car.

Logan didn't know how she did it, but even with all the gusty, rainy weather, Jean never had a hair out of place and her expensive, leather flats—today's color a brilliant, peacock blue— were unfailingly and completely dry, in spite of the morning drizzle.

Amazing.

Wednesdays had become something of a ritual for the three friends. A few years back, Tim christened them the Cormorant

Coffee Crew and gave them custom mugs for Christmas with the lucky fisherman's bird and their names printed on each.

Jean and her husband both ran busy medical practices in Lincoln City, but she wore her medical examiner's hat in Newport on Wednesdays. Sam's stories for the print edition had to be filed by Tuesday night, so midweek at Pirate's in Depoe Bay was perfect for the three friends to meet for breakfast.

Logan was the only one who didn't have a set schedule and she lived just up the street, so she could have joined them any day. Now that she and Ben were married, she usually only stopped for a coffee after her morning run, but on Wednesdays she indulged.

Jean ordered her usual large Americano and croissant before joining them at one of the three well-worn picnic tables across from the pastry case.

As she sat down, she eyed Sam's baby belly with a practiced eye.

"Hope you've got a bag packed," she said. "When's your next appointment with Grady?" Jean had recommended an OBGYN in Lincoln City.

"You takin' your vitamins?"

Sam's mouth was full, so she gave her a thumbs up while she finished chewing, then swallowed and said, "Friday."

Jean nodded her approval and took a bite of her croissant. *Again. Not a single crumb.*

Logan wiped the dribble of hot sauce off her chin and sighed.

For the next few minutes, they got caught up on each other's lives, including Jean and her husband's weekend getaway to Five Pines Lodge in Sisters, Oregon, a small town a few hours inland. They had stayed at the Serenity Cabin—Logan googled it while they were talking. OMG! A cute little cabin had been totally remodeled with slipper tub, a walk-in river rock shower, leather furniture, and a fireplace.

If you could be in love with a bathtub, Logan wanted to marry that tub! She made a note to see if Five Pines had openings for her and Ben's upcoming anniversary. Luxury accommodations, hiking trails, *and* good restaurants in town—sounded right up their alley.

"Where are you playing next, Logan?"

Logan broke away from her drooling and looked up her upcoming performance dates. She mostly composed music these days, but now and then she and her violin, Bella, made an appearance around town.

She told them about Ben's various house projects and then they asked Sam how crab season was going.

"Great!" Sam said, "Not a stellar year, and it'll be long days for a while, but at least we got a season—and Tim's *very* happy to be out on the water. If the weather's good, he should be coming in tonight, then back out in the morning."

The financial pressure of the delayed season starter was definitely a factor for Tim, but Logan also understood the passion he had for the work went beyond pay. She knew how he felt. If she wasn't composing music and playing Bella, she got cranky. Tim really loved what he did. Passions were visceral and difficult to explain to people who worked nine-to-five jobs.

"Did Tim ever decide what to do about finding another crewmember?" Logan asked.

"The half-share guy showed up, but the full-timer he was hoping to hire for the season ran his truck off the road in the fog last night. He'll be out for a few weeks at least.

"Everybody good has already been hired," Sam said. "Tim's looking, but for now, he and Francis and the half-share guy are handling it. The *Sara Lynn's* a small boat. They'll be okay."

Wanting to distract her friend from worrying about Tim being on the water with a skeleton crew, Logan asked her what stories she was working on this week.

"Follow-up stories, mostly. The animal shelter still doesn't have a new home since the old building was condemned for toxic mold in 2019, Newport's trying to get a cut of the money from the state to help with the homeless situation, the school district's superintendent resigned, and there's something of a disagreement about whether a national search is necessary when they have a good candidate here in the district already, and of course, Monday's floater."

It took Logan half a beat to realize Sam was talking about the dead body that had washed up and caught on the rocks in a narrow inlet called Shell Beach in Little Whale Cove (LWC), half a block south of town. She'd seen Sam's online post yesterday about the grisly discovery.

Logan knew right where Shell Beach was. She'd walked right past that spot several times when she stayed in her friend, Rita's house in the LWC neighborhood.

"Did they ever figure out who it is?" Logan asked.

"The short answer? No," Sam said, taking a sip of coffee.

"What's the long answer?" Logan said, turning to Jean, whom she knew as the Lincoln County Medical Examiner would have done the initial examination of any person who died of unknown circumstances. "Can't you use DNA or dental records or something?"

Jean pressed the lid down on her to-go cup, getting ready to leave.

"Normally, yes," Jean said, "we started there, but no one's reported anyone missing. I took samples, but until we have something to compare those samples to, he'll probably remain a John Doe."

She looked at Logan, then added, "I don't like it either, but it happens more often than you think. We'll keep him in cold storage for a while, but he'll get transferred up to Portland soon."

With that, Jean stood up, gave Sam a quick peck on the cheek, and told her to remember to take her vitamins.

LOST AND FOUND

Logan thought about the man who'd washed up onto the rocks Monday. Less than a week ago he had been a living, breathing person. Someone's father, brother, son, husband, friend. Someone must be looking for him. She knew Jean would do everything within her power to identify him, but that the chances of that happening were slim to nothing.

14

The next night, Logan sat in her favorite chair on the back deck, pale winter sun warming her face. Almost 50 degrees. Spring looked like it was arriving early this year. She watched Ben as he dug around in the dirt, prepping his garden, happy in his element. Since the soil was so poor and the hard ground was crisscrossed with tough tree roots, he'd opted for a raised bed option.

He already had Swiss chard, strawberries, kale, and snow pea seeds started in egg cartons on the kitchen windowsill. Logan offered to help, but he waved her off. Which was just as well; she knew less about gardening than she did about cooking.

Jotting down some phrases she was considering for her next musical composition, Logan was grateful he hadn't taken her up on her offer. This division of labor suited her just fine.

She didn't even need to get up and help with dinner. Sam would be here any minute and was providing their evening sustenance—fresh crab! Tim had delivered on his promise, then taken off again this morning to fill up the boat again. He wouldn't be back until late tonight or maybe tomorrow morning, depending on the weather. If the waves were breaking high, the Coast Guard could close the bar to all boat traffic, which meant whoever was still on the water stayed on the water until conditions cleared.

With Sam's delivery date less than a month away, Logan and Ben had promised Tim they'd be on call should the baby girl arrive early. Logan still didn't know if Sam and Tim had agreed on a name and was afraid to ask.

Needing to hear how the notes she'd jotted down fit into the composition as a whole, Logan went inside to retrieve her violin, Bella, and try it out. Bella was created out of a true, deep love between Logan's Appalachian great-grandmother, Norah, and Giovanni, an Italian immigrant running from the law back in Padua. The result was an exquisitely made instrument that rivaled a Stradivarius.

Sam arrived in the midst of Logan's musical stylings. So involved with visualizing the various threads of music and how they all fit together, Logan didn't hear her come in.

"Hey!" Sam called out. "Woman on the floor! And she's carrying fresh crab! If you two are screwing around, you may want to cover up!"

Logan laughed, put Bella away, and went out to help Sam roll in the cooler. The live crabs were kept on ice to keep them from thrashing around until they were ready to be cooked.

The traditional method for cooking crab was to plunge them into boiling water . . . *alive* . . . then crack them open and clean out the guts and gills.

But Logan had learned not everyone did it that way. For Christmas, she had gotten Ben a Crackn' Crab cleaner, a simple tool designed by a fisherman in Newport that dispatched a live crab in seconds. You grabbed all of the legs on either side to prevent it from pinching you or getting away, placed it over the Crackn' Crab tool, then smacked it hard so it cracked in half in one smooth motion. Then you shook out the guts and voila! Cleaned crab! Sam said it was probably more humane than boiling them first, then cleaning them, but really, it was a tossup. Either way, fresh boiled crab was delicious!

Logan liked hers steaming hot, dipped in melted butter, although if any was leftover, or Sam brought extra crab, as she did tonight, a cold crab cocktail garnished with Ben's special cocktail sauce of horseradish, lemon and ketchup was also awesome. His secret ingredient was a few dashes of Worcestershire sauce.

Serving was simple. Logan spread a few beach towels across the table, and everyone had at their crab with nutcrackers and little skinny metal picks Sam had given them to help dig out the big, meaty chunks in the legs and claws. For the next hour, everyone was busy picking out the best bits, piling the shells on a big platter in the middle of the table. All cleanup involved was gathering up the towels, shaking them over the deck railing for the raccoons, then throwing them in the washing machine.

Completely sated, they adjourned to the living room with Ben's lemon brownies.

Sam sank her fork into the sweet-tart lemon and powdered sugar glazed square Logan had put on her plate and took a bite.

She closed her eyes and declared, "If you weren't already married, Ben . . ."

Just then, Sam's cell rang. Instantly, she dropped her fork and sat up straight, "Tim?" she said, "What's up? . . . Okay, I'll give her a call. You just focus on getting yourselves home safely. Be careful, hon."

"What?" Logan asked, not liking the look on Sam's face. "Is everything okay?"

Sam held up her finger for Logan to wait, then found a saved number in her phone and hit dial. She waited while it rang.

"Penny? This is Sam . . . .no, don't worry, Francis is okay. They're on their way back, though. They were dealing with some rough seas, the crab block broke and caught Francis on his right arm . . . No, it doesn't look broken, but it's swelling up pretty fast. In case it's fractured, Tim has him resting down below with some ice on it to bring the swelling down. Yes, they're coming in now . . . Yes, he is a tough guy . . . Do you want me to call an ambulance to meet you at the boat or do you want to drive him in, it's your choice, just let me know what you want us to do . . . Okay, I'll meet you there."

"Why wouldn't she want an ambulance?" Logan asked. "They could give him something for the pain at least, until they got to the hospital."

"No insurance," Sam said. "Ambulance rides are $1,000 or more."

"Ahhh," Logan nodded. *The Great American Health Care System.*

Ever the protective male, Ben offered to give Sam a ride, but she politely declined. Before marrying Tim and moving to the slower-paced small town of Newport, Sam had been a tough, investigative reporter in Olympia, Washington, covering major crimes and politics—which, she said, were basically the same thing. Driving twenty minutes to Newport at night, even in rainy, winter conditions while very pregnant, wasn't beyond her capabilities.

Logan turned on the porch light while Ben went to get the to-go bag of brownies he'd made for Sam to take back to the crew.

"What happens if Francis can't work for a while?" Logan asked as Sam got in her car, "Will Tim be able to find someone else to help?"

Sam shrugged.

"Most everyone is already on a boat," she said, "We'll find someone. They just might not be a good someone, and we'll probably have to miss a few days before we can go back out."

15

Craig Peterson's heart filled with nostalgic pride as he approached his parents' house. 1407 Vista Drive had been in Craig's family for over seventy-five years, ever since Lars Bjørkland came to Newport, Oregon to ply the rich waters of the Pacific for crab, tuna, shrimp, rockfish, lingcod, salmon, and whatever else swam into his net, including squid.

Furnished simply with sturdy furniture and wide-planked floors, it was a solid home made to withstand generations of kids and dogs and tough people who wrested their living from the sea. It had been upgraded over the years—Trex decking, tile bathrooms, built-in closets, and gourmet kitchen, but the bones of the house were as Lars had designed it and still served them well today.

As an old man, Lars liked to tell anyone who would listen about the glory days, when regulations were few, Dungeness were double the size, and they caught 80 percent salmon and only 20 percent rockfish. He always expressed his sympathy for this generation, now that those percentages were reversed.

Lars reigned over the dinner table for most of Craig's childhood. He and Liv loved listening to Morfar (the Swedish word for maternal grandfather) Lars's stories. He'd named his fishing vessel after his beloved wife, *Freya*. *Freya* died shortly after giving birth to Emma, Craig's mom, so she and Lars never got to fill up the large house with children as originally planned. She left that up to the next generation.

When Emma grew up and married Walt Peterson, a good man from another local family who'd been crewing on Lars's boat for several years, it just seemed natural for Walt to move in. It worked out so well, they remained there even after the kids came along.

Craig had moved out when he'd married Roxy. They had a small house a few streets over, but still in the nice neighborhood where he'd grown up. Roxy had not grown up there. Liv still lived at home but took over Morfar Lars' independent living area over the garage, which had its own separate entrance. She and her mom got along well and liked to cook most meals together, so she still spent a lot of time in the main part of the house.

When people asked Emma if she'd ever thought of doing anything else, or wanted a different life for her kids, she just laughed. "No," she said, "the whole family has salt in their blood. Fishing was in their DNA."

Just as Lars had continued to mentor Walt, even after he got too old to go out on the *Freya* himself. Walt now kept a close watch on Craig.

Sometimes too close, Craig thought. But that was part of the price you paid to have all the benefits of a close family.

On the way home, Craig swung by his house to pick up Roxy, but she wasn't there. He checked his voicemail. Without thinking, he tapped play and put it on speakerphone. There was a cheerful message telling him she'd walked up the hill early to help his mom cook.

Roxy? Cook?

Roxy? Help?

He pretended this news didn't shock him and turned up the radio to drown out any snarky comments Liv might make. He did see his sister roll her eyes, though. He let it go.

This was definitely out of character for Roxy. First, getting up early and seeing him off at the *Freya* Sunday morning, and now helping his mom make dinner for everyone? He didn't trust the new Roxy, but she did seem to be sincere. Maybe she really was turning over a new leaf.

He curved up and around Vista and parked in front of the family home.

He and Liv unloaded the cooler of live crab on ice into the garage, then Liv jogged up the outside stairs to her place. She wanted to take a quick shower before dinner. Craig would do likewise, then they'd all meet for cocktails and snacks in the living room. Closing the garage door, he went back to his car, made sure it was locked, and went inside.

The front doors opened onto a huge great room, with a gourmet kitchen on the right and a short hallway leading to bedrooms on the left. Filled with oversized leather couches and generous easy chairs—there was plenty of seating for the adults and guests, plus running around room for kids and dogs.

A triptych of three large picture windows perfectly framed the Yaquina Bay Bridge, showcasing the fishing boats below, reflected in the still waters of the harbor. Large leather couches and oversized easy chairs were arranged to take advantage of the view.

One of eleven major coast highway bridges designed by Conde McCullough, the Yaquina Bay's distinctive art deco arches also made it the most recognizable. Although the overall length of the bridge was over three thousand feet, the navigable channel below it only measured four hundred feet, leading fishing vessels out to the infamous bar.

Every fisherman knew the inherent dangers of crossing the bar, where the power of the Pacific met the shallow waters of the harbor in a narrow channel between two rock jetties, often creating unpredictable, monster waves.

God bless the coasties. Every fishing family depended on the Coast Guard, stationed right at the mouth of the harbor, to guide them in over the bar and to be there to rescue them if they didn't make it.

Craig thought again of Roxy and her abrupt change in attitude. She'd said she realized she had been selfish, that now she wanted to give him a child. Lots of children! She could turn her store over to her assistant so she could be home with the baby.

The thought of another generation of little Petersons running around this house, being bounced on Grandpa's knee, licking the frosting spoon when making a cake with Grandma, having him, their dad, take them out on the boat, teach them what he knew, brought a deep joy to Craig's heart.

He entered the house with a lighter step.

Roxy saw him first, gave a little squeal and ran over to wrap her arms around him and give him a big kiss. His mom was carrying a large tray of snacks into the living room, so she simply gave him a huge smile and told him to hurry up or Walt would eat all the shrimp.

They'd wait to boil the crab until they'd had their cocktails.

16

The restorative powers of a hot shower and a fresh change of clothes lifted Craig's mood. Suddenly ravenous, he made a beeline for his mom's cheese dip before it was all gone. Roxy came over with a couple of beers and snuggled up next to him on the couch.

Liv was already there, sitting in a chair within easy reaching distance of the chips and guac, scratching their old chocolate lab behind the ears. Cocoa lay across Liv's feet, eyes shut in blissful contentment, his tail thumping on the rug. Liv was deep in conversation with their mom, while their dad was working through a plate piled high with smoked salmon, crackers, Tillamook sharp cheddar, and of course, his wife's cheese dip. Cholesterol was not a consideration in the Peterson family. They were all on the thin side.

Even Roxy ate big and never gained an ounce—but to give credit where due, it was because she worked it off like a fiend at the gym. Roxy was not blessed with the Peterson metabolism. She had to work at it.

Although Roxy and Liv were within ten feet of each other, it appeared no blood had yet been shed, so Craig relaxed his shoulders—a little—the night was still young. Hopefully, Roxy's new leaf included getting along with, or at least not antago-nizing, his sister.

Craig took a long pull of his beer and made a decision. He needed to stop borrowing trouble and focus on what he had. His family. Imperfect as they were, family was all you had and right now, he was surrounded by his. Life was good.

After many years of crewing, he was now captain of the *Freya*. He'd come in with a full hold—a huge mess of fresh crab—even with the lower prices this year, they'd make good money.

And Roxy had finally warmed up to the idea of starting a family—little Petersons to run around the house. He put his arm around his wife and gave her a squeeze, pulling her closer to his side.

The Shillings and the Zimmermans, two other long-time fishing families who lived just down the street, always joined them for this annual feast, so his mom put both leaves in the dining room table. Soon, she called them all in for dinner, platters of steaming crab arranged down the middle within everyone's easy reach, next to hot loaves of sourdough bread.

Finally, when everyone was seated, his dad offered a brief prayer, expressing gratitude for everyone's safe return after their first trip out.

Beaming at his family, Walt raised his glass, "May your pots be full, and your bilges be empty!"

Craig could drink to that.

For the next hour, everyone dug in. Occasional bits of shell flew off and landed on the floor, but Cocoa, who had parked herself under the table, was an experienced enough scrounger not to fall for those. She held out for pieces of sourdough or butter-drenched crab the kids sneaked her.

Cocoa did not go hungry.

Dessert was New York cheesecake with Lorinda Zimmer-man's wild huckleberry preserves drizzled on top. Everyone had to be out on the water again early in the morning, so the party broke up around nine. Walt walked the remaining guests to the door. Roxy, Craig, and Liv finished clearing the table while their mom started washing the pots. Craig and Roxy offered to stay and help with the dishes, but their mom shooed them away. Liv was kind of stuck because she lived there.

After Roxy washed the table, she went to get their coats. Craig and Liv removed the two leaves from the table and returned them to the hall closet where they were stored.

Suddenly, Liv clutched her stomach and doubled over. She made it to the sink just in time to vomit into one of the stock pots her mother had just washed.

Yuk.

Immediately, Mama Peterson went into action, pulling Liv's hair back into a rubber band to get it out of the way. Next, she ran a clean dishtowel under warm water and handed it to her daughter along with a trash can, then pressed the back of her hand against Liv's forehead.

"No temperature," she declared. "Anyone else sick?"

Craig texted the departing guests, but no one else reported gastrointestinal issues.

After putting Liv on one of the kitchen stools, Emma reached under the sink and pulled out the first aid box. She kept it well stocked for patching family members up from various fishing-related accidents. She had everything in there from hydrogen peroxide to ace bandages to splints for broken arms. There was even a hydrocortisone tablet or two left from unused prescriptions. No pain pill was ever wasted in the Peterson household.

"Food poisoning?" Roxy asked, sounding concerned.

"No, food poisoning takes several hours to show itself," Emma said, somewhat defensively. "Whatever this is, it's not that."

She continued to root around in the box until she found the thermometer. Before she could dip it in rubbing alcohol, Liv bolted for the bathroom, trash can in hand, her body determined to rid itself of every last morsel of food by whatever orifice provided the shortest route out. Violent, audible explosions could be heard by everyone in the room.

Poor Liv.

Craig's second thought was less generous—*Hope none of us get it*—followed by a realization that the crab derby wouldn't stop for a sick crew member. The *Freya* was ready to go. They had to be out on the water as early as possible tomorrow morning if they were going to grab their share of crab. Without Liv, he would have to manage with a two-man crew.

Liv opened the door of the bathroom, looking pale and shaky, "Don't worry, Craig, I'm sure I'll be okay once I empty ou—" Before she could finish the sentence, she slammed the door and continued retching.

Emma came into the living room, drying her hands on a clean dishtowel. She'd cleaned up the mess in the kitchen sink. "That girl's not going anywhere, Craig. Can you manage out there tomorrow?"

No one even suggested the *Freya* stay in harbor, even though they'd checked the weather station earlier and knew a big, winter storm was blowing in.

"We'll be okay," Craig said, although he didn't sound completely confident. "Doyle's solid—not as good as Liv—but good. I'll ask around to see if anyone decent shakes loose I can scoop up to fill in for Liv if she's going to be out very long."

17

oyle slid gratefully down into the scalding water. He had
boiled water on the stove to add to the tub so he'd have
enough hot water for a bath. He so needed this. Every inch of
him hurt.

It was Thursday and they'd been out for four days. Dropping
pots, pulling pots. Even with the help of the power-driven
winch that lifted them out of the water, each pot weighed 100
to 150 pounds. And each one had to be lifted by hand, emptied,
rebaited, and tossed back out—as fast as humanly possible—in
whatever weather mother nature decided to throw their way.
Last night she'd served up rain, sleet, twenty-foot waves and
biting, freezing winds.

His face felt numb, and he almost couldn't see in front
of his face to sort the crab. Male crabs measuring at least five
and three-quarters inches across the back were thrown into the
refrigerated hold down below. Females and small crabs were
tossed back into the ocean.

To keep up the twenty-four-hour schedule, they did a simple
crew rotation, spelling each other at night every few hours. They
got a few additional hours of rest when traveling from one line
to another to check pots that had been soaking.

At those times, one person could handle the deck while the others went below, grabbed something to eat and a few hours sleep. As captain, Craig stayed in the warm wheelhouse with the computer and maps, but he came out to help if needed.

He and Liv had the *Freya* reloaded with bait and made sure everything was ready to go back out in the morning. Mrs. Peterson, Liv and Craig's mother, was making a big family dinner tonight—crab, of course—so Doyle parted ways with them at the dock. All he wanted to do was sleep.

Saturday, Craig had spent the night on the boat, but he and Roxy seem to have made up sometime over the last few days, because when they'd pulled in Tuesday, she had been there to meet the boat, all smiles. She even remembered to drop off a pair of new work boots Craig had ordered for him on Amazon when he noticed Doyle's old ones were barely staying on his feet.

Craig hadn't said if they were a gift or a loan, so Doyle didn't know if they were coming out of his pay, but he didn't care. They made a world of difference on a pitching, icy deck.

Tougher than he was three years ago—muscles hardened, and soft midsection melted away—Doyle held his own on the *Freya*, but by the end of the day, he still felt every one of the ten years he had on Liv and Craig. He didn't see very many deckhands over forty. It was definitely a young man's game.

Slipping further down into the water until his head was submerged, he mentally counted this week's earnings.

Even at $2.50 a pound, his take for this trip out was $15,400. That would help replenish his anemic bank account. And when the check cleared and he had half a minute, he was going grocery shopping.

The crab would start thinning out in a few weeks, so that was five, maybe six trips . . . his share would be 8 percent . . . Craig had promised to bump it up to 10 percent now that he had more experience but said with the low price of crab this year, 8 percent was already stretching it. So even if they only made five trips out, or had a couple lighter loads, he'd gross at least $75,000. After taxes and living expenses . . . he might clear $30,000. He needed a lot more than that.

He could do people's taxes online, but tax season was right in the middle of crab season, so that wasn't happening. There had to be a way to make more money, faster.

Interrupting his thoughts, his cell phone, an older model iPhone Tim Pullman had given him as a bonus when he crewed on the *Sara Lynn* two years ago, started ringing and dancing across the bathroom counter where he'd left it. Doyle caught it just before it landed in the toilet. He answered it as he got out of his bath and toweled off. Since he'd been disowned by his sister and his mother and he wasn't exactly a social butterfly, he knew it had to be work.

It was.

"Doyle," Craig said. "I'm calling to give you a heads up. Liv's got some kind of bad flu bug, so it'll be just the three of us tomorrow unless she feels better in the morning."

"Is she okay?" Doyle asked.

The thought of Liv being sick was very upsetting. Liv was never sick. It wasn't just that they had established an easy rhythm working together—setting and pulling pots—but he had come to think of her as a friend.

"Oh, yeah," Craig said. "She'll be fine. It's probably just a twenty-four-hour bug."

Craig sounded worried, too, in spite of reassuring Doyle. "I was just calling to make sure you're there on time tomorrow. We leave at five."

Doyle had never been late, but he didn't take Craig's reminder personally. He knew how critical these first few weeks of crab season were.

"Don't worry, I'll be there," he said.

He didn't even bother asking if Roxy was going to help. Roxy didn't know aft from stern on any boat. Besides, she might break a nail.

18

After his bath, Doyle polished off the last TV dinner and dropped into bed. He was deep asleep in seconds. Even with only five hours of shuteye, he woke before his alarm and was at the *Freya* by 4:30 a.m., feeling surprisingly rested.

Craig was already in the wheelhouse, eyes glued to his laptop, checking conditions and deciding where to drop the rest of the pots this morning. Both men glanced at the darkening sky in the west, hoping to be across the bar before the storm arrived so they wouldn't get stuck in the harbor.

A 150-mile-wide storm was about to make good on its threat. They needed to get out—and hopefully back in—before it hit. Several other fishing vessels were already over the bar.

Doyle went below to stow his gear, reminding himself to thank Craig again for the new boots. When he came back, the other two crew members, Lonnie and Sean, came on board and Craig was talking to another guy. He could only see him from the back. Something about the way he stood reminded Doyle of the men he'd met in prison at the lower end of the pecking order. Sort of cowed.

Dark-blonde—or maybe just dirty—hair curled out from beneath the man's dark blue wool beanie. Hunched against the cold, his hands stuffed in the pockets of a North Face jacket that had seen better days, he didn't inspire confidence. A duffel bag lay at his feet.

Craig shook hands with the man, then with an eye to the charcoal-smudged horizon behind him, made hurried introductions.

"Everyone, this is Søren, off the *Sea Gypsy*. He'll be our bait guy until Liv gets back. Show him where he can stow his gear, then I want all of you back up here *tout suite*. Go ahead and cut her free, Lonnie, let's go catch some *crab*!"

With that, Craig went back into the wheelhouse, started the engine and when they were clear, pulled smoothly away from the dock, joining the other boats motoring toward the narrow channel between the jetties.

Doyle wondered why Søren wasn't on the *Sea Gypsy* anymore. It was rare for people to make a change during crab season. Had he been fired? If so, he doubted Craig would have hired him, even under these circumstances. Liv was only out temporarily.

The *Sea Gypsy* must be in for repairs, but there wasn't time to ask, nor would he. Minding his own business was a lesson he'd learned well in prison. Besides, the sky was getting darker by the minute. They didn't have time for idle chit chat.

Following the boss's orders, Doyle showed Søren where to put his bag, then everyone geared up and headed topside, grabbing donuts and thermoses of scalding, hot coffee on the way.

Doyle automatically reached out and tested a stack of pots as he passed to make sure they hadn't shifted. You didn't want to be top heavy. It didn't take much to unbalance and capsize a boat.

Last year, another fishing vessel only a little smaller than the *Freya* had gone down seven miles north of Newport. Of the four crew members on board, only one had survived, and he was so badly injured he was now confined to a wheelchair.

Because the wreckage was spotted by another fishing vessel shortly after it went down, the Coast Guard was able to respond quickly. They recovered the other three crew members' bodies before they drifted away, so at least their families had the small comfort of having their loved ones back, if only to bury them.

Doyle shook his head at the memory. No sense borrowing trouble. Stacking crab pots was an art and with a long crabbing history, the *Freya* had a five-hundred-pot crab permit, not all of them on deck at the same time, of course. They'd dropped most of their pots yesterday but still had about a hundred to drop today, so the deck was pretty crowded. Craig wanted all the pots fishing before they called it a night.

With the assistance of the Coast Guard and the outgoing tide, Craig got them across the bar ahead of the storm.

For the next few hours, they worked like dogs. In places that were fishing well, they dropped as many as fifty pots per string. Craig saved a few out to drop in an area he and his dad had fished before, hoping it still had a good, muddy ocean floor. It was several hours away, so by the time they set the test string, it was time to head back to see what they had in the pots they'd baited this morning.

They'd do crew rotations through the night if the weather held.

This morning's storm had blown off to the north, but another, larger one darkened the horizon and was moving their way, fast. Craig advised everyone to go below, get dinner, and rest up while they could.

Lonnie, the block guy, turned out to be a pretty decent cook. He fried up a platter of pork chops and put sour cream as well as butter in the mashed potatoes. After several helpings, Doyle was stuffed but made room for one of Emma Peterson's monster chocolate chip cookies. So much better than stale Cheerios.

Sean ran a plate up to Craig and relieved him for a few minutes so he could use the head. He offered to give him a longer break, but Craig laughed and said he'd sleep when he was dead. With a storm coming in, they assumed he probably didn't trust anyone else to pilot the *Freya*. It was his boat, after all.

19

Whatever the reason, the crew was grateful for the brief respite. They lowered the lights and within minutes everyone was either sleeping or on their phone. After helping Sean clean up, Doyle lay on his bunk and closed his eyes. For now, the weather was holding, so they'd start crew rotations when they got to the first string. Better catch some sleep now, while he could. He was second up, right after Søren.

Soon, the low rumbling of the engine and rhythmic lapping of water against the sides of the boat began to lull him to sleep. As Doyle drifted off, thoughts of a certain woman entered his dreams. A certain beautiful, unattainable woman.

Women like that deserved the best and being a Peterson, this one already had everything. What could he possibly offer her? Until he had the money to start his business, absolutely nothing. The thought depressed him immensely. At this rate, it was going to take forever to save enough money to just start his business, let alone have anything to offer his dream woman.

He punched his pillow. He needed to win the lottery. Of course, in order to win, he'd have to play, and he never wasted his money. He lay awake, staring at the ceiling, but soon exhaustion overtook him, and he dropped into a deep and dreamless sleep.

2:57 A.M.

Doyle woke with a start on a hard, wet surface, being assaulted by freezing wind and rain. Before he could make any sense of these sensations, a gush of water barreled into him, sweeping him—and everything else that wasn't nailed down—across the deck into the sea. He was saved at the last minute by some rope tangled around his legs.

He tried to get up, but a sharp stab of pain on the right side of his head, accompanied by a wave of nausea, made that a bad idea. He only managed to roll over and throw up most of his dinner. Furious winds kept him pinned to the deck, whipping salt crystals into his eyes. Laying still for a few minutes, he forced his freezing fingers to get a grip on the rope. Hand-over-hand, he slowly pulled himself toward the wheelhouse.

He couldn't see anyone else but did see the block swinging wildly off the rail, an empty crab pot dangling off the end.

Doyle felt the side of his head. His hand came away bloody. The last thing he remembered he had come up on deck to relieve Søren. Where was Søren?

The light from the wheelhouse pierced the darkness above him. He screwed his eyes open and shut a few times, trying to make them focus, but it was still mostly a blur.

It looked like Craig was yelling into the ship's radio, while desperately attempting to turn the boat and steer it into an oncoming wall of water. Doyle stared, stunned. It was like watching a silent disaster movie in slow motion.

Forcing his limbs to work together, Doyle inched his way toward the door. Suddenly, it was wrenched open. Someone untangled him from the rope and dragged him in. Immediately, he was flooded with warmth and sound. It was as if someone has turned off the mute button. His rescuer had gone back to the radio. Panicked shouting filled the small space.

LOST AND FOUND

"*. . . Yes*, this is this *Freya . . .* the captain . . . Craig Peterson . . . overboard . . . no, I can't see him. I can't see *anything* but huge goddamned waves! *. . .*"

Ninety-mile-an-hour winds pinned the door shut, essentially trapping both he and Søren inside. They could only hope that Lonnie and Sean were still down below. They watched helplessly as the awesome power of the sea hurled everything it had at the *Freya*, tossing her around like a flimsy, toy boat. All they could do was hunker down and ride it out.

Even the coasties couldn't help them now.

20

SATURDAY MORNING, JANUARY 21

PACIFIC MARITIME HERITAGE CENTER

NEWPORT, OR

After refilling her coffee mug from the catering urn, Logan joined Sam at a table in front of the large, bay windows of the Pacific Maritime Heritage Center. It was the first time either of them sat down in the last couple of hours. The Newport Fishermen's Wives, unfortunately very familiar with organizing such events, had swung into action last night to support friends and family waiting for news or actively out on the water, assisting the Coast Guard in the search. The room was filled with food, radios, and lots of hugging.

Most of them had been up all night. Logan wondered if any of them would get any sleep today. Probably not. Not with one of their own missing at sea.

Even though she and Ben couldn't help directly with the search, when Sam called, they came to do what they could.

When they got the call, Ben had just finished making and freezing another week of meals for the *Sara Lynn*, so they had those to donate to the cause. He was down at the dock, now, delivering the packages to Tim.

Logan and Sam reported to the Heritage Center to help serve breakfast just as a catering crew began setting up chafing dishes of scrambled eggs, sausage, and bacon for everyone, along with a waffle station for the kids. It being a Saturday, there were quite a few preschoolers and toddlers underfoot, blissfully unaware they were supposed to be sad. All too familiar with the dangers their fathers faced on the water every day, older children and teens were more subdued.

Looking out the window, Logan couldn't tell which boat was the *Sara Lynn*, but the Coast Guard must have cleared the bar, because several boats that had been waiting were now heading out. It was a beautiful sight, their prows slicing the silky blue water, motoring smoothly beneath a pale winter sky. Not a breath of wind.

Such a contrast with last night's storm. Winds up to eighty miles per hour in Depoe Bay had knocked down an old shore pine in town and sent it crashing through the window of one of the tourist shops. And it had still been dark and nasty out when she and Ben got on the road earlier this morning. Logan had to drive carefully to avoid hitting downed branches and other detritus on the highway.

But looking out on the harbor now, it was like the storm had never happened.

Everyone wanted to get out earlier but had to wait until the Coast Guard assigned search areas and cleared the bar.

In addition to being there to support the search effort, Sam was on the job. She would post an online story today, then a more complete version would come out in the weekly print edition on Wednesday. She filled Logan in on what they knew so far from the rough draft on her computer.

LOST AND FOUND

At 12:47 a.m., a distress call came into the Coast Guard over VHF radio—emergency channel 16—from the Freya. *Søren Vestergaard, a crew member, reported their captain, Craig Peterson, went overboard in the storm. They were able to return to Newport safely, but it wasn't until the early morning hours that the storm abated enough for the* Freya *to limp back across the bar into port. All remaining crew members on board were safe and accounted for.*

According to crew member Lonnie Jacobsen, the Freya *had been coming back to check on the majority of their pots from setting a test string several hours away. The captain began crew rotations, with the majority of the crew sent below to rest while they could.*

According to temporary crewman, Søren Vestergaard, he was on deck when the winter storm that had been brewing all day overtook them and Captain Craig Peterson was swept overboard.

One crew member, thirty-eight-year-old Doyle Jefferson, was also on deck at the time, but had been knocked unconscious. When they returned to port, Jefferson was treated for a head injury, but is expected to make a full recovery.

Currently, the Coast Guard SAR unit has been activated, drafting search patterns, coordinating all vessels, volunteer and official. Local operations unit has deployed forty-seven-foot motor lifeboats (MLBs) and a SAR helicopter was on its way.

Experienced in these types of emergencies, Newport Fishermen's Wives immediately activated their phone tree and set up an ersatz command center at the Pacific Maritime Heritage Center. It is unknown how long the search will last.

While Sam went back to her computer to finish and post her story, Logan arched her back and stretched, looking up. She hadn't noticed it before, but remnants of sheer, white chiffon streamers were draped in a starburst pattern from the ceiling—probably left over from a recent wedding. The incongruity struck her. If only these walls could talk. This room must have seen its share of both joyful and tragic gatherings over the years.

She fervently hoped this gathering had a happy ending.

Finally, Sam hit send and closed her laptop, reaching for her coffee with one hand, pushing her cat-eye glasses up on her nose with the other. Since her nose was as diminutive as the rest of her, this was a constant battle.

Logan handed her the sugar, then leaned in and voiced the question that had been on her mind.

"What are Craig's chances? How long can someone last out there?"

Sam shrugged, "Depends on a lot of factors. Water temperature, what he was wearing, if he was injured when he went in . . . tides, currents . . ." She took a sip of coffee and looked out to sea, then added quietly, "Unless someone spots him soon, not long."

"Did anyone see him go in? Do they know if he was injured?" Logan asked. "Is that why he fell?"

"No, not as far as anyone knows. Lonnie and Sean were down below in their bunks——Doyle and Søren, the other two, were on deck. Doyle—the man you sort of met the other day—he was the one who got knocked out, and Søren, a new guy they brought on to cover for Liv, was the one who sent out the distress call on the radio. Neither of them actually saw Craig go in the water.

"My contact at Yaquina was the one who took the call. He said no one really knows what happened. One minute, Søren said he saw Craig standing on deck, the next, he was in the ocean."

"Why was Craig on deck?" Logan asked. "And where was Doyle?"

She assumed the captain would stay at the wheel during a storm, steering the boat or manning the radio or doing whatever it was a captain did to get his boat and crew home safely.

"Don't know," Sam said. "Doyle says he came up to relieve Søren and do his shift, then must have gotten knocked down in the storm and hit his head on the deck. Craig was already gone when he came to. Maybe they'll figure it out later, but right now, all efforts are being focused on the search."

They watched as a red dot approaching from the south turned into a Coast Guard rescue helicopter that turned right and headed out to sea over the tops of the search vessels.

Sitting back, Sam spotted Ben over Logan's shoulder. She pointed him toward the food, indicating he should get a plate first, which he did before walking over and pulling up a chair next to Logan.

"How'd it go?" Logan asked. "Did Tim get out okay?"

"Yep," he said. "Fully fueled and stocked. They're on their way. He says they'll stay out as long as they can, searching, until either the weather turns, or they need to refuel."

"And now we wait," Sam said.

21

Søren slid onto his favorite barstool and ordered a shot of tequila. It felt great to be on land, warm and dry. For five days he'd been out on the water, freezing his butt off, but finally the Coast Guard called off the search.

The bartender delivered his shot.

Toasting himself in the mirror, he tossed it back, then ordered his usual.

Tuesdays were slow, so he got his whiskey right away. He took a long pull and set the glass back down. He could afford something off the top shelf but asked for Jack Daniels out of habit. Next time. Besides, he wasn't rich yet. Not as rich as he was going to be.

Søren smiled and flagged down the bartender to bring him another drink. He wet his finger and ran it around the top of his glass like he'd seen James Bond do in one of those movies.

It was time to part ways with the *Sea Gypsy*. He'd learned long ago not to be greedy. Greedy was how you got caught. Never do the same job twice. Besides, the pay hadn't been that good, especially compared with the penalty if they'd been caught.

No, it was time to move on. He'd thoroughly enjoyed his romps with Roxy, but she was getting a little long in the tooth. As soon as he'd helped her spend all of her dead husband's money, he'd find the next rich bitch. She shouldn't have any complaints. He gave her her money's worth.

Again, just being careful. Pigs get fed; hogs get slaughtered. Words to live by. His needs were simple. Once he was in Vegas, there were many, many opportunities for someone like him. He was beginning to see where his talents lie.

Just then, a thin blonde walked in and hiked herself onto the stool two down from him. Purple lipstick; tight, fake leather pants. Sparkly top; ratty jacket. Somewhere between thirty and dead. She looked rode hard and put away wet.

The woman lowered her eyes and gave him her best come hither look, exposing tobacco-stained teeth in a practiced smile. There was a black hole where one of her molars should have been.

Meth addict.

Throwing a twenty down to cover his tab, Søren pulled on his jacket and jerked his head toward the door, as if to take her up on her thinly-veiled offer.

She slid off her stool to follow, but Søren leaned down and whispered in her ear as he walked by, "You really hit the ugly wall at ninety, didn't you, sweetheart?"

He laughed all the way out the door.

Awkwardly pulling together the last shreds of her dignity, the woman climbed back onto the stool.

The bartender brought her a free drink.

22

NEWSTIMES
"NEWPORT FISHERMAN LOST AT SEA"
JANUARY 25
SAMANTHA BADGER

Late Tuesday evening, the Coast Guard announced it had suspended the four-day search for Craig Peterson, captain and owner of the F/V *Freya,* who went missing last Friday night at sea and is presumed dead.

According to surviving crew member Søren Vestergaard, who was on deck at the time, the captain was swept overboard sometime between midnight and 1:00 a.m. Friday, January 20 during high-wave, winter storm conditions, 15 miles west of Newport, Oregon, on their second trip of the 2023 crab season.

"The decision to suspend an active search and rescue case is never made easily," said Yani Blevins, Yaquina Bay Coast Guard Search and Rescue Program Manager. "Multiple factors are carefully considered before making that call. We will of course immediately resume the search if any credible information that Craig Peterson has been located is received."

"Our hearts are aching for the family at this very sad and difficult time. These men are like family to each and every one of us at the Yaquina Bay station. We know how dangerous it is out there. It's like we've lost one of our own."

Craig Peterson came from a long line of commercial fishermen here in Newport. He grew up on the *Freya* and after proving himself over the years, had recently taken over as captain from his father, Walt Peterson, who was in turn trained by his father-in-law, Lars, one of the many Scandinavian and Scotch-Irish immigrants to the area who established the commercial fishing community here on the central Oregon coast. The sixty-four-foot F/V *Freya* was named after Lars' wife, *Freya* Bjørkland.

A memorial service for Craig Peterson will be held this Sunday, January 29, at 1:00 p.m. at the Gladys Valley Marine Studies Building at 2030 Marine Science Drive, Newport, Oregon.

*****

OBITUARY

Craig Lars Peterson, 32, of Newport, Oregon passed away Friday, January 20, 2023, when he was swept overboard in a winter storm and lost at sea.

Born in 1991 in Newport, Oregon to Emma and Walter Peterson, he was born and raised on the tall tales of his grandfather, Lars, around the Peterson dinner table. Craig was a hard worker. He and his younger sister, Liv, could be found cleaning fish and baiting pots from the time they were "knee high to a grasshopper," said his mother.

Survived by his wife, Roxy Peterson, his sister, Livia Peterson, and both his parents, Walt and Emma Peterson, Craig's final resting place is at sea.

"He died doing what he loved," his sister said, "and will be missed by many."

A memorial service will be held Sunday, January 29 at 1:00 p.m. at the Pacific Maritime Heritage Center at 333 SE Bay Blvd, Newport, Oregon. In lieu of flowers, the family requests all donations go to the Newport Fisherman's Wives who do so much to support and sustain our fishing community families.

Craig Peterson's name will also be added to the Fisherman's Memorial Sanctuary plaque in Yaquina Bay State Park and along Fisherman's Memorial Walk located in the Bayfront District.

23

WEDNESDAY, JANUARY 25

Doyle wiped the steam off the bathroom mirror and checked his head wound. They'd put Steri-Strips on it and it looked like it was healing. He couldn't remember what they told him about washing it or keeping it dry, but after four days, he had taken a chance and soaped it up in the shower. It looked okay, but he should probably get some rubbing alcohol or something. He couldn't afford for it to get infected. Doctors were expensive.

He sighed. He couldn't afford much of anything right now. He had some savings, but he needed to get with another boat and soon. Rent was due in a week, and he needed groceries. He was even low on peanut butter. He'd have to get to the store today.

Drying off quickly, he threw on some clothes and went into the kitchen area for a glass of water. It was mid-week, so most of his neighbors were at work. Still, it wasn't exactly quiet. Whoever built the Orchard Palace Apartments had not spent a lot on insulation. The walls weren't exactly what you'd call soundproof.

Sitting at his kitchen table, he tried to concentrate. He needed to remember what had happened on the *Freya*. But his memories of that night were still confusing. He tried to put together the series of events.

The first day out had been a good fishing day. They'd filled up fast with meaty crab, gone in, unloaded, then Craig sent everyone home to rest up for the next day. He'd gone back to the apartment and Craig and Liv went to their annual family dinner.

Later that night, Craig called to tell him they were going to be short-handed because Liv had the flu or something, and to be sure and get there on time.

Wincing at the morning light coming in the window, Doyle squeezed his eyes shut to focus, which made his head hurt. He'd gone over this in his mind so many times already, but he took it slow and tried to visualize everything as it had happened.

When he got to the *Freya* that morning, Craig had managed to find a new guy, Søren, to sub for Liv. He put him on bait until she got back. The rest of the day was uneventful. They had a pretty good haul and were headed back to check on the pots they'd dropped that morning.

Craig stayed in the wheelhouse and started crew rotations, telling everyone to rest up while they could. Søren was up first, then Doyle, then Lonnie and Sean. Lonnie made dinner and then they all settled in for the ride back.

Then . . . that's where the playback of his memory stopped. He remembered laying down and drifting off to sleep, then the next thing he remembered was waking up on deck in the middle of a raging storm and a huge wave almost sweeping him into the ocean. If it hadn't been for Søren, he'd have gone over for sure.

No one else was on deck, so Craig must have just gone over. After pulling him inside the wheelhouse, Søren was on the radio calling the Coast Guard for help. You couldn't see anything in those conditions, let alone get anywhere near a man in the water without running over him or getting everyone else killed by one of those monster waves. The Coast Guard told them to come back to port, which they managed to do.

The next morning, after the storm passed, the Coast Guard started organizing everyone down at the docks, but when Doyle had finally felt steady enough to go down to the *Freya* to join the search, Walt Peterson cut him off and told him curtly his help wasn't needed.

He hoped Mr. Peterson would tell Liv he had at least offered to help in the search.

Doyle had been raised with the Mary Poppins admonition 'Never complain, never explain,' so he didn't bother to tell Mr. Peterson he would have been there earlier, but he couldn't hardly stand up without getting dizzy and falling down. Besides, he needed to cut the man some slack. His son was missing at sea. He had enough on his plate.

*****

A short, staccato knock broke into Doyle's gloomy thoughts. Opening the door, he was surprised to see Søren standing outside with a six-pack of beer in one hand and a McDonald's bag in the other.

"Hey," Søren said. "I came by to see how you're doin'. You gonna let me in or am I gonna have to drink this beer all by myself?"

Doyle stood aside to let him in.

He was afraid to ask why Søren was here and not out on the *Freya*, searching for Craig. Maybe they'd just brought the *Freya* back in to refuel.

Along with the beer, Søren had brought breakfast. It was only nine o'clock, so Doyle passed on the beer but ate the Egg McMuffin and hash brown patty gratefully. He hadn't realized he was so hungry.

"How's your head? You seemed pretty confused when the EMTs were working on you, and you sure weren't making any sense in the wheelhouse. You were hit pretty bad. How'd you get hit, anyway?"

"I don't know," Doyle said. "All I remember is waking up on deck. Thanks for pulling me in, by the way."

"That was nothin'," Søren said. "You're one lucky son-of-a-bitch, though. That was some storm!"

The thought floated in the air between them that Craig had not been so lucky.

Finally, Doyle worked up the nerve to ask.

"Have they found him yet?"

"No," Søren said, putting down his beer. "The Coast Guard called off the search last night. They have some kind of formula. When they plug in all the numbers, like time missing, water temperature, currents, stuff like that, it tells them when to quit."

Damn. Doyle hadn't been close to Craig, but he was a good guy. And now he was gone. Just like that.

"How's Liv taking it?" Doyle asked.

"I wasn't there when she got the news, but she's okay, I guess," he said. "Once the Coast Guard called off the search, we came back in. The *Freya's* in port for a few days. She's helping her parents with the memorial service."

"When is it?"

"Sunday, I think," Søren said. "Liv said she will have all of our checks ready by Saturday. We can stop by any time after 2:00 p.m. to pick them up. She'll be at the house."

Søren asked if he could use the bathroom, then left Doyle with the rest of his day. Doyle forgot to ask him when the *Freya* was going back out again, or if it was. At the earliest, he assumed probably not until the thirtieth, the Monday after the memorial service.

24

Cindy saw her boss pull up out front and quickly threw her gum in the trash. She hadn't expected her boss to come in today—the memorial service for her husband was tomorrow.

Roxy was driving her Range Rover. Nice car. Cindy didn't have a car yet. She only worked part-time, so her mom usually dropped her off, but if it was a nice day, she lived close enough she could walk.

The bell over the door jangled when the boss came in. No one else was in the store. Of course, it was early yet, but really, it was never very busy. Sometimes they'd go a whole day and never see one customer. She wondered how they stayed in business.

"Hi, Mrs. Peterson," Cindy said, "what are you doing here? You didn't have to come in today. I can cover the store until after tomorrow. I don't mind at all."

"Oh, I know you can handle things, Cindy, and thank you," Roxy said, putting her purse on the counter. "But I haven't been able to come in much this week and I wanted to get you your paycheck."

"I wouldn't have minded if you just mailed it," Cindy said. "I would have understood." Usually her boss wasn't so considerate, but Cindy was getting low on money, so she didn't protest further.

From the drawer under the register Roxy pulled out the business checkbook. Placing it on the counter, she started filling it out. "I'm putting a little overtime pay in here, Cindy. I appreciate you filling in for me this week. It's been a little crazy . . ."

"Oh, I know, Mrs. Peterson," she said. "I'm so sorry . . . my mom said to tell you that if you need anything, the Fishermen's Wives are there to help."

Roxy nodded her thanks, finished writing the check briskly, then tore it out and handed it to Cindy.

"I'm not sure what the schedule will be next week," she said. "Everything is kind of up in the air right now. I'll call you."

She put the checkbook back in the drawer, glanced around the store at the displays with a critical eye—that's more like her usual self, Cindy thought, worried she hadn't stacked the t-shirts well enough. Mrs. Peterson liked them exactly centered on the tables.

A series of muffled dings sounded from within Roxy's voluminous leather purse. She fished her phone out and looked at the screen, then stumbled over to the stool and sat down, laying the phone on the counter like she never wanted to touch it again, like it was contagious with some dread disease or something.

Cindy just stood and stared.

Wow, was her tough-as-nails boss *crying*?

"Mrs. Peterson!" Cindy said, finally rousing herself. "What happened? What's wrong?"

Roxy shook her head, then reached for a tissue and blew her nose.

"I'm sorry, Cindy," she said. closing her eyes. "I thought I could handle this. I just want him to leave me alone."

LOST AND FOUND

Cindy's backbone straightened. The oldest of five children, she knew how to take charge when someone needed help. She picked up the phone, half expecting her boss to object, but Mrs. Peterson just sat there, limp.

"Here," she said. "Let me see."

She scrolled up but couldn't find the beginning of the text thread. Except for an occasional "Leave me alone!" reply from Mrs. Peterson, the entire thread was rapid-fire, rambling, and one-sided.

". . . Call me! Why won't you call me back? . . . I LOVE you! Haven't I proved that? . . . I did this for US . . . for YOU! I know u love me too! . . . what do I have to do? Answer me!"

"How long have you been getting these messages, Mrs. Peterson?" Cindy asked.

"Two . . . three weeks," Roxy said.

"Do you recognize the number? Do you know who it is?" she asked.

"No," she said. "I don't recognize that number."

Cindy heard the hesitation in her boss's voice. She'd heard the same tone often enough from her younger siblings when they were trying to hide something.

"But you do know who's sending these, don't you?" she said. "It's gotta be the same guy—the one you caught sneaking around your house."

Roxy looked away. "Well, probably, but I'm not sure," she said. "It was dark, and I didn't get a good look at him. I don't want to get him into trouble if it's not him. I just don't know what to do."

"Well, I do," Cindy said. "You need to call the police. I read somewhere where guys like this don't stop. When they obsess about a woman it gets worse, not better. I mean, when you look at it all together, it looks pretty bad."

"I know," Roxy said. "I know. I just can't think straight. First the prowler . . . he was right outside our bedroom window!

Then losing Craig, then these texts. I get them night and day. I use this number for work, but I'm going to have to go down to Verizon next week and get it changed. I just can't handle this right now."

"You know that's not enough, Mrs. Peterson," Cindy said. "I mean, what if he gets really mad and comes after you? You need to tell the police. Let them protect you. You need to file a restraining order on him. My cousin had to do that when her husband got crazy jealous and tried to beat down her door when she locked him out. They had to replace the door."

"It's just that Doyle has a record," Roxy said. "Craig took pity on him and hired him even though I told him not to—I haven't told anyone—I figured everyone deserves a second chance, a clean slate. He served his time, but, well, Doyle is a convicted felon."

"OMG!" Cindy said.

"I know. I can't believe Craig hired him, but he was always helping someone out, giving them a job, teaching them. I just accepted that, so I tried to treat Doyle the same as anyone else. I am always nice to everyone on the boat, but I guess my being nice to Doyle backfired. He must have taken it the wrong way, twisted it in that criminal mind of his.

"I should have told the police, but I am pretty sure it was his face I saw that night outside my window. But I wasn't 100 percent positive and well, Craig liked him, said he was a good worker. The *Freya* was going back out the next day and he needed every crew member on that run."

She grabbed another tissue from the box on the counter.

"I should have said something, but I didn't want to be the bitch everyone says I am! They all hate me, especially Emma, Craig's mom! No one understands how hard it is to be a woman in business. You *have* to be tough! Men are tough and they're praised out the wazoo! If a woman gets ahead . . . well, we're all harpies!"

LOST AND FOUND

Roxy dissolved into tears again, totally breaking down.

Cindy, emboldened by her boss's new vulnerability and the fact that she had confided in her, put her arm around Roxy's shoulder and said, "You need to tell the police. It's the right thing to do. Do you want me to call?"

25

Not wanting to be too late or too early, Doyle showed up at the Peterson residence right at two o'clock Saturday afternoon. Since the *Freya* had been docked last week while the family prepared for Craig's memorial service, he'd taken Tim Pullman up on his offer to crew for the *Sara Lynn* for a few days.

Tim's right-hand man, Francis, was out hurt. It was good to work with Tim again. The pay wasn't as good, but it was better than nothing, which is what he would have earned staying in his apartment all week, listening to Wheel of Fortune through the walls with the deaf guy.

He'd seen in the paper that the memorial service for Craig was tomorrow. He was sure the family still had last minute preparations for that. They may even have out of town family coming in, although Liv had never mentioned any relatives who didn't live right there in Newport.

He was startled out of his thoughts when Walt Peterson yanked open the door. "Oh, it's you," he said. "Wait here, I'll get Liv."

Surprised to be left standing on the doorstep, Doyle hadn't quite wrapped his head around Walt's attitude when Liv appeared at the door.

She looked tired. She gave him a warm smile, but instead of inviting him in, she stepped outside. Shutting the door behind her, she handed him an envelope. Lowering her voice, she said, "I'm sorry, Doyle, but this is the last check. You're going to have to find another place, another boat."

Doyle took the envelope, folded it, and put it into his pocket.

"Oh, okay," he said, a little confused. "Are they grounding the *Freya* for a while out of respect for Craig?"

"No," she said, looking very uncomfortable. "It's not that. It's our business. We have to fish. We're going out first thing Monday, but Dad doesn't want you on the boat."

Doyle let that sink in for a minute.

"For now . . . ," she added quickly. "I'm trying to work things out on this end, but I just wanted to tell you as soon as possible you'll need to find other work . . . for now."

Doyle's face burned. He couldn't bring himself to look Liv in the eye.

Of course. His past come to haunt him again.

He had always been upfront. He hadn't hidden anything. He told Tim and then Craig about his felony conviction, and he knew Liv knew, but maybe Craig hadn't told his parents. Maybe Walt Peterson hadn't known his son hired a convicted felon. Maybe he had gone through Craig's business paperwork this week and just found out.

Not wanting to prolong the agony of this mortifying conversation, Doyle thanked Liv for the check and walked away. He didn't even have a car to get into. He had to walk down the street like a drunk with a DUI. Might as well have a bicycle.

LOST AND FOUND

Whenever he saw a grown man on a bike not wearing neon spandex, he assumed it was someone whose license had been taken away.

When he finally let himself into his apartment, he was still shaking, but he forced himself to stop. After today, he was under no illusions his past would not continue to drop down like a huge boulder in his path whenever he tried to move forward.

But he couldn't change the past, so moving forward was his only option. Work like a dog and save money until he had enough to start his business and work for himself, where no one could look down on him. At least Tim and Sam trusted him. He'd give Tim a call and see if he could still use a hand on Monday.

26

Walking into the Gladys Valley Marine Studies Building, Logan felt like she was back in college. Spacious and modern, the GVMS was all glass and open spaces, with ocean-themed murals and a scattering of low open seating options near the elevators, taking full advantage of the location near the harbor.

She wished they were there for a happier occasion.

Following the signs for the memorial service, she and Ben found their way to the auditorium and joined a group of people funneling in at one of the doors. An usher handed them a two-page printed program as they went in.

Scanning the room, Logan spotted Sam four rows up. Waving, Sam pointed at a couple of seats between her and the aisle she had saved for them. Tim was on her other side, reading his program.

They took their seats and Logan looked over the crowd. Most of the room was filled and more people were still arriving. It seemed the entire fishing community was in attendance. Several generations were represented, with quite a few young families. All had the solid look of people who worked for a living and much of that outdoors.

Some looked like they'd just come in off their boats, others fresh from church. It being Sunday, Logan hadn't been sure what to wear, so opted for a pair of black slacks, a dark green turtleneck, and low-heeled boots.

Someone flicked the lights and the remaining people quickly found seats. Down in the front row, Logan recognized Roxy's cap of platinum blonde hair. She assumed the two older people on Roxy's left were Craig's parents, Walt and Emma. Mr. Peterson sat staring straight ahead. Beside him, his wife was crying softly.

At her mother's other side, a young woman with shoulder-length, light brown hair was handing Emma tissues as needed. Sam whispered that that was Liv, Craig's sister. She hadn't been on the boat when her brother went overboard because she'd been too sick to go out that day.

Logan felt for all of them, but particularly the mom. She couldn't imagine losing Amy. The very thought made her tear up. Ben gave her shoulders a squeeze. Ben had no children but had a sixth sense when it came to Logan. He always knew the right thing to do.

Taunette Dixon, president of Newport Fishermen's Wives, walked up to the podium and waited for everyone to settle. Her confident, calm presence did the job. She started by thanking everyone for coming and conveying the family's deepest gratitude for the valiant efforts of the Coast Guard and all the friends and family who either had a boat out on the water or supported the search for Craig from home. She then introduced Pastor Terry Buchanon of the Resurrection Lutheran Church, who at the family's request would be leading the service.

To the right of the podium, propped on an easel, a poster of a smiling Craig Peterson beamed out at the group of friends and family who had gathered to honor him. The candid shot was obviously cropped from a larger photo of him at the helm of the *Freya*. It was the same photo as the one on the cover of the program.

LOST AND FOUND

Several large flower arrangements were grouped along the front and sides of the podium. After a short summary of the disaster at sea that took Craig's life, Pastor Terry invited everyone to bow their heads and join him in prayer, asking comfort for the family and safety for all those continuing to go out in this winter weather to make their living and support their families.

Lights were dimmed and a screen lowered to show a brief photo montage someone in the family had put together. Following a solo rendition of Amazing Grace by one of the Fisherman's wives, Pastor Terry invited anyone who would like to share a *brief* memory of Craig to come forward and do so, keeping in mind how many of his friends and family may want to speak.

For the next twenty minutes people filed up to the mic. It seemed everyone in town had either gone to school with Craig or worked with him out on the water. There were stories of joy rides, good years, bad years, busted boats, and Walt's strict, but effective training on the *Freya*. Tim shared an underage drinking story, when he and Craig significantly depleted Walt's liquor supply one night when his folks had gone to visit Liv at her sixth grade science camp in the mountains.

Finally, it was the family's turn. Only Roxy came forward.

Gone was the brash, leather-clad dynamo Logan had seen barreling down the Bayfront a week ago, giving them the finger. Dressed in a subdued ensemble of modest black dress, dark grey jacket, opaque tights and plain boots, the widow stepped up to the mic, a wad of tissue gripped in her hand. She looked out at everyone with a pale face and red-rimmed eyes. Any makeup she'd started the day with had long since washed away. She started to speak, but nothing came out, so she cleared her throat and tried again.

The room got very quiet.

"This all feels very unreal, still. I can't believe he's gone, but Craig died doing what he loved. He loved the *Freya*, he loved fishing, and he loved his family. Like most of you, he did what he did for his family . . ." She paused for a minute to compose herself, then continued, "I just wish that we had been able to have a child before . . . before we lost him. Craig would have been a great father!"

Quietly sniffling, she made it back to her seat before burying her face in her hands. Several people nearby reached over to pat her shoulder or back as she took her seat.

The family did not.

27

On Monday morning, Logan stopped by the front office to pick up the files Abe Mitchner, the vice principal and the person in charge of tutoring, had promised to leave for her. Cheryl Meece, the school secretary, had the three manila folders ready to go.

After hearing how Cheryl's granddaughter, Rebecca, was doing in her first year participating in the Paralympics—she took second place in the slalom—Logan wished her the best of luck and promised to send another contribution to her GoFundMe site. She'd met the cheerful fifteen-year old last year and was impressed with her determination to not let the loss of her leg slow her down.

"How was Craig's memorial service?" Cheryl asked. "I just got back last night and couldn't make it."

Logan assured her it was very nice and gave her a brief rundown. Just then a parent came in who needed Cheryl's help, so they waved their goodbyes and said they'd catch up more later.

Tucking the student files under her arm, Logan left the office and headed down the main hall to her assigned room. The gauntlet of metal lockers immediately transported her to 1987, her junior year in high school. That's when Jack, the handsome jock who lettered in just about every sport, had zeroed in on the auburn-haired, straight-A math whiz/musician. He'd swept her off her feet and made sure every boy and man in fifty miles knew she was his. Jack always got what he wanted. She hadn't stood a chance.

Logan smiled at the memory. That shy young girl seemed so far away from who she was now.

Since the official tutoring center was currently being expanded and reconfigured, volunteer tutors were tucked in all over the campus, wherever enough space and a modicum of quiet could be found. Logan had been assigned a tiny room at the end of the main hall. Tucked between two classrooms, the seven-by-seven space had been used by a variety of speech therapists and school psychologists over the years.

No window and just large enough for a table, two chairs and a filing cabinet, Logan kind of liked it. The only thing it lacked was a caffeine machine, so she'd picked up a coffee maker at one of the outlet stores last week. It held pride of place on top of the two-drawer filing cabinet on her left.

She dropped her shoulder bag into the bottom drawer, pulling out a couple of mugs first. She didn't know if her tutees drank coffee, but assumed they did—at least if they were anything like Amy and her friends were at that age.

Her first student, Vanessa Pérez, was set to arrive in fifteen minutes.

Placing the three, blue file folders neatly along the left edge of her desk, she took a sip of coffee and opened Vanessa's.

Last year's school picture was stapled to the upper left-hand corner of the first form. Thick, dark brown hair fell straight, framing a warm face. Small gold studs and a simple, cross neck-lace were her only ornamentation. Logan liked that her smile, even though subtle, reached her eyes. The overall impression was of quiet strength.

Home address, no landline, but there was a cell phone number for the father. Lincoln County school records going back to kindergarten. Good grades, from what she could see. No red flags.

Before she could read the rest of her file, there was a knock on the open door. Other than cutting her hair so it just skimmed her shoulders, Vanessa looked much the same as her school picture. Adjusting her backpack, the young girl stepped halfway into the room.

"Is this tutoring?" she asked.

"Yes, temporary digs, but you're in the right place," Logan said. "I'm Ms. McKenna, one of the new volunteers, but you can call me Logan."

Vanessa gave her a respectful but appraising look.

Something about the girl looked familiar, then it came to her. "Hey, didn't I see you last week at the Maritime Center? You were part of the catering crew delivering breakfast for the search party volunteers, right?"

Vanessa said yes, it was one of her part-time jobs. She picked up a few hours here and there, working for the restaurant whenever her schedule would allow.

Small talk over, the girl got right to business.

"Do you know much about math?" she asked Logan. "I mean, most of the volunteers we get are great. They're pretty good with reading and grammar and things like that, but not very many can help me with math. Did they tell you what I'm working on?"

She sounded doubtful.

Logan smiled. She liked this girl already.

"Nope," she said, "but why don't you tell me what you need, and I'll be honest about whether I can help you or not."

With a double major in music and math, Logan was more than qualified, but she could tell her knowledge would count more with this girl than any degrees or letters after her name.

Vanessa decided to give her a chance and they got to work.

By the end of the first half hour, Vanessa's reserve had melted away. Logan helped her hack through a particularly knotty equation and then moved on to mapping out her big project. They'd also polished off the entire pot of coffee, Vanessa matching her mug for mug, although she added tons of sugar and creamer, while Logan took hers black.

They spent the last five or ten minutes arranging their schedule for the rest of the semester. Vanessa's mom worked as a housekeeper at a motel down in Yachats and Vanessa picked up shifts now and then to help, so they penciled in Mondays and Wednesdays for tutoring.

After her happy charge left for lunch, Logan sat back in her chair and grinned. She hadn't had this much fun in a long time. After her accident, she had tried teaching seventh grade full-time down in Southern California, but school politics and the whole bureaucracy of the public school system made the job less than a good fit. She had no patience for the bullshit.

But she loved the students. She didn't realize how much she'd missed the creative energy of teaching—that 'aha' moment when a student got it was pure gold.

Since she had confidential student files on her desk, Logan locked the door before leaving for lunch. Halfway to the cafeteria, she spotted Vanessa standing in the middle of the hallway, frowning down at her phone.

"Everything okay?" Logan asked.

Vanessa's head jerked up and she slipped her phone into her pocket. Logan noticed it was an older model Samsung in a beat-up case.

"Yeah," she said, "Yes, everything's fine."

Just then the bell rang, and students started spilling out into the hall, chattering with friends, all hurrying to get to the cafeteria, use the bathroom, and get to their next class in the 45 minutes allotted for lunch.

"Okay then," Logan called out to her. "See you Wednesday? Don't forget it's last period that day, not at eleven."

Vanessa mumbled something in the affirmative, then hunched her shoulders and joined the current flowing river toward the cafeteria. Within seconds she was swallowed up in the crowd.

The girl's complete 180 from enthusiastic and engaged student, her eyes alive with the joy of learning, to worried and distracted girl made Logan wonder, but she chalked it up to teenage hormones. She'd be okay. Probably boy trouble or more likely, some drama between friends. She remembered those days well.

"Are you my first best friend, or my second-best friend? Because Sally said . . ."

Logan cringed at the memories. Many women tried desperately to turn back the clock to what they thought of as the carefree days of their youth, but Logan was not one of those women. She *remembered* high school! You couldn't *pay* her to go through that again.

28

PIRATES COFFEE

DEPOE BAY, OR

A young woman with her hair pulled back in a blue bandana finished scrawling February 1 on the daily menu board, then turned toward the door when it jingled. When she saw who it was, she called out, "The usual?"

"Yep, fully loaded and the strongest coffee you've got on tap," Logan said, shaking off her wet jacket in the entryway, hanging it on a hook by the door. Logan loved living in a small town. Kathy was her favorite barista, and she made a great breakfast burrito.

Sam had already grabbed a table. She waved Logan over impatiently.

When she saw the luscious cinnamon roll on Sam's plate, Logan caught Kathy's attention and had her add one to her order. She'd put in her three-mile run this morning. What's a few extra calories? A girl's gotta eat.

"What's up?" Logan asked Sam as she sat down.

"Remember Doyle?" Sam said.

Logan furrowed her brow. "The guy from the *Freya*? The one who got knocked out during the storm? Is he okay?"

"That's him. And no, he's not okay. His head is fine, but he spent the night at the police station," she said.

"What? Why?" Logan said, laying her bag on the bench next to her. "What for?"

"The police picked him up Sunday, while everyone was at the memorial," Sam said.

Logan was so stunned she couldn't even formulate the next question. Sam answered it for her.

"They didn't come out and say it, but from the questions they were asking, Doyle says he thinks the police believe Craig Peterson's death was not an accident, and that he had something to do with it."

Kathy delivered Logan's gargantuan breakfast burrito, coffee, and a heavily-frosted cinnamon roll, then went back behind the register to take the order of the next customer—a local worker by the look of his Carhartts and boots.

Logan finally regained her ability to speak. "I thought Craig had a fishing accident. At the memorial they said he fell overboard during the storm. Lost at sea, right? There were huge waves. Did they find his body? I mean, what makes the police think he was murdered?"

"No, Craig's body hasn't turned up. Nothing like that. He is still considered lost at sea, but the police think he had a little help getting there," Sam said. "Doyle said they didn't come out and say that directly, but that's what they kept asking him about."

"Why? I mean, even if the police knew somehow that Craig had been murdered, what does Doyle have to do with it? Logan asked.

"That's just it," Sam said. "From what I've been able to gather, they're not telling Doyle much of anything, yet. Their *looonng* chat Sunday was very one-sided."

Logan took a bite of her burrito and chewed thoughtfully. Her brother being a cop, Logan knew a little about how these things worked. Talking to the cops was never a good idea, innocent or not.

"Have you talked with him? Where's Doyle now?" she asked.

"He's back home. Very upset," Sam said. "He called us as soon as they'd let him make his phone call, which was *way* after he'd talked with them for hours without an attorney. Tim gave him a ride home to his apartment. Tim said it was a mess; apparently, the police searched it when they took him in."

Frustrated, Sam ran her fingers through her jet-black bob, which fell perfectly back into place. "Who knows what he said to them before they let him go."

Not good.

Logan was well aware of the wisdom of not talking with the cops, even if you were innocent. Her kid brother, Rick, a K-9 police officer back in Jasper, although loyal to his brothers in blue, had repeatedly taught Logan to be careful if ever questioned by the police. Cops knew all the tricks civilians did not, and some were more interested in making and closing a case than uncovering the truth.

"I assume he doesn't have an attorney," Logan said.

"No, at least he didn't Monday," Sam said. "He may have retained someone since, but we haven't heard, and I doubt he has the funds."

"Okay," Logan said, her logical mind taking over. "Doyle used to work for you guys, right?"

"A couple of years ago, yes," Sam said. "Tim was the first one to hire Doyle when he moved here. He gave him his first shot. Took him on at half-share that first year, trained him. He took a chance."

Logan picked up on the slight change in Sam's tone of voice. "What do you mean, took a chance?"

Sam looked her straight in the eye.

"Doyle's a convicted felon," she said. "White collar crime, but still."

"Wow," Logan said. She hadn't seen that coming. She didn't know what she expected convicted felons to look like, but Doyle didn't fit her mental image. He seemed so normal looking.

"Any history of violence?" she asked.

"Not that we know of," Sam said, her voice sounding tired. "Doyle was very upfront with us about his criminal past. And he's never even lost his temper on the boat and there are plenty of reasons to. Things happen all the time. No, I can't imagine Doyle hurting a fly. He's quiet, keeps to himself, works hard."

"Why'd you fire him, then?" Logan asked.

"We didn't. We were sorry to lose him, but the *Freya*'s a bigger boat, so bigger money. We didn't blame him for wanting to go to work for the Petersons. Tim even gave him a glowing reference."

"What else do you know about him?" Logan asked.

Being nosy was in Logan's bones. She knew people weren't always what they seemed.

"Not much," Sam admitted. "He only worked for us a year. He showed up on time, took instruction, learned fast. Didn't drink or do drugs. That's considered a stellar work record around here."

"Did the police give Doyle any idea why they think Craig was murdered?" Logan asked.

"No, they didn't come right out and say that, and he doesn't know what evidence they have," Sam said. "We'll have to see if Jean knows anything when she gets here . . . if we can pry it out of her. She gave me a statement for the story, but she must know something—she knows almost everybody in law enforcement in Lincoln County."

"That's true," Logan said. In her job as part-time medical examiner, Jean had established good working relationships with law enforcement not only in Lincoln County, but all around the state. But she was also a stickler for following the rules. She may not share.

Getting back to her original question, Logan asked, "If Craig *was* murdered, why did the police want to question Doyle? Did they question all of the crew members?"

Sam shrugged.

Just then, the front door opened, letting in a blast of cold air.

Jean stopped at the counter for a *pain au chocolat* and a café Americano, then joined them at the table, tucking leather-clad feet under the bench. Today's brilliantly colored flats were electric lime. And dry, of course, in spite of the rain.

"What?" she asked.

Over the next few minutes, Logan and Sam grilled their friend, but Jean had little to share. Or little she *would* share.

"You know I can't tell you anything at this point," she said. "If I hear anything I can share, I'll let you know."

Logan's mind switched gears. She searched her brain for the name of the Newport police detective she'd met a few years back who had investigated a young woman's murder at her family's 1930s hotel in town, a vestige of Depoe Bay's colorful, rum-running past.

"Monson!" she said, finally remembering his name. "Detective Monson, is he in charge?"

If so, Doyle stood a chance. A few years ago, Logan had met Monson when he questioned her in connection with another case he was working on. He was solid. A good man. At least Doyle would get fair treatment if Monson caught the case.

"No, the state's taking this one," Jean said. "Some hotshot from Salem. Quill . . . Quail something . . . Real gung-ho."

That didn't bode well for Doyle.

There didn't seem to be much else to say, so the conversation turned to less serious topics, like the weather and how Jean's rental in Eugene was doing. She and her husband had leased it last fall to an economics professor and her husband. Neat freaks, no kids, no pets, and the husband knew how to change a lightbulb and unclog a toilet without calling for help. Jean was ecstatic.

After her sister-in-law left for work, Sam raised her eyebrows, reached for her laptop, and gave Logan a look.

"Shall we?" she said.

Logan knew exactly what Sam had in mind.

29

WEDNESDAY, FEBRUARY 1

Logan got a refill for her coffee and settled in. Pirate's was between the breakfast and lunch rush, so she and Sam had the place pretty much to themselves.

Sam pushed her glasses back up on her nose. "Where do you want to start?"

What Sam had in mind was a deep dive into what the police wanted with Doyle and why they suspected Craig's death was not an accident.

"Well," Logan said. "we need to learn everything we can about Craig, Doyle, and the rest of the crew. Did Craig and Doyle have any interactions outside of work other than Craig being his boss on the *Freya*? What could the motive possibly be? And if Doyle didn't do it, who else had a motive to murder Craig? If he was indeed murdered. And opportunity? It has to be someone on the *Freya* that night."

As the acknowledged Excel queen in the group, Sam created a basic timeline, starting from when the *Freya* left Newport the morning of their second trip out, Friday, January 20, until the emergency call went out to the Coast Guard, early the next morning. According to her notes for the story she'd posted to the *News Times*, the call came in at 2:57 a.m.

Now they needed to know who was where, when, and what each crew member was doing each one of those twenty-one hours. The murder—or accident—whatever it was, occurred ostensibly right before the emergency call, but something that day had led up to it. Maybe Craig got into a fight with one of the other crew members. They needed to narrow down the options.

And, Logan pointed out, there was no exact time of death for Craig—and without a body, no way to get one—so they left that blank, along with how long Doyle had been knocked out on deck.

In the first column on the left, Sam listed each crew member on the *Freya* that was onboard during that run. Craig, Doyle, Sean, Lonnie, and Søren, the half-share guy filling in for Liv.

There wasn't much else they could do for now, but it gave them a framework at least. They agreed the next step was to talk with Doyle and the sooner the better. Logan had tutoring that afternoon at the high school but was free for the next few hours. Sam called Doyle and set it up.

Logan was half-surprised when Doyle answered the phone. Being a felon, he could still be on parole. If so, his parole officer could have yanked him back to jail at any time. She wasn't sure what the requirements were for that.

They decided to grab a large pizza to bring with them. People always opened up better when well fed. Sam closed her laptop and slipped it into her messenger bag. "Tim and I promised Doyle we'd figure out some way to help him," she said. "I just hope we can."

Logan admired her friends' loyalty to Doyle, but she wasn't so trusting. She needed to know more. Logan was after the truth, no matter what it was or how well it was hidden.

LOST AND FOUND

12:15 P.M.

ORCHID PALACE APARTMENTS

APARTMENT 109

NEWPORT, OR

Almost immediately after Sam's knock, Doyle opened the door. and motioned to the chairs at the kitchen table, where he had placed three mismatched plates and some folded paper towels.

"Sorry for the mess. The police didn't exactly clean up after themselves. I still haven't found my computer, and I have no idea where my right boot is. They just threw everything everywhere."

They offered to help him straighten up.

"Do you know what they were looking for? It should have said in the search warrant," Logan said.

"They showed it to me and even read it out loud, but I was so scared I didn't listen very well. I should have, I know." He looked miserable. "I'm sorry, but I don't have anything to offer you to drink, either. I only have one mug for coffee—they did leave that in the cupboard—so not even water."

"No worries," Logan said, pulling a six-pack of Coke out of her bag. "We stopped at the mini-mart for beverages on our way."

"Unless you're a Pepsi man, and then you're out of luck," Sam said, twisting off a can for herself.

Logan opened up the pizza box and everyone helped themselves. Pepperoni and Coke. The classics were the best.

When they were done eating, Doyle cleared the table while Sam pulled out her laptop. Over the next hour, Doyle told them what he knew and what he could remember about that night and the day leading up to it.

127

"And that's it, really," he said. "I wish I could remember more, but the first part of the day was nothing unusual. We always do crew rotations when we're going to be putting in long hours. I was down below with Sean and Lonnie. Søren was up first. Craig was in the wheelhouse, bringing us back to Newport to pick up the pots we'd dropped earlier."

"Was the weather bad when you went below?" Logan asked.

"The first storm passed us by," he said. "The second one was coming in, but things were calm when I went below."

"Were you awake or asleep?"

"I went to sleep after we ate . . . at least I think I did," he said. "I just don't know. One minute I lay on my bunk and the next I was out in that storm, drenched, freezing, sliding across the deck. If it hadn't been for some rope I somehow got tangled in, and for Søren grabbing me, I would have gone over, too."

"Could you see anything?" Logan asked.

"The only light came from the wheelhouse," he said. "I saw someone at the wheel. I thought it was Craig. Turned out it was Søren, not Craig inside. He was on the radio with the Coast Guard, trying to get help. When he saw me, he helped me in."

"And you didn't see anything else in the wheelhouse?" Logan asked. "Where were Sean and Lonnie in all this?"

"Down below," he said. "I was next up. I must have come up to relieve Søren, but I can't remember."

Logan pointed to the bandage on the side of Doyle's head.

"Do you know how you got that?" she asked. "Looks like you got hit pretty hard."

Doyle gingerly touched the taped, white square of gauze. "It's okay," he said. "I don't know how I got it, must have banged it against something when I got knocked out by a wave or wind or . . ."

Or while wrestling with your captain to throw him overboard . . . ?

Logan kept her doubts to herself and asked Doyle what questions the police had asked him.

Doyle said the police hadn't really asked him very many direct questions. Whomever the state detective was, he was good. He hadn't given Doyle any clue as to why he was there or how they thought he was involved. He'd just kept asking him to tell his story over and over again until he was too tired to think straight anymore.

Logan was aware of that tactic, too. By getting a suspect to repeat a sequence of events multiple times during a long night, discrepancies between each telling—even small ones—were bound to occur, which could later be used against them. If they had recorded the session, the police could easily make Doyle seem like a liar. Which he may be. The vote was still out on that.

But even liars deserved adequate representation. Doyle said he had the money from his first trip out on the *Freya*, but that was all. And he still had food and rent to pay in the meantime. Sam reassured him if the *Freya* didn't go back out right away, she was sure Tim could use him on the *Sara Lynn*.

He hadn't retained an attorney yet, so he asked Sam if she knew of any lawyers in town she could recommend. She promised to put together a list and call him later. There might be someone in town available, but he may have to go to Salem or Eugene to find someone.

Until then, Logan reminded him not to talk to the police again without one. They could take him to the station, but they couldn't force him to talk without an attorney present.

30

Logan and Sam made their way to their cars. Since Tim was out on the boat, Logan suggested Sam come over for dinner.

"I should be done at the high school by four," Logan said. "Ben's home cooking, so you can show up anytime. I'll meet you there."

"Thanks, I'll take you up on that," Sam said. "Oh, I almost forgot to ask. How's the tutoring going?"

"Great," Logan said. "I've got three students. One's a junior, Vanessa Pérez. Smart girl. Then I've got a senior and a freshman, both boys."

"What are they in for?" Sam asked.

"The two boys just need help with basic math, but Vanessa could teach the class. She's light years ahead!

"If she's good at math, what does she want to do? Engineering? Medical school?" Sam asked.

"You'd think, right?" Logan said. "But no, she actually wants *your* job."

Sam pushed her glasses back up onto her nose and gave Logan a look.

Logan laughed. "Yep. I tried to tell her there aren't many jobs in journalism anymore—at least not in print, right? She needs some good career advice and it's not my area. What should I tell her? Oh, and if you have any recommendations for good schools or scholarships, let me know. Since Amy graduated, I'm completely out of the loop."

"I'll do better than that," Sam said. "Have her meet me down at the paper. I'll show her the ropes and answer any questions she has about the field. I think it's still a viable career choice—if she's willing to hustle."

Sam sidestepped a puddle and struggled to open her car door against a sudden gust of wind and drizzle. When she got inside, she rolled down the window and patted her tummy, "But tell her to come down soon. Once I pop out Miss Magnolia here, I'll be home for a while, drowning in diapers."

"Will do," Logan said, getting into her own car. "I'll see if I can find out what her schedule is when I see her today. Not sure what her hours are this week. Her mom's a housekeeper at a motel south of here. She helps her out sometimes, but I'll give her your contact info."

*****

The high school parking lot was full, so Logan had to park on the street. By the time she got inside, she was soaked. Welcome to Oregon! If you don't like the weather, just wait ten minutes and it will change.

Even after shaking off her jacket as best she could and visiting with Cheryl up at the office, Logan still had a half hour to kill before Vanessa's tutoring time. While she was waiting, she made a very strong pot of coffee and caught up on email.

There was one from Amy, telling her all about Ian's new teacher. A retired woman who subbed part time, she started in January when the other teacher was out for maternity leave. Ian took one look at the woman's wrinkled face, then innocently asked her what all those lines were for! Amy was mortified, but the woman had been teaching kindergarten for thirty years and wasn't offended at all.

Logan was on her second cup of coffee when Vanessa walked in the door.

Immediately, Logan knew something was very wrong. There were shadows under her eyes, and it didn't look like she'd washed her hair. Logan tried to get her focused, but the girls eyes kept darting around the room. She doubted Vanessa could add two and two together, let alone work on the intricate, difficult math project she'd been excited about just two days ago.

After a few minutes of this, Vanessa gave up. Her face crumpled and tears welled up in her eyes. Holding it together long enough to reach back and close the door for privacy, the seventeen-year-old then buried her face in her hands and sobbed.

Pushing her laptop aside, Logan refilled the girl's mug and sat back in her chair, giving her time and space to collect herself.

What the hell was wrong?

Ben would have had three different kinds of tissue at hand, but Logan wasn't in his league. She did have plenty of coffee filters, so she thrust a few of those across the desk at Vanessa, who accepted them gratefully, blowing her nose.

Logan ran through all the possible options for her student's distress. Was she pregnant? Were her parents getting divorced? Maybe her boyfriend broke up with her or slept with her best friend. According to her file, she wasn't flunking anything—she was a straight-A student.

When Vanessa had pulled herself together, Logan put her mom hat on.

"Look at me, hon. Whatever is wrong, I may not have an answer, but there's always a way to deal with it. Talk to me. I promise to hear you out and help if I can."

The relief on the young girl's face was immediate, even though the deep worry remained in her eyes. She blew her nose again and took a deep breath.

"It's my dad," she said. "He's missing."

"Missing? What makes you think he's missing?" Logan asked.

Vanessa teared up again.

"That's okay," Logan said. "Just start at the beginning. How long has he been gone?"

Vanessa took a deep breath. "Since January 5. Almost a whole month! Dad is *never* gone that long. My mom's been sick, and he is *always* home at night to take care of her."

"Wait, slow down," Logan said. "What does your father do for work? Is he a fisherman? Maybe he's just out on a boat, crabbing. It is crab season. Maybe he got a job on a boat."

Even as she suggested this, she knew that didn't make sense. Even the big boats weren't out for a month.

"No, my father works for a restaurant in town, a nice one . . . ," Vanessa hesitated. "He works very hard."

Logan didn't challenge her, although on this point, Vanessa seemed defensive.

"Have you asked his work if they know where he is?" Logan asked.

"Yes, they don't know either," Vanessa said. "He said he was going to be out for two days, but obviously it's been longer than that. They haven't heard from him, either."

"Okay," Logan said.

"Dad sometimes takes on extra work, but he's never gone overnight. He told us someone told him about a well-paying job. It was out of town, but he'd be back the next day, with enough money to pick up mom's prescription at Walmart. We don't have insurance, so he has to pay cash. Mom's medicine is expensive."

"I gather he didn't pick up the prescription?" Logan asked.

"No," Vanessa said. "I got it. I used some of the money we've been saving for college, but Dad never came home! He's still not home and we haven't heard from him!"

"Okay, hon," Logan said. "Have you notified the police? After forty-eight hours your mother can file a missing person's report at the police station—or even sooner if you suspect foul play."

Vanessa's eyes filled up again with tears.

"She can't! My mom and dad are both undocumented. She's afraid if she goes to the police for help, ICE will find out and she'll get deported, and my dad, too, if they find him.

"I was born here, so I have citizenship, but I'm only seventeen, still a minor. Mom worries about what will happen to me if she gets deported. They've worked so hard for my future. They have such big dreams for me . . . If I stay, I will have to go into a foster home until I turn eighteen. And if I went back to Mexico with my mom—which I would do . . . she's sick and I'd never let her travel alone—then I couldn't go to college like she wants. Dad said this job would help pay for whatever college I got into.

"I have to find out what's happened to my dad. He's *never* been gone like this, *never!* I don't know what to do!"

Logan's heart went out to her. She was so very young and, in many ways, very alone.

Logan reached across the desk and took both of the girl's hands in hers.

"I don't either, hon," she said. "But let me do some thinking about this tonight. There must be something we can do without alerting ICE. Let me work on this, okay?"

"Okay," Vanessa said.

"Okay," Logan said. "Look, there's nothing you can do right now. Why don't you go home, have some dinner, get some rest, and take care of your mom. I'll call you tomorrow."

They exchanged cell phone numbers.

Logan wished she had answers for her, but right now, all she had was questions. But one way or the other, she was determined to help. Someone must know where Vanessa's father was.

31

Her mind full of thoughts about Vanessa's problems, Logan headed home. She felt the girl's worry deeply. It brought back painful memories from Logan's own past. She had been thirteen and Rick had been nine when their mother disappeared. One morning they woke up and she was gone—just left—for reasons Logan wasn't sure she'd ever fully forgive her for.

A few years ago, her mother showed up on her doorstep with an explanation of sorts. For Amy and Ian's sake, Logan had decided to let her mother back into her life, but only on a trial basis. So far things had gone well, but she was taking it slow.

She hoped Vanessa's father would return soon and hadn't decided to ditch his family like her mom had.

About halfway home, a deluge of rain slashed across Highway 101, causing Logan to put her windshield wipers on high. Even then, she could barely see the road. But as quickly as the downpour began, it lessened to a sprinkle, opening up a panoramic, watercolor vista of charcoal clouds, slate seas, and white-capped waves, punctuated now and then by the silhouettes of inky cedars and pines.

For the next few minutes, all worries about missing fathers, mothers, and possibly murdered fishing boat captains receded to the back of her mind. Nothing like nature to soothe the soul. We're only here for a blip, Logan thought, which makes our problems seem very small in relation to the history of the planet, or even of all of human history.

The rain started up again just as she pulled up to the house, leaving room for Sam to park closest to the door when she arrived. Logan pulled up her hood and hustled inside.

Immediately, she was enveloped with the sights and sounds of home. A warm fire crackled in the fireplace and delicious smells drifted out of the kitchen. She'd sent Ben a text, letting him know Sam was joining them for dinner, so the table was set for three.

Sloughing off her jacket and hanging it on a hook by the door, Logan removed her wet boots and padded into the kitchen, where Ben was stirring something lemony on the stove.

Sliding her arms around his solid, warm body in a fierce hug, she pressed her cheek against his back until he put down the spoon, turned around, and gave her a proper welcome home.

Gratitude filled her heart. This is how marriage was supposed to be. She was so lucky Ben had not been deterred by her reluctance to take a chance on love again.

Just then, she heard Sam come in. She must have been right behind her.

"Jeez, guys! Get a room!" Sam teased.

Sam handed Logan a bottle of white wine, then eased her very pregnant self down into a chair at the table.

"When's dinner? I'm starved!" she said.

She didn't have long to wait. After handing Sam a bottle of Perrier, Ben poured the wine for Logan and himself, and dished up one of his new specialties—pan-fried cod with *Meunière* sauce, served with rosemary red potatoes and a tossed salad made with greens from his garden.

As they sat down, Logan asked Sam if she'd heard anything more from Doyle.

"Just briefly. He didn't get pulled in. Luckily, his parole officer has too many cases to manage as it is. So he's safe. At least for now, but the PO is making him check in more often. He also told him to stick to his plan and keep working, so Tim's putting him on the *Sara Lynn* for sure so he has steady employment.

"Francis is back, but he's supposed to take it easy—like that's possible on a crab boat—so it's a win/win all around," she said.

During the meal, Logan filled them in on Vanessa's revelations in her office that afternoon.

"I understand they're afraid of ICE, but isn't there anyone else she can go to besides the police to try and find out what happened to her dad?" Ben asked.

"Not that I can think of," Logan said as she got up to clear the table while Ben got the ice cream out. "I was hoping you guys would have some ideas."

Sam's fork stopped halfway to her mouth.

"How long has he been missing?" she asked.

"About two weeks," Logan said. "She said he took a job on Friday and was supposed to be home the next morning . . . January 14, I think."

Sam stared at Logan until her own lightbulb went off.

"January 14? . . . oh my god," Logan said. "You don't think . . ."

"The timing certainly fits," said Sam.

"Fits what?" Ben asked.

Sam plowed ahead as if she hadn't heard him.

"Jean said the body had been in the water two to three days before that man and his dog found him."

"Found who?" Ben asked. "What body?"

"The floater," Sam said.

Ben still looked confused.

"Remember Sam's story about the guy's body that washed up on the rocks in Little Whale Cove?" Logan explained.

"You think that was your student's father?" asked Ben.

"Well, like Sam said, the timing sure fits, and the circumstances. No one in Lincoln County has reported a missing person and we know that even though Vanessa's dad *is* missing, her mother was too afraid to call the police."

"That'd be one hell of a coincidence if it's not him," Ben said.

Logan didn't believe in coincidences.

"There's only one way to find out," she said.

Turning to Sam she asked, "Did Jean send tissue samples in for DNA testing?"

"I don't think so, since they have nothing to match it to," Sam said.

The wheels in Logan's brain started turning.

"What if we got her something to compare it against? Do you think she'd send both samples in, then?"

Knowing how Jean disliked loose ends, they agreed it was worth a try.

While Ben did the dishes, Logan and Sam sketched out a plan.

The plan required a visit to the Pérez home and minimal lying. Normally a very truthful person, Logan had discovered she had a secret talent for stretching the truth when the situation called for it. And Sam? An award-winning investigative reporter from Olympia, she'd been trained on the job.

Logan would call Vanessa in the morning and see if her mom would mind if she brought Sam over to help. Being a reporter, Sam had contacts in town and could make discrete inquiries without directly involving the police. All of that was true. Sam would and could do that. But the real reason was to collect something that would have Vanessa's dad's DNA on it.

They just hoped that neither Vanessa or her mom would see the article in the *NewsTimes* and come to the same conclusion they had. Sam's update hadn't included the detail they'd learned from Jean, but Vanessa was a very smart girl. If she read the article, and they went in tomorrow asking directly for one of her father's combs or a toothbrush, she would put two and two together and know her father might be dead.

Logan had no intention of putting that kind of devastating news on the girl or her mother until they knew for sure that the dead body in cold storage at the funeral home was all that remained of Mr. Mateo Pérez.

32

Logan's GPS took her the wrong way down Benton, but she looped around in front of Mai's Market and got back on track, arriving at Vanessa's place a few minutes before eight. Vanessa's first class started at ten and it took her mom over an hour on the bus to get to work, so they'd agreed to meet early. Sam was already there, parked in front.

Redwood brown with forest-green trim, the Pérez family home was a neat, one-story duplex tucked behind an auto repair place, next door to another similar rental.

White, plastic blinds at the windows were closed. A narrow, concrete walkway led through a scrubby yard up to the front door, which was flanked by a metal mailbox on one side and a pot with red, plastic flowers on the other. Before they could knock, Vanessa opened the door and invited them in.

As her eyes adjusted to the dimly lit interior, she saw they were standing in the living room. To the left was an open doorway to the kitchen and a short hallway on the right led to what she assumed must be bedrooms and bathrooms.

A low couch with wide, roll arms, upholstered in fabric that probably had been green at one time, along with two mismatched chairs and a coffee table and a TV on the opposite wall, created the conventional seating area.

Sitting nervously at the left end of the couch, hands clasped in her lap, sat an anxious looking woman somewhere in her forties or fifties. Dark brown hair curled at the collar of a stretched-out cardigan sweater, worn over a blue shirt with small, white buttons. Dark pants and comfortable shoes completed what were probably her work clothes. Her only jewelry was a small, gold cross and a plain wedding band. Mrs. Pérez. She didn't look sick, but maybe she had misheard Vanessa yesterday.

Taking a seat next to her mom on the couch, Vanessa made the introductions. Logan and Sam each took one of the two side chairs.

While Sam got out her computer, Vanessa's mom turned to her daughter and poured out a volley of Spanish, then looked expectantly at her guests.

"Mom wants to know if you would like some coffee," Vanessa said. "She made some."

Although fully caffeinated already, Logan accepted her host's offer. Mrs. Pérez popped up and went into the kitchen. Within seconds, she was back with a fully loaded tray, mugs, packets of powdered creamer and sugar, and a plate of cookies.

While accepting her coffee, Logan used her limited Spanish to tell Mrs. Pérez what a great student Vanessa was "*Muy intellegente!*" and then "*Lo lamento . . . ,*" how sorry she was to learn about Mr. Pérez being missing.

With Vanessa translating, she then explained who Sam was and how she might help, reassuring Mrs. Pérez multiple times that neither she nor Sam had shared what Vanessa had confided in her or would share anything she said with anyone unless she asked them to. In other words, no one was going to report this to ICE.

Sam, it turned out, knew quite a bit of Spanish, which sped things up and put Mrs. Pérez more at ease. Nibbling on cookies and sipping her coffee, Logan listened as Sam skillfully encouraged Mrs. Pérez to give her some background information. "The more we know about your husband, Mrs. Pérez, the better. I worked on a story about immigration in Lincoln County a couple of years ago. One or more of the people I interviewed back then may have worked with your husband or know of him through other Spanish-speaking friends."

"Please, Gabriela," Mrs. Pérez said. "Where you want me to start?"

"How about at the beginning," Sam said. "When did you arrive in this country and what area in Mexico were you from? Do you have connections with anyone here who came from the same town?"

For the next fifteen minutes, Gabriela told the story of how she and her husband had fled their small fishing village and made the long journey north. Her husband found work here and there around the docks, finally landing a full-time job doing dishes in the back of one of the restaurants. For the first year, until they'd saved some money, they'd stayed with another immigrant family in their apartment, but the landlord didn't like that many people living in one unit, so eventually they had to move. Just in time, too, because by then, she was pregnant with Vanessa.

Proudly, she told them how her husband had worked several jobs in order for her to stay home with their baby daughter. It wasn't until Vanessa entered school that Gabriela started looking for work. She found a housekeeping job at a hotel close enough to walk to, but when a friend told her about a motel in Yachats that paid decent wages, she got a ride down there with her one day and got the job. On days she couldn't ride share, it took over an hour to get there by bus, but the pay was good and speaking good English was not required.

Both she and her husband believed in the value of a good education, so they didn't even own a car. Not only did it save money, but they were also too afraid to apply, even though Vanessa told them the laws had changed and they could get a driver's license without a green card. They were determined that Gabriela would have the opportunities they did not. Being deported would ruin everything.

Vanessa looked at a clock on the wall, which hung next to a red and gold picture of Christ with a crown of thorns. She said she needed to leave for school soon, but waited until Sam had the name of the restaurant where her father worked. Neither mother nor daughter knew any of his friends.

"Dad always came home every night. If he wasn't at work, he was here at home," Vanessa said.

"With us," her mother added.

Neither of them knew what the job was that Mr. Pérez had taken that would keep him overnight, or who had offered it to him.

While Sam asked a few more questions, Logan asked if she could use their restroom. After three cups of coffee, the need was actually legit. Vanessa pointed down the hallway, "First door on your right, Ms. McKenna."

After availing herself of the facilities, she flushed the toilet and turned the water on in the sink, letting it run to camouflage any noise she might make carefully opening cabinets and drawers. It's a good thing they only had one bathroom. She didn't know what plan she would have come up with if she'd had to search two.

It didn't take long. There were only a few items in each of the two drawers—a couple brushes and a comb—but she didn't know whose was whose and none of the strands of hair she found had the follicle still attached on the end, which she knew from one of the CSI TV shows was necessary to extract any DNA.

She'd almost given up when she opened the mirrored medicine cabinet above the sink. It looked like each family member had one shelf. The one with the mens' shaving cream looked promising. The other two had a woman's pink roll-on deodorant, some bobby pins, and a tube of lipstick.

Knowing her absence would become obvious soon, Logan turned the plastic Ziploc baggie she'd brought with her inside out and grabbed the razor. Carefully, she pulled the bag back over the razor, sealed it and shoved it deep into her jacket pocket. Hopefully, there would be enough skin cells or a spot of blood for Jean to test. She almost grabbed the toothbrush, too, but at the last minute, decided against it. Too many missing items would be suspicious.

33

With the plastic baggie containing Mr. Pérez's razor snug in her jacket pocket, Logan drove straight to Lincoln City. She'd called ahead and Jean said she had a break between patients a few minutes after eleven; she could see her then. If there was a way to identify the corpse cooling his heels at the mortuary, she was all for it. And yes, she understood it all had to be done quietly, due to Mr. and Mrs. Pérez's immigration status.

While driving, Logan mulled over the Pérez family's problem. Where could Vanessa's dad have gone? What kind of job had he taken that involved being away from home overnight and that he couldn't share with his family?

GPS brought her to Jean's office at 10:47 a.m. The receptionist must have known she was coming, because she sent her back right away, where Jean was waiting in her office.

Logan removed the baggie from her pocket and handed it to Jean. "I hope I did this right," she said. "And thank you for doing this."

"No problem," Jean said, making herself a cup of green tea. "Want one?" she asked Logan.

Never having developed a taste for pond scum, Logan declined. While she had Jean's attention for the next few minutes, she asked for an update on the investigation into the death of Craig Peterson.

"Do the police still think he was murdered and that Doyle did it or was involved somehow?" she asked. "Tim and Sam think he's innocent."

"Well," Jean said. "They may want to rethink that, Logan."

Logan was all ears. "Why?"

"Quayle has Doyle in his sights, front and center. The only reason Doyle's not in jail right now is that Quayle wants to build an airtight case before picking him up."

"But why? There isn't a shred of evidence that Craig was anything but swept overboard in the storm. And Doyle almost met the same fate. They have no body; what are they basing it on?"

Jean set her mug of tea back down on her desk.

"I don't like Quayle, but he does have some reasons—good ones—to be looking at Doyle."

"Like what?" Logan asked again.

"I don't know what else he has, but there is at least one piece of physical evidence I've seen that links Doyle directly to Craig." She took another sip of her tea. "And before you ask, no, I can't tell you what it is."

"Wow," Logan said, sitting back. Sam was not going to like this news.

"Let me get this straight," Logan said, ticking the points off on her fingers.

"One: *The Freya* left port for their second crab run early in the morning on Friday, January 20. During a lull, they did crew rotations—Craig in the wheelhouse and the new guy, Søren, taking the first shift on deck. Everyone else, Doyle, Lonnie, and Sean, got some shuteye below."

Jean nodded. Logan continued.

"Two: sometime that night, Doyle is supposed to have gone up on deck, thrown Craig overboard, then knocked himself out—all without the other crew member seeing it—in the middle of a huge storm."

Jean raised a finger to interrupt, "There's no way to tell when Doyle received his head injury," she clarified. "We only have his word for it that he was injured on deck. And even he doesn't know how long he was unconscious—if he ever was."

Logan conceded the point and continued.

"Three: Another crew member calls the Coast Guard to report the man overboard and takes the wheel, bringing them back to port. Not sure when the other two crew members come back up on deck or if they do.

"Four: the storm is so bad, and due to winter currents and everything, after an intensive four-day search, Craig's body remains lost at sea, and he is assumed dead."

Logan wrapped it up. "Where in that series of events is there any hint of murder?"

"You're going to have to trust me on this one," Jean said. "I know you want to know everything yesterday, but you need to stay out of this one, Logan. Quayle won't stand for any interference, and if Doyle is guilty, you want him to pay for his crime, right?"

Logan folded her arms. Well, there was *that*.

Jean sighed. "Look, they found a couple of things when they searched Doyle's apartment."

Logan remembered Doyle mentioning the police showing him a search warrant, but he hadn't read it. He was scared and wanted to be cooperative, so he told them they were welcome to look around—he had nothing to hide.

"What did they find?" Logan said. "If they have evidence, why haven't they arrested him already?"

"Because," Jean said, exasperated. "I'm only telling you this so you'll let it go . . . you are not to share this information with anyone, even Ben. One of the things they found in Doyle's apartment was what *might* be the murder weapon. When they were executing the search warrant."

"And . . . ?"

"And it had dried blood on it," Jean said. "The blood type is A-positive, same as Craig's."

"Millions of people have the same blood type. My blood type's A-positive—I think. Don't they need more than that?"

"Yes," Jean said, "Which is one reason, I assume, that Doyle was only questioned, not arrested. The hammer came from a tool set on the *Freya*, but there are no useable fingerprints on it. What they need is something more definitive to arrest him. That's why they gave it to me. I submitted some of the blood from the hammer for DNA matching, but that usually takes several weeks. The actual testing takes less time, but there's always a waiting list."

Answering Logan's unasked question, she tapped the plastic baggie on her desk. "This little guy is going to a different lab. One that owes me a favor."

"Have you told Sam?"

"No, and don't you tell her, either," Jean said. "I know she thinks she's invincible, but she's eight months pregnant with my niece and should be reducing her stress, not adding to it. I don't want her and Tim worrying about Doyle until I know for sure.

"Although, I don't know why I try to protect her. When the results come back, I won't be able to keep it from her, anyway," Jean said. "Sam's got eyes and ears all over the courthouse for her job. Someone will probably spill the beans before I do."

Logan had a ton more questions, but for now, she let Jean get back to work. She needed to think about this for a while. What she really needed to do was decide if she should break Jean's confidence and tell Sam that the man she and Tim thought was innocent may very well be a killer.

34

Roxy reluctantly shimmied into the boring black dress and looked in the mirror. Ugh. After today, this one was going in the trash. She topped her ensemble with a puffy jacket. Another soon-to-be-discarded clothing item. She wouldn't need heavy coats where she was going. And nothing waterproof!

Not bothering to lock the front door, she walked out to the car and strapped herself in. For almost a week she had stayed home, patiently playing the part of the grieving widow, but today she was getting out of the house. She had shit to do.

She revved her engine. First stop was the bank. She needed some cash. Craig normally did all the banking, but Craig wasn't here anymore, was he? And besides, it was her money now. There was no one to tell her she couldn't transfer all the money from the business account into the checking account. It was all *her* money, now!

Someone at the bank was sure to tattle to Emma that Roxy was being greedy, thinking about money right after losing her dear departed husband instead of staying home, devastated, crying in her soup, but really, it didn't matter what anyone thought. Once she had the money and the title to the *Freya*, she was out of there.

Which reminded her. She groped inside her purse on the passenger seat and felt around. Good. It was there. Craig kept the key to their safety deposit box taped under the drawer of his nightstand. She'd never bothered to see what was in it. Probably baseball cards. But she hadn't been able to find the title to the *Freya* anywhere at home, so that's where it must be.

She was selling the house, selling Craig's beat up truck, selling the boat, and leaving! She'd trade in her Range Rover for a sleek, new convertible. Cherry red . . . or black . . . gold would be nice . . .

She hadn't decided where she was going yet, but it was either Florida or Las Vegas. Someplace sunny and warm, with lots of action! Søren preferred Vegas.

Roxy pulled her mind back to her to-do list.

After the bank, she was driving straight to Portland. She planned on spending the whole weekend doing whatever she wanted. She so needed some downtime. She'd earned it!

She had already booked a room and a massage at The Nines and told Søren to meet her there tomorrow night. She could have had him join her tonight, but Saturday was just for her. Spa day and shopping! And maybe some new clothes and a good haircut for Søren. If she was going to be seen in public with the man, he needed a makeover.

The only fly in the ointment was that the police had only questioned Doyle, not arrested him. But, with everything she and Søren had set in motion, she was sure it was only a matter of time.

She smiled at how she had engineered Liv's 'flu' the night of the family dinner so Craig would need to hire someone to take her place the next day on the *Freya*. Then Søren just *happened* to show up that morning looking for work. It was the perfect plan. A few drops of Visine in Liv's cheesecake worked like a charm! How she had loved watching Liv clutch her stomach and run to the bathroom.

The plan had been brilliant. Everything had gone smoothly, but the police were either really stupid or brain-dead. What did she have to do, hand-deliver the guy? The police had the texts, they had the burner phone, the 911 report-of-a-prowler call, they even had the murder weapon! What more did they need to arrest Doyle's ass?

The police had picked Doyle up for questioning while everyone was at the memorial, but then let him go home. Roxy tapped the steering wheel. Søren said there was no way the cops could have missed the bloody hammer when they searched his place. He made sure it was way in the back, but still in plain sight.

The cops were probably waiting for the DNA test on the blood or something. She wondered how long that took. When the results came back as Craig's, which they would, that should be the last piece of evidence the cops need to arrest and convict Doyle of murder.

She smiled when she remembered the sob story she'd given Cindy.

"That horrible man has been bothering me, threatening even! Do you really think he could have pushed Craig overboard just so he could have me for himself?"

And Cindy bought it hook, line, and sinker! So had the police. She'd even let it slip that Doyle was a convicted felon. That's why she hadn't come forward sooner—didn't want to get him in trouble . . . yada, yada, yada. Oh, brother.

She always knew she could act. Maybe she should look at LA. It checked all the boxes. Warm, sunny, and lots to do. Yeah, LA. She could see herself in LA. If Søren didn't like it, he could leave. Now that he'd served his purpose, she was already getting tired of him, anyway. Probably lots of boy toys in LA.

Dreaming of tanned muscle men on Venice beach, Roxy parked and practically skipped up to the bank, dazzling the security guard with a smile. An old guy with manners, he opened the door for her and watched her sashay up to the counter. Even in this frumpy dress, Roxy knew how to rock her walk.

Being a Friday, each teller was two or three deep, but that was okay. Check-in at The Nines in Portland wasn't until four. She pulled out her ID and got in line.

While she was here, she'd have to ask them to set her up with online banking. Craig was old school. He liked coming into the bank and talking with everyone, but she liked quick and simple. Besides, she didn't plan on schlepping over to the bank every time she wanted a latte. She'd open a new account wherever she moved to, but for now, online would be more convenient.

"Next, please!" The second teller from the left waved Roxy over.

35

Roxy hurried up to the teller's window and asked for the balances on both personal and business accounts. She had an ATM card for their personal checking account, but wanted one for the business account, too. She found the business checkbook in a drawer at home, so had the account number handy.

While the teller tapped the account number into her system, Roxy waited impatiently. Finally! It was all coming together. Craig could no longer keep all that money for his precious boat! She couldn't wait to get her hands on the funds. This was going to be a *great* weekend!

The teller hesitated, then turned back to the window.

"I'm sorry, Mrs. Peterson," she said, "but you don't have access to that account."

"Of course, I do," Roxy said. "Check again."

The teller did but came back with the same message.

"There are only two signers on this account, and I am sorry, but you are not one of them."

Roxy glared at her.

"Maybe you could have your husband add you to the account? Would you like a signature card?" the teller asked sweetly. Producing one from her drawer, she slid it across the counter to Roxy. "Just have him fill this out and sign it and you'll be good to go."

Roxy did a slow burn. She spoke slowly and clearly, enunciating every syllable.

"My husband recently passed away," she said. "Surely you can make an exception in this case."

"Well, I think we have to wait for the proper paperwork to come through before we can do anything," she said. Seeing the look on Roxy's face, she got the manager.

A short man with dull, brown hair came over and reaffirmed what his teller had already told her. "I'm sorry, ma'am. We'll contact the other signer on the account and see if they can help you."

Roxy clenched her teeth.

"Who might that other person be?" she asked, furious and embarrassed that someone else had access to money that was hers!

"I'm afraid that information is confidential, Mrs. Peterson," the manager said, his tone becoming more official and distant. "I'm sure you understand. We value and protect our customers' privacy. As soon as you have the death certificate and everything passes through probate, we can get this all straightened out. In the meantime, is there anything else we can help you with?"

Stuffing the now useless business checkbook back in her purse, along with what was left of her dignity, Roxy dug the safety deposit key out from the inside pocket of her purse. At least Craig hadn't blocked her access to that. *Probably because he hadn't thought of it . . . yet,* she thought.

The manager did his best *maître d* impression and escorted his customer back to the vault. After instructing her on the procedure, he made himself scarce so she would have some privacy.

Roxy placed the long, narrow, metal box on the table and started going through it. At least she'd have the title to the *Freya*.

That was the big prize. She didn't really need whatever money was in the business account. There was enough in their regular account for her weekend in Portland.

Once she sold the *Freya*, she'd have plenty. Crab permits were the real prize, and they were attached to the fishing boat. She wouldn't just get money from a boat sale, but hundreds of thousands of dollars for the crab permit! That's where the real money was. She'd found brokers online. She wouldn't have any trouble selling the *Freya*. Then she'd be out of here!

The title hadn't been anywhere in Craig's things at home. It made sense for him to keep it safe in a bank vault. Not wanting to miss any stocks or bonds or whatever else was worth selling, Roxy took one item out at a time and laid it on the table. First on top was a dogeared greeting card that looked familiar. She opened it and saw it was one she had given Craig on their first anniversary. All mush and crap.

Next up were a few pics of Craig as a boy on a camping trip with a super young Walt and Emma and a little brat that must be Liv. Weird how people aged.

High school ring, some other stuff, then bingo! Not the title to the *Freya*, but a Mutual of Omaha life insurance policy. A measly $50,000—better than nothing, but not the score she'd been expecting. *Her* money. The money she needed to make a fresh start.

Anger roiled in her gut. She wanted to throw the damned box across the room, but that wouldn't help. The title to the *Freya* had to be somewhere. Craig must have it squirreled away at home someplace. Maybe he had a safe buried under a floorboard. What an idiot. Now she'd have to go home and hunt for it. Why was nothing ever easy for her? She'd had to scrap and fight for everything she ever got. She took a deep breath. This was no different.

Calmly, she returned everything but the life insurance policy to the box and locked it. After exiting the bank, she sat for a minute in her car. She needed to think.

No reason to change her plans for the weekend, or to tell Søren anything. If she canceled, he might wonder what was going on. She had already realized she needed to dump him— she didn't need to drag old business into her new life—but not yet.

Nope, she needed a break and Søren was good for some strenuous stress relief, which she sorely needed. She'd enjoy herself for a couple of days, then come home and search for the title. If she had to, she'd tear that entire awful house apart, one board at a time, until she found it.

36

FEBRUARY 7

ICU, ADVENTIST HEALTH HOSPITAL

TILLAMOOK, OR

At 5:00 a.m. Bethany Lenox entered her patient's room and proceeded efficiently through her end-of-shift routine. She had performed these tasks for this and other patients many times before. The blips and beeps soothed her.

She'd promised her seven-year-old she'd drive her to school this morning, but there was no hurry. She'd already laid out the first grader's clothes and made her lunch, and she had gassed up the car on the way to work last night. No need to rush.

She checked her patient's catheter, jotted down some notes, then tightened the elastic band on the stubby ponytail at the nape of her neck.

Bethany had her own system. Sure, there was a daily checklist of the basics, like fluid status, labs, tests, sedation, and if a central line was present, but over the years, she had developed her own, more detailed plan of care. If you were lucky enough to be one of Bethany's charges, you were very lucky.

Even after a long shift, her scrubs were unwrinkled, unstained, and her shoes were completely clear of bodily fluids. Nursing was often a messy business. She kept a few changes of everything in her locker.

Meticulous to the core, when she'd entered an ICU unit seven years ago, during her training, she knew that was where she belonged. Not in the ER, where everything was crazy and medicine was practiced in a seat-of-your-pants way, both doctors and nurses reveling in the chaos, but here, in this calm, controlled environment.

ER did the intake. They patched 'em up and sent them home—or to the morgue, depending. Only the really critical cases were sent up here. Up here where attention to detail counted. Up here where you had to know your stuff. Up here . . . lives were saved.

She glanced at her patient's chart.

His condition was stable, but critical. Due to his traumatic injuries resulting in increased intracranial pressure, the medical team had decided to put him into a medically induced coma, but he was still alive. He still had a chance.

She wished they knew who he was so they could contact his family, but he'd come in with no ID. Sometimes, just the presence of a loved one could help a patient heal better than any medicine or treatment they could offer.

Bethany wasn't family, but she did what she could. She always kept up a cheerful one-sided conversation while she attended to his medical needs, telling him about her daughter and their dog, a German shorthair pointer named Freckles. Freckles liked to hunt. They lived in an unincorporated area of Tillamook, so people could keep farm animals like chickens, goats, or rabbits. Unfortunately, Freckles predilection to chasing anything that moved meant that neither Freckles nor their neighbor's chickens were allowed to roam freely in the yard anymore.

She had lots of Freckles stories to share. She even asked her patient questions, like did he have a family or any pets. So far, Mr. Doe had not responded, although she did think he may have moved his left hand one day. Hard to tell.

She glanced at the chart again. Admitted January 14, brought up to ICU on the fifteenth.

Janet, one of the ER nurses, was a friend of Bethany's. She was there when he came in. According to Janet, who got the story from the EMTs, on his way back to port, a small fishing boat had spotted a man about a half a mile from shore, struggling to stay afloat. After several tries, two of the crew members were able to drag the half-dead man onboard. No life jacket, no wallet or other ID.

Even more strange, there was no boat anywhere in sight. If the man had fallen overboard, wouldn't someone be looking for him? None of the fishermen had any formal CPR training, but one of the guys had been a lifeguard years ago, so remembered enough to roll the man onto his stomach, then press on his back and pull back on his shoulders repeatedly to get the water out of his lungs. He said the man spouted seawater like a fountain.

Dazed and disoriented when he came to, the man hadn't been able to put a sentence together, let alone tell his rescuer what had happened. As he slipped into and out of consciousness, the captain wrapped him in a blanket and called it in. An ambulance was waiting when they docked.

Janet had told her it was a wonder the man had survived. By the looks of things, he hadn't been in the water long, but in the freezing temps, hypothermia had set in. Even without the cracked ribs, multiple contusions, and a bad bash on his head, he was in terrible shape. One eye was still taped shut.

Bethany shook her head and looked down at the man, hooked up to various machines that for now were probably the only things keeping him alive.

The neurologist had left a note on the chart. The swelling in John Doe's brain had gone down enough that the doctor recommended trying to bring him around as soon as possible. The longer a patient remained in a coma, the less likely they were to fully recover. Even those who were only in a coma for a few days were sometimes left with volatile changes in personality, confusion, trouble speaking, or seizures. Last year, a woman managed to rip her IV out and give one of the doctors a black eye before she could be subdued.

She just hoped things would go better for this patient, but his odds weren't good. Less than seven percent of people recovered completely without long-term residual effects.

Before she left, she reached out and squeezed his hand.

"Good luck, Mr. John Doe," she said. "Tomorrow's a big day for you. Hopefully we'll be able to swap dog stories soon."

37

Lengthening her stride for the home stretch, Logan picked up the pace and sprinted the last forty yards. *God, that felt good!*

Since the rain let up this morning, she'd logged a few extra miles, making it almost to Fogarty beach before turning around and heading back to Depoe Bay. Good thing she left early, because just as she pulled open the door to Pirate's, the sky let loose.

Logan looked around. Kathy was busy helping a couple of guys at the counter, but other than a woman at the first table, the place was empty. Neither Sam nor Jean was there yet. Before she could hang up her jacket and get in line, Logan got a text from Sam.

Can't make it this morning—lunch okay? 12? Jean will meet us at the Horn.

Sam put most of her stories to bed on Tuesday night before her deadline for the print edition, but something must have come up. She texted back.

Sure, see u at the Horn at 12

Logan's schedule was flexible, but she was surprised that Jean could rearrange hers. Wednesdays were her medical examiner days in Newport. Maybe she was only working a half day.

As long as she was there, Logan picked up a couple of breakfast burritos for her and Ben before walking back up the hill. They ate in front of the fire. She had the sausage one. It was delicious.

The rest of the morning Ben cruised YouTube videos looking for a solution to a problem he'd run into with his water catchment project, while Logan worked on a new song she'd been noodling with the last few weeks. Intermittent strains of violin music, keyboard tapping, and crackling logs joined the bass line of steady rain on the roof.

Around noon, Sam texted she was on her way.

Be there by 12:30.

It was still raining, so when Ben left for Ace Hardware, Logan had him drop her off at the Horn.

Still full from breakfast, Logan ordered a coffee.

When Sam came in, she wasn't smiling. Putting her laptop down at the table, she held up a finger for Logan to wait. The server came over. She ordered an iced tea and a cheeseburger and fries with all the fixings. That sounded good, so Logan said make it two.

When the server left, Sam pushed her glasses back up her nose and said, "They arrested him."

"Doyle?" Logan said. "When?"

"Yeah," Sam said. "Last night."

Logan's heart fell. The test results on the hammer Jean sent in must have come back a match. Damn. She wanted to tell Sam, but even if that's what got Doyle arrested, it wasn't her news to share. If that's what had happened, Jean would tell them when she got there, but it made Logan uncomfortable. She didn't like keeping secrets, especially from friends.

Instead, Logan asked, "How'd you find out?"

"I would have found out this morning anyway," Sam said. "I cover the court, but Doyle called us last night. He wanted to let Tim know because they were supposed to go back out today on the *Sara Lynn*."

"Did Tim go out?"

"Yes, I pushed him out the door. There's nothing he could do here, and everyone needs the money. He found a guy to fill in for a couple of days. Francis's family has medical bills. Every day they miss, someone else is scooping up the crab. It seems heartless, but it's the way it is."

Logan understood the sometimes cruel realities of life.

"So getting back to Doyle. I thought they didn't have enough evidence to charge him," Logan said. "What's changed between when they brought him in for questioning and now?"

She hoped one of Sam's contacts had already spilled the beans about the hammer.

"I don't know," Sam said. "But whatever it is, the DA must think it's strong enough to stand up in court, or they wouldn't make the charge."

"What is the charge?" Logan asked.

"Murder one," Sam said, pushing her glasses back up again.

"Wow," Logan said.

"Yeah," she said. "His arraignment was this morning. I just came from court. That's where I was when I texted you."

"Isn't that kind of fast? I don't know much about how these things work, but isn't there usually more time between an arrest and an arraignment?" Logan asked.

"Usually, but they can if they can pull everybody together and get it on the docket," she said. "And they did."

While Logan was digesting this news, her phone burred. It was Vanessa.

"Ms. McKenna?"

"Yes?"

Maybe this was good news. She could sure use some.

"Have you heard from your dad? Did he come home?" Logan asked.

"No," Vanessa said, "not yet. But I wanted to ask you about something. I was reading some *News Times* stuff online for my government homework, and I saw a story your friend wrote about the body of a man they found . . . in Depoe Bay . . . it says they haven't been able to identify him. I was wondering if you could ask your friend if she knows if they've been able to find out who it is. The dates are so close, do you think . . . I mean . . ."

Vanessa cleared her throat. Logan dreaded the next words out of her mouth.

"Do you think it could be my dad?" she said in a very small voice.

Logan kept her voice calm and tried to project comfort and confidence.

"I don't know, hon," she said. "It's possible, but, let me do some checking and I'll call you back, okay?"

Logan knew that the man in the morgue was almost certainly Vanessa's father, Mr. Pérez, but before she threw that grenade into Vanessa and Gabriela's world, she needed to be sure. She doubted the test results from the man's razor would be back this soon, but she'd ask Jean when she got there.

She reassured Vanessa again as best she could, then disconnected the call and filled Sam in on the other half of the phone conversation. Sam agreed they should wait until the DNA results came back and they knew for certain.

In the meantime, Sam told her about that morning's arraignment.

Logan asked who Doyle had for a lawyer or if he represented himself.

"Public defender," Sam said. "Local attorney. He didn't do much. Of course, there isn't much to do in an arraignment. All they do is tell the defendant what the charges are and see how he pleads."

"I assume it was not guilty?" Logan asked.

"Yes," Sam said. "But it was so sad, Logan. He got the words out, but it was so flat the way he said it. The judge had to ask him to repeat himself. You should have seen him. He just looked so defeated—like he'd already given up hope."

When Jean arrived, Sam immediately grilled her about what evidence the DA had on Doyle.

"What happened?" she said. "What have they got?"

Jean filled her in about the search warrant turning up the hammer on the floor in the back of Doyle's closet. Logan was relieved. At least she wouldn't have to keep that secret anymore.

"The DNA clinched it," Jean said, accepting the coffee Kathy brought over for her. Everybody else had to go up to the counter. But Jean always got her food delivered. "The sample I sent in came back a 99.8 percent match. That's Craig's blood on the hammer. And it was found in Doyle's closet, way in the back, but not hidden, so technically, they could take it. If it's in plain sight, they can collect it, even though it wasn't mentioned explicitly in the search warrant."

They talked a few more minutes about Doyle's case, but until Sam had a chance to talk with either Doyle, his lawyer, or one of her contacts at the jail, there wasn't much more they could do.

Logan thought about it. If Doyle had murdered Craig Peterson, he deserved whatever he got. But if he didn't do it, she couldn't think of anything much worse than an innocent person being locked up for life.

As they threw their trash away, Jean turned back to Logan and said, "Oh, I almost forgot. I also got results from that razor you dropped off last week, Logan."

Logan was all ears. This would confirm Vanessa's father was not coming home. She dreaded having to tell her, but she knew the girl and her mother had a right to know.

"That one was *not* a match," Jean said.

"Say again?" said Logan. Had she heard her correctly?

"It's not a match. That DNA from the tissue sample I collected from the body they brought in last month does not match the DNA from the skin tissue on the razor you brought in."

Logan took in that information. On one hand, she was relieved. She wasn't going to have to tell Vanessa her dad was dead. But that didn't mean he was alive, either. She spoke her next thought out loud.

"So who is the guy in cold storage and where is Mr. Pérez?" she said.

38

Bailiff Nichols had a bit of a crush on the cute reporter, Sam Badger, who covered the courts, so yesterday, when she asked if he would help set up a private meeting with Michael Witcomb, the local attorney serving as Doyle Jefferson's public defender, he was happy to be of service. He and Mike were friends from way back, having gone to school together until Mike went off to college, and he got a job to support his girlfriend's bun in the oven. Four kids and twelve years later, they were still going strong.

Since the DA's office was just down the hall, Nichols did suggest that Sam meet Mike at his office in town. People at the court already knew he and Mike were friends—he couldn't afford to be viewed as taking sides.

FRIDAY MORNING, FEBRUARY 10

LAW OFFICES OF HANLEY & WELLS

Susan Bloodstone, the sixty-something office manager for Hanley & Wells, waved a cheery hello to Mike Witcomb as he emerged from the elevator.

Tall, dark, and handsome, just the way I like 'em.

She continued to appreciate the young man's swimmer's physique—inverted triangle shape and tight butt—all the way down the hall until he entered his office, removed his jacket, and sat down behind his desk. He glanced up and caught her looking at him. She pretended to look at the clock over the door.

Oh, that skin and those dreamy, ebony eyes.

She swore law school was pumping them out younger and better looking every year.

Ignoring Susan's obvious but harmless drooling, Mike smoothed his tie as he sat down behind his desk, placed his to-go coffee down on his right, and opened the file he'd left on his desk after last night's meeting with Samantha Badger and her friend, Logan McKenna. He was glad Nichols had set up last night's meeting with the two women. The file he'd been given on his new client was still pretty thin, so he was willing to take any opportunity to have a leg up before meeting with his client this morning.

Logan McKenna would be here soon, and he wanted to have the details fresh in his mind before they left for the jail. He needed to get his client to open up. To that end, he had planned on taking Samantha Badger along with him, as she was a closer friend of his client, but he knew her job as a reporter might set off red flags for the prosecution, so he'd decided to take Logan, instead. He would bring her in as one of the firm's defense investigators. And in a way, that's what she was. From what the two women told him last night, they'd already begun investigating on Doyle's behalf.

Hopefully, Logan might get his client to open up. He sure hadn't talked much yesterday. Then again, the man was probably in shock after the arraignment and who wouldn't be? It's not every day one is accused of murder.

He skimmed through the file. Doyle Jefferson. His client had a prison record, but that was for embezzlement, a non-violent crime. That neither cleared nor convicted him in Mike's mind. His client's guilt or innocence really didn't matter, though. Mike gave every case he was assigned as strong a defense as possible, given the allocated time and resources, which were never enough. The prosecution had access to a hell of a lot more.

He didn't know yet what the prosecution had on Doyle, but from what Alan hinted at, it must be pretty damning. Given his criminal record, a plea bargain was probably going to be Mr. Jefferson's best bet.

The only thing his client had said in their brief meeting was that he didn't murder his boss, Craig Peterson. But he hadn't seemed all fired up and ready to fight either. He said he was innocent of the embezzlement charge that had sent him to prison last time, too, so didn't have a lot of confidence in the justice system. He seemed to have already given up hope.

That didn't mean his lawyer had to give up though. Mike's job was to mount the best defense and that was what he was going to do. He continued through the file. The next few pages were his notes from Wednesday afternoon and the legwork he'd fit in yesterday.

The best place to start in any defense, he had learned, was knowing everything there was to know about your client. He'd already spoken to Doyle's parole officer, who said he'd been a model prisoner, no fights or problems, and he had kept his nose clean and worked steadily ever since his release.

When he asked her about Doyle's family, she'd told him yes, he had a mother and sister, but they'd long since cut off all communication. No idea where the dad was, and he wasn't married. No one had visited him in prison.

He'd spoken with Doyle's landlady and neighbors. Landlady said he was a decent tenant. Paid his rent on time, mostly. And the neighbors said they didn't know him better than just to say hello to. Other than last week when he had two sets of visitors, he lived alone and didn't bring any women home or have parties, for which both neighbors and landlady were grateful.

Since he didn't seem to have any friends, girlfriends, or boyfriends, the only people left to interview were the people Doyle worked for and with. His most recent employer, Craig Peterson, was lost at sea, presumed dead by the Coast Guard, and presumed murdered by the prosecution, so that was a dead end. He smiled to himself at the pun.

He had appointments to speak with the other crew members who had been onboard the *Freya* that night, including Liv, the victim's sister, even though she had been home sick. She might know something.

The only other employers Doyle had in town were Sam and her husband, Tim, the owners of the *Sara Lynn*. They were the first ones to hire him when he was fresh out of prison and showed up down at the docks. They had already given him a brief statement.

Mike checked his watch. Almost time.

He'd gone over the ground rules with the McKenna woman when she and Sam Badger came to see him last night. The main purpose at this point, was to gain Doyle's trust. He needed to get Doyle actively helping in his own defense, and that meant sharing things he might not want to share.

First, though, he needed to hear Doyle tell his story and listen carefully, then ask questions to fill in any holes. Logan McKenna would take notes, help his client relax, tell him she was there for moral support, that Samantha and Tim had sent her to find out if he needed anything.

The more comfortable his client felt, the more he would share. And in this game, Mike knew, information was power.

39

Even though she didn't have to meet Witcomb until nine-thirty, Logan was up, showered, and dressed by seven. She came into the kitchen just as Ben was putting the finishing touches on breakfast. Eggs benedict, her favorite. She grabbed the Tabasco sauce from the fridge, and they carried everything over to the kitchen table. After cleaning their plates, Ben refilled their coffee mugs and they talked about her upcoming trip to the jail.

Ben didn't like the idea of her going, just on general principle, but he trusted her instincts and after his initial objections, he supported her decision. Last night, she'd told Ben about the hammer and the DNA test, but to protect Jean, neither she nor Sam had shared what they knew with Witcomb yet.

"When does the DA have to tell Doyle's attorney what they have in the way of evidence?" Ben asked.

"Hopefully today," Logan said, "but Sam says they'll wait as long as possible."

She took another sip of coffee. "We're going to meet up afterwards for lunch. I should be home mid-afternoon. Need anything from Newport?"

Ben said no, so they kissed goodbye, and she got on the road. She should have offered to help with the dishes, but she was anxious to get there.

What Ben didn't know was that she and Sam had one more stop after lunch. The Lincoln County Animal Shelter. Even though the main shelter was closed, they still operated out of a small trailer near the original site. Through a phone line and limited drop-ins, they took in abandoned or lost animals like before, but mainly housed them in pet foster homes. The new procedure was to fill out the paperwork, then set up an appointment time for a meet and greet.

When Sam told her three new dogs had come in, Logan hesitated at first. Would Ben want to raise another puppy, or would an older dog be better? For that matter, he'd probably want to pick out the breed. Would he want another Greater Swiss Mountain dog, or would that make him miss Purgatory even more?

The three dogs available for adoption were a five-year-old female pit bull mix named Fawn, a tiny dog they warned had a biting problem, and Dixon, a two-year-old Australian cattle dog/lab mix.

She already regretted making the appointment, but Sam made a good point. She said that after COVID, when everybody adopted a dog to keep them company during lockdown, there weren't a lot of dogs available for adoption, so she might want to take a look at these before they were snapped up. So Logan filled out the paperwork online and made the appointment at one. She'd just get it over with, then she really needed to sit down with Ben and ask him if he even wanted another dog.

*****

She'd arrived at Witcomb's law offices early, so she filled up her car with gas first before pulling into a parking space in front of the building and calling to let him know she was there. The jail was only a few blocks away and parking was sometimes tight, so she offered to drive. They arrived a few minutes before ten.

Logan had only been inside the Newport County jail one other time; she knew what to expect, but that didn't make it any easier. You never got used to the smell. The minute you walked through the entrance, you were engulfed in a unique stench of unwashed bodies and industrial food.

She tried not to breathe as they worked their way through the lobby, then a set of double doors that let them into booking, and finally arrived at one of the small rooms on the right used by attorneys to meet with their clients. Witcomb introduced Logan as his defense investigator, and they let her through.

Inside there was just a metal table and three chairs. Two on this side and one on the other, she assumed for the prisoner. Witcomb took the first one, Logan hung her jacket on the back of the next one, and they sat down to wait.

40

Logan was glad she hadn't had a second cup of coffee. She didn't want to have to interrupt their meeting with Doyle to find a bathroom. For now, she focused on Witcomb's instructions.

"I'll start things off, but jump in whenever you see an opening," he said. "If you can get him to talk with me, maybe I can mount a defense, but right now, he's not even trying."

Although it seemed longer, they only had to wait a few minutes before Doyle was brought in. He looked as if he'd aged ten years since she'd seen him on the deck of the *Freya*. The orange jumpsuit made him look guilty already.

After the guard left, Witcomb reassured his client that the conversation was privileged and totally private, so he could speak freely. That included anything he said in front of Logan. Doyle was okay with that. He remembered her from the pizza delivery and asked her to be sure to thank Sam and Tim again for all their help.

Logan said if he needed anything, to tell her and she would let them know. She was just there to take notes and if he wanted her to, to share what was going on with Sam and Tim. He said sure, he had nothing to hide. They were his only friends here. He also said to thank them for the offer of help, but he had no pets to feed or plants to water. The only thing he needed was to get out of here. He asked his lawyer about bail.

"Doesn't look good," Witcomb said. "I'll keep asking, but with your criminal record, and the murder charge, the judge won't be inclined to grant it."

"Well, did you find out why I'm in here?" Doyle said, suddenly more animated. "Why do they think I had anything to do with Craig going overboard? I was knocked out myself and only came to after it happened. I didn't even see it happen."

"I know it's hard, Doyle," Witcomb said, "but you'll have to be patient. The DA has to tell us what they have, but not all at once. They'll dole it out in bits and pieces—drag it out as long as they can. And they don't have to tell us their strategy, only the bare bones evidence. It's my job to figure out what they're going to do with that evidence, how they're going to present their case, and then build your defense."

Doyle slumped back into his chair.

"That said," Witcomb reassured him, "when I leave here today, that's my first stop. I'll get whatever I can. By the next time we meet, I'll have a better idea what we're facing. We'll know more soon, I promise."

Logan watched Doyle's face. His frustration seemed genuine. If he was innocent, this must be pure hell. Especially if he was innocent of his former felony conviction, too. To be imprisoned for five years for something you didn't do and then be facing a murder charge. She couldn't imagine what that would do to your mind and soul.

On the other hand, she knew about the bloody hammer. What was an innocent man doing with what was almost certainly the murder weapon in the back of his closet?

As if in answer to Logan's unasked question, Doyle added, "And for the record, I wasn't guilty of embezzling, either. My partner framed me. I was only guilty of being stupid. I believed everything Blaine said, and then one day, he left the country and the police showed up at the office. Done. So forgive me if I don't have a lot of faith in the system."

Witcomb asked Doyle to go through everything that happened that Friday, January 20, the day of the storm when Craig went overboard.

Doyle rubbed his eyes with his knuckles. "I've been through all this twenty times with the detectives."

"I know, but let's make it twenty-one. I need to hear it from you," Witcomb said.

Witcomb recorded everything, so Logan really didn't need to take notes, but she did so for herself and Sam. For the next hour, Doyle went over the events of the fateful day.

The fishing was good, the weather was holding, but dark clouds were gathering on the horizon. They'd headed back to the strings they'd set earlier that day to scoop them up and cross the bar before the big storm hit. Craig started crew rotations, sending everyone below to get some grub and rest. Søren had first watch, then Doyle was next up. Søren was supposed to come down and get him when it was his turn to go on deck. He didn't set his phone alarm because he didn't want to wake up Lonnie and Sean before he needed to.

The rest of the night was where his memory got patchy. Sometime during that next couple of hours, the storm arrived in full force. Doyle said he woke up on deck, lashed by wind and rain, almost getting swept overboard himself. His legs getting tangled in a rope saved him and he dragged himself back to the wheelhouse, hand over hand, with Søren's help. If he hadn't been wearing his new work boots with the better grip, he might not have been so lucky.

No, he didn't remember seeing Craig anywhere. The only light piercing the darkness was coming from the pilothouse and Søren was at the wheel, not Craig. He was calling the Coast Guard. After he made it inside, Søren got them back to port. There was no chance to even look for Craig in that storm, let alone rescue him. Lonnie and Sean stayed below the whole time. He didn't know if they were awake or not, but they couldn't safely have come on deck in that weather, anyway.

"And you don't remember how you got that bang on your head?" Witcomb asked.

Doyle touched the side of his head. The bandage was gone, but it hadn't yet healed completely.

"Not really," he said, "I do remember a jolt of pain, but not what caused it. This morning I remembered coming up the stairs to relieve Søren, but I'm not sure if that memory was from another day or what. Everything's pretty jumbled. I don't remember waking up in my bunk or anything for sure before I came to on deck in the middle of the storm."

"That's okay," Witcomb said, "you did fine."

He clicked off his pen and turned off his phone, which had been recording their session as he took notes on his legal pad. "I think we've done all we can for now, and I need to get back to the office and start working on all this. If you think of anything else, let me know. And don't talk to anyone, not a fellow inmate, not a guard, no one—no matter what."

Doyle nodded, then looked up at his attorney.

"There isn't much hope, is there?" he said.

Witcomb hesitated as he put the file in his briefcase.

"I mean, I'm a convicted felon," Doyle said, sitting back in his chair. "Everyone assumes I'm guilty already."

For a minute, no one said anything, then Doyle sat up straight and looked them both in the eyes. "I didn't kill anyone. If you can prove that, I promise I'll do both your taxes for free for the rest of your lives."

41

Sam couldn't get there until twelve fifteen, so they decided to grab some lunch from the taco truck on the corner and eat on the way. They took Logan's car. While she drove, Logan gave Sam the reader's digest version of her and Witcomb's meeting with Doyle.

"I got a better sense of who Doyle is," Logan said, "but he didn't tell Witcomb anything more than he told us the other day."

"What about the evidence?" Sam said. "Witcomb know any more about that?"

"Nope," Logan said, swallowing the last of her taco and wiping her mouth with the takeout napkin. Sam held the trash bag open for her and she wadded it up and tossed it in. She took a long drink of her Coke before continuing.

"He said he'd have something soon," she said, "but the prosecution hadn't shared anything yet."

"Not surprised," said Sam, "Getting anything out of the DA's office is like pulling teeth."

"Doyle doing okay?" Sam asked as she pulled up to the trailer serving temporarily as the Lincoln County Animal Shelter headquarters. Two cars were parked out front. A white SUV and an older model Honda Civic. The SUV was backing out. They waited until it was clear, then took that spot and got out of the car.

"As good as can be expected," Logan said, walking up to the door. "He said to thank you and Tim for all your help, giving him a ride back from the station after they questioned him the first time and offering to help straighten up his apartment after the cops went through it."

"Did he ever find his boot?" Sam asked.

"No, but he said he still had his old ones," Logan said. "Witcomb said he doubts the judge will grant bail, so he won't be needing any of his clothes for a while."

They opened the door and went inside. A young woman behind the counter named Kaylee was expecting them. She volunteered for the shelter and was excited someone had come to see one of the animals in her care. She put them in a windowless room with a tile floor and plastic chairs and went to retrieve the dog.

As she waited, Logan started getting kind of excited. Sam looked up the breed mix on her phone. "They're called labraheelers," she said.

"Really? I didn't know that was a thing. I've heard of labradoodles, but not labraheelers," Logan said. "Let me see."

"Yeah, Australian cattle dogs are also called heelers."

Sam started to show her some images, but just then the real deal trotted in the door with a middle-aged woman who introduced herself as Marla, Dixon's foster pet parent.

A little smaller than most labs Logan had seen, the first thing she noticed about the two-year old dog, besides the attractive silver-gray and black, short-haired coat, was the way he held himself. Compact and muscular, he sat calmly by Marla's side and waited for further instructions. Triangular ears straight up, he laser-focused his intelligent, black eyes on Logan. She swore the dog was reading her mind. It felt like he was sizing her up.

LOST AND FOUND

Marla told them a little bit about the characteristics of the two breeds. She said this one seemed to have more cattle dog than lab. "They are very active, smart, and need lots of mental and physical stimulation. They are not lap dogs. If you want a lap dog, you should wait for a pug. They rarely move. Of course, it's because they can barely breathe through those smashed noses . . . don't even get me started!"

To get Marla back on track, Sam asked how Dixon had done in foster care and whether he was potty trained.

"Yes, that's not an issue. I have a small, fenced yard. I let the dogs out back first thing in the morning to let them do their business. This one's never had an accident in the house."

"How did he come to be in the shelter?" Logan asked.

"Dixon here was picked up down at Nye Beach a few weeks ago. Someone called in a stray, but it took a while for us to catch him. He wasn't very trusting and outsmarted our animal control officer more than once. We thought maybe he got left behind accidentally when someone was here on vacation, but he's not chipped and no one's claimed him, so, eventually, we cleared him and made him available for adoption. The vet gave him a clean bill of health. Mixes are usually healthier, anyway. They haven't been overbred. You want to walk him?"

Logan hadn't planned on walking the dog, but he looked well-behaved enough. When they got outside, Marla handed her the lead.

"Just try to keep it up behind his ears and give it a gentle tug if you need to," she said. "But you won't need to. Dixon responds very well to basic verbal commands."

"But only when he wants to," she added, "Stubborn comes with smart."

Logan didn't know what basic commands were, besides "sit" and "don't-get-yourself-run-over-by-a-car," but Ben was going to be in charge of all that. For now, she'd wing it. Short walk, take a picture, show Ben. Let him decide. He had to make the final selection.

They got as far as the far end of the parking lot when Kaylee, the girl who manned the front desk, popped her head out the door, looking flustered.

"Marla! Phone call!" she yelled.

Marla excused herself and said she'd be right back.

42

Sam waddled a few feet away to listen to a voice message. She was still on the clock. Her boss told her she could start maternity leave anytime, but Sam said she felt fine. Logan remembered her saying she'd work as long as possible, because after she used up her regular sick leave, the rest of her maternity leave would be unpaid. She wanted as long as possible with little Magnolia once she arrived.

Logan stood there, shifted her weight, and adjusted the yellow lead in her hand. Dixon remained motionless. Should she walk him without Marla? Was that allowed?

Marla was taking a while.

Finally, Logan got tired of standing and went to lean against her car. Dixon trotted behind, then took up his position on her left.

Impressive.

She could definitely see this dog jumping into Ben's truck, playing catch with them at the beach with a piece of driftwood. And running. He looked like a dog who could go flat out and never get tired. He'd be a fun running buddy. She pictured him loping beside her up Highway 101 and back to Pirate's. They allowed dogs at the picnic tables. Wonder if he liked breakfast burritos? While she was lost in her imagination, Dixon clinched the deal. He leaned against Logan's leg and gazed up at her with trust and love.

Oh my god.

"Looks like Ben might have to find himself his own dog!" Sam laughed, coming back over. "This one's claimed you for his own."

Logan reached down and scratched the dog behind his big ears. Dixon closed his eyes in pure contentment. She could have sworn he was smiling.

Just then, the door opened and Marla swooped out. She did not look happy.

"I am so sorry, Ms. McKenna," she said, "but—there's no other way to say this, there's been a mistake. I didn't know this, but Dixon has already been adopted. We normally would have called you, but the paperwork got mixed up and the morning volunteer didn't tell the afternoon volunteer . . . this never happens, but we're short-handed and not in our usual facilities. I am so sorry."

Logan looked down at the warm body waiting patiently to go home with her.

Marla rattled on, "We had several people interested in Dixon and two of you qualified. We take applicants in the order and well, she already came by this morning and adopted him. She is coming this evening after work to pick him up and take him to his new forever home."

Logan looked down at the dog she'd already taken for a run on the beach in her mind. To her surprise, her eyes filled with tears. She furiously blinked them back and handed back the lead, feeling her heart wrench as she did so.

Marla accepted it and again apologized.

"I'm sure we can find you another dog," she said, as she led Dixon back inside. "Have you met Tinkerbell, our teacup chihuahua?"

"Uh, no, thanks," Logan said, getting back in the car. She didn't look back. She didn't think she could bear looking at that little face again.

"That sucks!" Sam said, lowering herself into the passenger seat, buckling in.

Logan started up the engine and backed out a little too quickly, spitting gravel. There wasn't much else to say. Wisely, Sam changed the subject.

"Look, it's only two o'clock," she said, pointing to the clock on the dashboard. "Unless you have something else to do, let's try to make some headway on Doyle's case."

Logan agreed. Anything to keep from thinking about making a fool of herself over that dog.

"Who haven't we talked to yet? So far, we talked with Doyle, and you said you spoke with Lonnie and Sean."

"I did, but they didn't have much to contribute. They were down below when it all went down. Didn't see anything."

"Well, if it wasn't an accident and someone murdered Craig, it has to be someone who was on board that day."

They both thought for a minute.

"We haven't talked with Liv yet," Sam said. "She was home sick that day, but she might know something. She and Craig were close. She knew everyone. She was part of the crew. Maybe she has an idea."

"Yeah, what about the temp guy they got to stand in for Liv while she was out? The one who made the emergency radio call to the Coast Guard? What was his name? Saren or Søren? Something like that."

"Yeah, Søren, I think," Sam said. "I'll check my notes later. Doyle says he's a good guy. He didn't like him at first, but if it wasn't for Søren, he might have gotten washed overboard himself, and after calling for help, he got the *Freya* safely back to port in the storm, went out and helped in the search for five days, then stopped by to see how Doyle was doing, brought him some food, made sure he knew where to go pick up his check."

"Does Doyle know where he is now? Is he still on the *Freya*? They might not even be out this week."

Some of the larger boats, Logan knew, had already moved on to other fisheries. Once the crab started thinning out, it made the most financial sense.

"I don't know the answer to either of those questions," Logan said. "If Liv's home, we can talk to her first. If she had to cut him a check, she would have his first and last name."

Sam pulled out her phone to see if Liv was available. While it was ringing, Logan asked, "You can say you're working on a follow-up story, but what excuse will we have for me being there?"

"Trainee," Sam grinned. "Wanna be a reporter?"

43

Logan was surprised Liv agreed to see them. If Logan's little brother, Rick, had just died, she wouldn't want to talk with a couple of nosy reporters.

But Liv had not only agreed but said now would be a good time. The *Freya* was in port for a few days. She was home catching up on paperwork.

Liv met them at the door and invited them into the open living room. Large picture windows overlooked the harbor. On the coffee table, a plate of chunky, homemade chocolate-chip cookies sat next to a stack of napkins. Liz accepted Sam and Logan's condolences, then sat her two guests on the couch nearest the cookies. She took a seat in a chair at right angles to the couch, nearest to Sam, who was getting out her computer.

"Thank you for seeing us on such short notice, Liv," Sam said. "We'll get some more background information for the tribute and a brief update on the latest developments. Most of this is verifying information we already have. We'll be out of your hair as soon as possible."

Liv nodded, then stood up. "Can I get you anything? Coffee? Soda? I'm afraid we're out of real cream, but I've got creamer and sugar if you want, or the fake stuff. We're kind of wiped out after all the people we've had here this week."

Logan said yes to coffee, black was fine, and Sam settled for a 7-Up. Liv doctored her own mug with sugar. Everyone took a cookie.

Someone in the Peterson house was a talented baker, Logan thought. She wondered if it was Liv or her mom. *Or her dad,* she auto-corrected her politically incorrect thought.

"This is actually a good time to talk," Liv said. "Mom and Dad are in Salem, doing a Costco run."

Laying her untouched cookie down on a napkin, she spread her hands on her knees and said, "Look, I know you have a job to do, and I know you and Tim are friends of Doyle . . ."

Logan wondered how Sam was going to handle this. She assumed Liv knew by now Doyle had been arrested for Craig's murder, but they didn't know how she felt about that.

"No worries, Liv," Sam said. "Doyle worked for us, and yes, we are friends, but I can do my job objectively. Today my focus is on Craig's tribute piece. The other events are still very new, and we don't know everything yet. Someone else is actually going to be taking lead on that story. I promise the facts will be reported as they develop, and we won't take sides."

"No, that's not it," Liv said. "I'm glad you and Tim are looking after Doyle. I know the police arrested him, but I don't think he had anything to do with Craig's murder."

"So you *do* think your brother was murdered?" Sam asked, ". . . But not by Doyle?"

Logan wanted to know the answer to that question, too.

Liv nodded.

"What do your parents think?" Sam added.

"Well, when they found out Doyle was a convicted felon, they were against him, especially Dad—he wouldn't even let him help us in the search," she said. "And they don't want him back on the *Freya*. I know he was very hurt by that. Mom and Dad were right there within hearing range. I couldn't do anything but deliver the message when he came to pick up his check. Thanks to you and Tim, at least he had work last week."

"We were happy to help," Sam said. "And Doyle's a good worker."

"The thing is, Craig was an experienced fisherman," Liv said. "He knew every inch of the *Freya*. He grew up on her, just like I did. I just can't see him going out on deck during a storm without taking precautions. We have procedures we follow. We've been in plenty of winter storms and never lost anyone, mostly because Craig insists on everyone being safe. He made sure we all had those life jackets that keep your head above water.

"Craig would have worn his life jacket, so even if he did go over, he probably would have survived. Those things will keep you afloat for at least three days. The weather cleared up that whole search week. Even if he was injured and went into the water unconscious, someone would have spotted that jacket."

She put her head in her hands, "But nothing."

"Have you talked to the police about this?" Logan asked.

"No," Liv said. "They already arrested Doyle for murder, and this would just give them more ammunition to convict him. I know in my bones it was not an accident—which leaves murder. But I know just as surely that Doyle did not do this, and I can't imagine why the police think he did!

"I know you've talked with him. Do you know if the prosecution has told him yet what evidence they based his arrest on?"

Sam and Logan shared what they could, which was nothing, since they still could not divulge the information about the hammer Jean had shared with them, not without jeopardizing her job. They had to keep their mouths shut until the DA disclosed it in discovery, which would hopefully be very soon. Logan hated having to remember who was supposed to know and who wasn't.

Logan did promise to give Doyle's lawyer Liv's contact information and let Doyle know she supported him. Apparently, he had called her once from the jail already, but they only gave him a few minutes to talk.

To Logan's trained mom ear, Liv seemed to care for Doyle a bit more than just as a fellow crew member. She doubted either of them had done anything about it, but if the two had feelings for each other, it made the whole situation even sadder.

"Was Craig's life jacket on board?" Logan asked.

"No," Liv said. "We keep them in the storage area under one of the seats. We never found it.

"I just don't know what to do," Liv said, "Doyle couldn't have done this. He wouldn't have hurt anyone, let alone murdered Craig."

"Then who do you think did?" Logan asked.

44

"If it wasn't an accident," Logan continued, "someone on board the *Freya* killed Craig and pushed him in, or just pushed him in and let the ocean do the rest. And there were only five people on board: Craig, Doyle, Lonnie, Sean, and the temp guy, Søren."

"I don't know," Liv said, looking miserable. "But if we don't find out, they're going to convict him and with his record, he'll never get out of prison."

At this she broke down and cried.

Logan was a woman who liked hard facts, but sometimes you had to go with your gut, and hammer or no hammer, her gut was telling her Liv was right.

"If Craig was murdered," Logan said, "there has to be a reason. There are really only a few reasons why people kill other people. Did Craig have any enemies from work? Any former employees who felt cheated or rival boat captains who wanted him out of the way?"

Liv pulled herself together. "No one on the docks had a beef with Craig. Sure, there were disagreements about lines or whatever, but nothing to kill over. Everybody pretty much stays in their own lane."

"What about other people? Anyone *not* from work get into it with Craig? Did he belong to any political organizations? Anything that might have made him a target?" Sam asked.

The way the world was getting, Logan thought that was an excellent question. These days people were getting shot over which camp they were in. Craig could have been involved in some fringe group online.

"No, Craig only thought about fishing and his family," she said. "He wasn't into in politics. None of us are."

Speaking of family . . .

"Who benefited from Craig's death?" Logan asked. "Financially, I mean."

"Well, Roxy will get the house, but it still has a mortgage, and they didn't put much down. It's appreciated some, but it needs a lot of work. Craig always meant to remodel it but hadn't updated it yet."

She looked out of the window at the boats in the harbor, then back at Logan. "I don't know if Craig had life insurance. She'll probably lose the lease on that store of hers. Craig was subsidizing that."

"What about the *Freya*?" Sam asked. "It comes with a crab permit, and that's worth a lot, even if Roxy sold it, which she will do as soon as she can, I'm sure. That's where the bulk of their money was, right?"

"Oh, that," Liv said. "The combination of the *Freya* and the crab permit is probably worth several hundred thousand dollars. And there's a black cod permit, too. But Roxy doesn't get those."

"Why not?" Logan asked. "As Craig's wife, doesn't she automatically get them? Even if he doesn't have a will and it has to go through probate, it will be hers eventually."

"No, the *Freya* didn't belong to Craig. It came through mom's side. The Bjørklands kept it in the family. Grandpa had no sons, so he left it to his daughter—our mom, Emma. My dad was trained by Lars and eventually became captain, but not the owner. Dad didn't want people knowing his wife owned his boat, so she didn't broadcast it. She has always taken a back seat in public to Dad, but Mom runs the show. And they are both okay with that. They make a good team."

Logan couldn't imagine Ben ever having that frail an ego. If he did, they probably wouldn't be married. But to each their own.

"I didn't even know the *Freya* was in Mom's name until Craig married Roxy. Mom did not approve of the marriage. She never liked Roxy. Figured Craig would come to his senses sooner or later and they'd get divorced.

"When they didn't, she confided in me that she owned the *Freya* and would be passing it down to me, not Craig, in her will. Surprisingly, Craig was okay with it. He was going to get the house and the rest of their estate when they go—stocks, all that, so it was split up pretty evenly. I'm sure Craig must have told Roxy, we just never talked about it."

Liv finished her coffee and put the mug back on the table.

"And before you ask," Liv added, "none of the crew stood to gain anything by Craig's death, either. In fact, they all lost a good week or two of fishing, right at the beginning of the derby."

They no longer needed an excuse to be there, but Sam verified some details for her story and told her she'd send Liv an email to request the pictures she needed. As far as Doyle's arrest and trial, someone else was covering that story, but she would do her best to make sure more than one point of view was represented. But she warned Liv, they could only print what they could back up with facts.

When they were done, Sam put her computer away and Logan accepted a cookie wrapped in a napkin for Ben. Liv walked them out.

At the door Liv stopped and said, "You know, even though Roxy's a despicable human being and I wish Craig had never married her, she has a rock-solid alibi. She wasn't there."

As they pulled out of the driveway, Logan said, "We're pretty much back to square one."

"Yep," said Sam, "We have each crew member's version of events. They all say they don't know anything, but unless a stranger snorkeled in and climbed on board to do the dirty deed, one of them has to be the killer."

45

Bethany waited impatiently in the elevator, rocking back and forth on her feet. A large work tote, containing her lunch, some snacks for the nurse's station, and a fresh set of scrubs, was slung over her left shoulder.

Wednesdays and Thursdays were her weekend, so this was her first night back.

Her husband said he'd put their daughter to bed tonight so she could leave for her 8:00 p.m. to 5:00 a.m. shift early. The man was a jewel. He understood how attached she got to her patients. She had even called the police station a couple of times on her days off, but they said they still hadn't received any missing persons reports matching the description of her John Doe.

When the doors opened, she hustled out and went directly to Room 3 to check on her patient.

Over the past two days, the medical team had been slowly tapering him off the propofol. If all had gone well, he should be conscious.

If all had gone well.

When she got to bed three, she was glad to see it was still occupied and her patient was even awake, his one good eye open, although he said nothing and didn't seem to recognize her. They'd also removed the trach, so he looked less like a Frankenstein monster or someone on permanent life support. She was used to the lines and equipment that helped keep people alive in the ICU, but family members often freaked out when they saw them.

Yang, the physiotherapist, was already there, gently but firmly putting the patient through a standard set of mobilization exercises.

After laying in a hospital bed for several weeks, patients' muscles atrophied. The exercises helped them regain flexibility and strength.

Yang finished with the arms and hands, then put loose, drawstring shorts on his patient for modesty before lifting his left leg straight up into the air. He held the heel and pressed down the toes with his other hand to extend the hamstring stretch and arch, before lowering that leg, then walked around the hospital bed and started in on his right one.

Bethany placed her bag on the visitor's chair and picked up the chart.

"Well, hello, Mr. Doe! Good to see you in the land of the living! I see Yang's putting you through your paces. When he's done beating you up, I have another Freckles story for you."

Mr. Doe drifted back to sleep.

"How's he doing?" she asked Yang, skimming the entries on her patient's chart.

"Very good, considering," Yang said. "Jules said he got agitated when they first brought him up, but he's better now, although he's still pretty out of it. When I came in, he tried to talk, but I couldn't understand it and he can't hold a pencil, yet. I think it was Spanish, though."

Spanish. Half the world spoke Spanish; that didn't exactly narrow it down. He could be Mexican, Venezuelan, Guatemalan . . .

Bethany tried to swallow her disappointment. She'd been hoping for more, much more. The TV ending where the man wakes up from his coma—totally recovered—sits up in bed and orders a steak and a two-olive martini, his loved ones by his side, was not going to happen here.

That's okay, she told herself. It just meant her work was cut out for her. If he did well the next few days, they'd be moving him to a step-down unit on the second floor. She set to work revising her schedule. Knowing how the bean counters worked, she didn't have much time. Even step-down was expensive. They wouldn't keep him very long. If he had no family, they'd ship him out to a state nursing home as soon as possible—if not sooner.

She needed to at least get him well enough to find out who he was.

EARLIER THAT WEEK

He was there, but not there. Floating, not connected to anything, but also unable to move away, from, or toward anyone or anything. Sensations. Lights. Sounds.

Other than dark, blurry smudges and vague shapes, he couldn't see, but he could hear. People moving around, talking to each other, using a lot of words he did not know. Doctor sounding words. Occasionally, he felt a sharp jolt of pain or the sensation of cold, but most of the time he felt nothing.

Right now, he felt wrapped in a warm blanket. He didn't know if it was a real blanket or the warm, summer sand he and his sister used to burrow themselves in at the beach when they were children. The sand felt oh so good.

In his dream, Maria was piling the sand up . . . higher and higher . . . it was so heavy he couldn't move . . . he tried to tell her to stop, but she couldn't hear him . . . he couldn't move, he couldn't get out! He couldn't breathe!

Then another voice, a nice woman's voice, pushed into his dream, and the universe shifted. Soft hands rubbed his arms. He had arms! At least that made sense. Having arms was wonderful.

The cheerful voice continued, ". . . you should have seen that dog standing there with that chicken hanging out of his mouth. So proud of himself! Then Mrs. Daspitt came running over! I mean, there was no way I could pretend someone else took one of her chickens. And how was Freckles supposed to know they weren't there for him? He thought it was his own private buffet!

"I paid her for the chicken, of course, but we have to keep him inside now. I tell you, Freckles is getting to be one very expensive dog . . . Do you have any pets, Mr. Doe?"

46

Logan couldn't put it off any longer. She'd known for two days that the body in cold storage at the funeral home, the one that washed up on the rocks in Little Whale Cove, was not Mr. Pérez. On the one hand, this was good news—she wouldn't have to tell Vanessa and her mother that he was dead. But on the other hand, she couldn't give them good news, either. They still didn't know what happened him.

For all she knew, he could have run off with another woman or been kidnapped and forced into labor somewhere where he couldn't get to a phone. The fact that he hadn't told his family what the job was, or where, was suspicious. It was probably something illegal, and if it was and something happened to him, they'd never find out.

She didn't know which was worse. Knowing for sure he died, or never knowing where he was or what had happened. There were a lot worse things than dying.

Ben agreed the best thing was to share what she knew with the family and then hope the man came home on his own, or if he had died somewhere, that his body would be found so Vanessa and her mom would have some closure.

Sam said she'd come along for moral support, so Logan swung by and picked her up on the way. Gabriela had to be to work at the motel in Yachats Fridays at 10:00 a.m., so she said for them to come by early.

Armed with a box of donuts and four coffees, Logan and Sam knocked on the door at 7:30 a.m.

Vanessa answered.

"Please, please come in," she said. "Did you hear anything about my dad? Do you know where he is?"

Vanessa looked nervous. Apparently, she hadn't told her mom about the article she read regarding the body that washed up in Little Whale Cove a month ago and had not yet been identified. The poor girl had been dealing with this worry all on her own.

While Sam put the box of donuts on the coffee table and passed out the coffees, Logan got right to the point.

She gently explained to Gabriela about the article Vanessa had seen online and her concern that it might be her dad.

Gabriela's hand flew to her mouth, "Oh!"

"No, no," Logan said. "Please don't worry, that man was not your husband."

Vanessa's body slumped with relief, then her face tightened with worry as she realized that only meant that dead body was not her father. They still didn't know where he was. She reached out and took her mother's hand and scooched next to her, then asked Logan, "How do you know this for sure?" she asked.

Logan confessed to stealing Mateo's razor from the bathroom when they were there and giving it to a friend who sent it to a lab for testing. The DNA results were incontrovertible. The tissue samples did not match.

Vanessa translated this for her mom.

"I am so sorry we had to deceive you," Logan said. "But I didn't want to worry you more than you already were until we knew for sure."

This didn't need translation.

LOST AND FOUND

"*Yo comprendo, gracias,*" Gabriela murmured, "*Gracias por todo.*"

Sam reassured them that they were going to keep looking, that she had feelers out around town and would let them know if she heard anything from any of her contacts.

Not wanting Gabriela to go to Yachats upset, Logan made her best attempt at small talk. She asked Vanessa how her classes were doing and asked what she wanted to cover in their next tutoring appointment. Gabriela asked Sam when her baby was due and how she was feeling.

Sam said fine—she'd had some Braxton Hicks contractions on and off, but that was to be expected, as the doctor said her baby was probably going to be late. They'd adjusted her due date to seven to ten days from now.

"So what's on your agenda, today, Vanessa?" Sam asked. I've got some free time if you want to come down to the paper. I can show you around, give you that tour I've been promising.

Vanessa looked disappointed. "I'd love to, but I'm working today."

"Doing another catering job?" Logan said. "I think I saw you at the memorial service for Craig Peterson. Do you know the family or were you working the event?"

"No, I wasn't working that one," Vanessa said. "Mom and I went to the memorial service out of respect for Mrs. Emma Peterson."

"Yes," Gabriela said, comfortable enough with her guests now to speak in broken English. "She is good woman. She help . . . so many. I am sorry her son *es muerto*. We go for her, *no para la esposa, la puta . . .*"

Logan waited for the translation.

Vanessa filled in the blank. "*Not* for his wife, Roxy Peterson." She didn't translate every word her mother said.

Gabriela nodded vigorously and clamped her mouth shut.

"Everyone knows Mrs. Peterson," Vanessa said. "The mother. She doesn't just help with Newport Fishermen's Wives families, but she drops off boxes of food and clothes to families in our community, then drives away before anyone comes to the door to see who it is. She's kind of a Secret Santa.

"We don't see Roxy in Newport very often," she added, "but we do in Yachats, she meets a man at the motel Mom works for. I've seen them, too, when I'm there helping Mom."

Gabriela let loose a volley of Spanish.

Vanessa laughed, "Yeah, Mom says Roxy is always complaining about something, always leaves a mess, and never tips. Mom said to tell you that if that woman was grieving her husband at the memorial, she will eat your hat!"

Logan looked confused.

"Mom doesn't always get English idioms right," Vanessa explained.

Gabriela muttered a few more choice words.

"True," Vanessa translated. "The guy is really sleazy looking."

Something made Logan curious. "What's his name? Do you know who it is?"

Vanessa shrugged. "I don't know. Roxy always gets there first and signs for the room, although Mom says she hasn't seen either one of them in the last week or two, since the husband was lost at sea."

Her voice raised a notch and she looked at Logan wide-eyed. "Do you think she had anything to do with her husband's death? I mean, what if it wasn't an accident? Roxy didn't do it herself, but maybe she paid somebody to get rid of him so she could be with the man she meets at the motel!"

"What does this guy look like?" Logan asked.

"A little taller than you, kind of thin, dark blonde hair, didn't smile much," Vanessa said.

Logan turned to Sam, who had been uncharacteristically quiet, "Do you think it could be . . . ?"

LOST AND FOUND

But Sam wasn't listening. She half stood up and looked at Gabriela, wide-eyed, "I am so sorry, Mrs. Pérez, but I think my water just broke!"

47

SAMARITAN PACIFIC COMMUNITIES HOSPITAL

NEWPORT, OR

After Sam's water broke, Logan thought she was going to have to deliver a baby on the Pérez couch, but with Gabriela and Vanessa's help, she got Sam into the car and raced to the hospital. Sam called her obstetrician on the way.

It's a good thing Sam knew how to get there, because Logan couldn't punch the address into the GPS while driving. She made a note to do a better job of learning her way around town. She should really know where the hospital is.

When they arrived, Logan started to follow the signs to the main entrance, but Sam said you had to go through the emergency room to get to the Birthing Center.

Tim was out on the *Sara Lynn*, but had kept within cell phone reach all week, just in case. Sam's call went through. She put him on speaker phone and told him not to worry, Logan drove her to the hospital.

"You better get here quick, hon," Sam said. "you're about to be a daddy!"

"I'm headin' in, babe! And Logan, hold my wife's knees together if you have to until I get there! I don't want to miss this!"

Sam started to laugh and then doubled over with a contraction and handed Logan the phone. Not Braxton Hicks this time!

Logan promised Tim she'd take good care of Sam until he got there, then followed the entourage into the elevator up to the third floor to the Family Birthing Center. Sam was in Room 324. While they were getting Sam settled into her bed and getting her prepped, Logan looked around.

Wow. Room 324 was bigger than her first apartment.

Called a private birthing suite, the nurse explained that Sam would spend labor, delivery, and recovery here. There was the usual hospital bed you would expect, but instead of one or two plastic bucket chairs and paper cups with ice chips, there was a full couch, a comfortable, upholstered side chair, soft lighting, real paintings, a flat screen TV, DVD player, and even a jetted bathtub where Sam could relax during labor. And for the newborn, there was an infant warming area, wraps, and a crib filled with snuggly baby things and a going home outfit.

OMG.

When she had Amy, she remembered going through labor in a small box of a room, with another woman not five feet away. When she was dilated enough to justify pulling her doctor away from his golf game, they wheeled her to a delivery room—which definitely did not come with a jacuzzi tub.

Labor was still labor, though, and the anesthesiologist told Sam there wasn't time for an epidural. Her labor was too advanced. Even doing it old school, though, Sam was a trooper. Logan held her hand until Tim got there, then turned over the birthing coach duties to Dad, who did a great job. He'd gone to the classes.

Logan was happy to fetch ice cubes, pour water, flash Sam a thumbs-up periodically, and generally stay out of the way.

LOST AND FOUND

Three hours later, Miriam Magnolia Pullman made her grand entrance, with all her fingers and toes accounted for. Tim had won the arm-wrestling contest for the formal first name, but since Sam always called her Magnolia, everyone else did, too.

Logan took some pics of the proud parents and sleeping beauty for Facebook before leaving the new family to bond. She texted Ben in the lobby and told him all had gone well and that she was on her way home.

It had been a very eventful day. A few hours ago, Sam and Tim were just a young couple. Now they were a family. They had no idea how their lives were going to change, but she knew they were up to the task. Magnolia didn't know how lucky she was, but that baby had landed herself a very good gig.

By the time she got home, Ben had lunch ready. She was filling him in on the amenities of the private birthing suite when her phone rang. She dug it out of her purse and looked at the screen. It was Doyle's attorney, Mike Witcomb.

"Logan," he said. "Glad I caught you."

"Oh, I'm so sorry, Mike," she said. "Were we supposed to meet today to go talk with Doyle again? I didn't even check my calendar, but Sam went into labor. I just got back from the hospital."

"Not to worry," Witcomb said, "We hadn't set up a definite time. Oh, and you'll have to congratulate Sam and her husband for me, but that's not why I called."

"Did you want to reschedule?" she said, swiping over to her calendar.

"Maybe," he said. "I need to talk with Doyle first. The DA gave me a call last night, just as I was leaving the office."

"Did they come through with discovery?" she asked. If so, he would now know about the possible murder weapon found in his client's closet.

"Not formally. The official paperwork won't come through until next week, but as a courtesy, he wanted me to know the bulk of what they have.

"I am sorry to have to tell you this, I know Doyle is a friend of yours and Sam's, but it's not good," he said.

He quickly added, "Of course I'm still going to present the best defense possible, but if the DA offers a plea bargain, given what they have, Doyle may want to consider taking it."

Logan sat back down and put it on speaker so Ben could hear. "Why? What do they have?"

Witcomb sounded tired. And pissed. He gave a sarcastic summary of what the DA had shared with him.

"Well, a murder weapon for one. A ball peen hammer. Looks like it came from a tool kit on the *Freya*. Right there in Doyle's closet. With blood on it and everything. Dried blood that belonged to Craig Peterson. They took some personal items in Craig's home and sent it all in. The DNA test came back a 99.8 percent match."

Logan's heart sank. She knew this, but it sounded so much worse coming from Doyle's attorney.

Witcomb continued, "And there's more. There was a burner phone, left lying on the counter, right out in the open, with a history of text messages from Doyle to Craig's wife, Roxy, all but confessing to killing her husband so he could have her. Nothing on his regular phone. So, this points to premeditation. All the more ammunition for the DA.

"There's more, but you get the gist," he said.

"What does Doyle have to say about all this?" Logan asked. She had really started to believe Doyle might be innocent, but she hadn't known about the burner phone or his fixation on Roxy.

"I haven't talked with him yet," Witcomb said. "I'm going over there today. I'm sure he'll say he's innocent, but there's no way he can make all of that evidence go away."

"I'm sure you're right," Logan said, but her mind was whirling, trying to think of other explanations. Things were not always as they seemed.

"Look, I am going to lay it all out for him, give him a chance to explain all this. Then I'll advise him to let me make a deal for him. With all they have, not guilty is a sure ticket to life on death row. With a guilty plea, I might at least be able to get him the possibility of parole, but no matter what, unless we can find new evidence or discredit what they have, I think Doyle's going away for a very long time.

"And between you and me, if he's guilty, he should," Witcomb added.

Logan had nothing to say. Witcomb was surprisingly forthcoming for an attorney. But then again, he was young. Seasoned lawyers probably didn't share their feelings so honestly.

Witcomb said he'd let her know what Doyle decided to do after he met with him today, but to let Sam know he didn't hold out much hope.

"You know, this shouldn't surprise me," he added.

Logan could hear him leaning back in his chair, making it squeak. "But I really bought this guy's story—hook, line, and sinker. My bad."

48

ICU, ADVENTIST HEALTH HOSPITAL

TILLAMOOK, OR

It was the end of Bethany's shift and being a Sunday, things were quiet. She smiled down at her charge. He looked good.

In just two days, after being brought out of his medically-induced coma, John Doe had made great progress. His broken ribs were still painful and made it difficult for him to move freely, and his right arm was in a cast, but his head wound was healing, and the bruises had faded from nightmarish purple and black to a washed-out yellowish green.

The ophthalmologist had even removed the patch from his left eye. It remained somewhat swollen and still sported a few stitches along the brow, but he could open it now and his chart said it would not require surgery. How much or what he could see was still unknown.

Bethany remembered a patient she had last year who was 95 percent blind, even though all of the physical parts of her eye worked perfectly. What didn't work was the optic nerve. It had been damaged in her car accident and no longer carried information about the images received from light, passing through the various structures of the eye to the brain. Optic nerves could not be repaired. Nothing they could do for her.

Yang had just finished putting John Doe through his physio routine. He and Bethany exchanged floor gossip, then he made his notes and moved on to the orthopedic ward where he was helping a young veteran get used to using his new prosthetic. It was better than the old one but was still giving him trouble.

When he left, Bethany had her patient all to herself. She raised his hospital bed a little and handed him a large plastic cup of ice-cold Gatorade with a lid, bending the straw sticking up out of the middle so he wouldn't have to lean forward. He still couldn't hold the cup by himself.

When he was through, she made a note on his chart. Fluid intake, 127 milliliters. She checked his other vitals, then hung the chart back on the bed and put her hands on her hips.

"Last day, mister," she said. "They're moving you to step-down this morning."

The man looked at her and tried to speak, but only raspy squawks came out and he started coughing. She reached over to the side table for the bottle of Cepacol and got him to let her pump a few sprays in the back of his throat.

"I know it tastes awful," she told him, "but it'll numb it for a while. You need to let your vocal cords rest, don't try to talk."

"*No habla*," she added, a little louder, as if volume would help.

She silently thanked Mrs. Rodriguez, her Spanish teacher, for the few phrases she remembered.

He nodded and lay back on his pillow.

The man still didn't have enough small muscle control to hold a pen, let alone write, so no one knew who he was or what had happened to him. But there must be a way to communicate. This man had a long road of healing ahead of him and most of that would be done at home. If he had a family, he really would need them in the months to come.

She looked into the man's eyes. She was as frustrated as he was. Then she held up a finger and said, "Wait! I'll be right back!"

A few minutes later, she returned with a small white board and a dry erase marker. In large, clear print she wrote the digits zero to nine across the top of the board, leaving the bottom blank. Reaching for her phone, she waggled it in front of him and pointed to the keypad, then at the ten digits on the board.

He looked at her blankly.

She propped the board up on the blankets with one hand and with her thumb and index finger gripped her phone and held it on top of the board, facing him, so he could see both.

With her free hand, she pointed at the digit 1 on the phone's keypad and the digit 1 she had written on the board.

A light went on in the man's eyes and he tried to reach for the phone, but only succeeded in knocking both phone and board out of her hand.

Patiently, she set it all up again, this time, patting his arm to indicate he should remain still and let her do all the work.

He nodded.

Good.

With the marker, Bethany pointed to the digit nine, then looked at him expectantly. He shook his head.

Okay . . .

She crossed out the digit nine, then repeated the sequence with the digits eight and seven with the same results. Maybe he didn't understand what she was trying to do, after all.

When she got to the digit six, he vigorously nodded his head up and down and barked out a happy sound—or a word, she couldn't tell which.

Yeah!

Bethany wrote the numeral six in the first position on the far left. John Doe shook his head no, then got his left arm to move jerkily to the right.

She got it.

Six was not the first number, it went somewhere to the right. Okay . . . she quickly added ten long dashes, like in the game hangman, and wrote the six on the second line.

Nothing.

When she got to the seventh place, her patient's face lit up and she got the emphatic up and down "yes!" nod again.

It took another twenty minutes, with a lot of erasing and rewriting, but finally, Bethany had ten digits neatly printed on the board that were approved by her patient.

541 555 6403

She still didn't know her patient's name or anything about him. Hopefully, whoever answered this number, did. And the area code 541 was Oregon, she was pretty sure, so maybe they were close by.

Spent but joyful, the man squeezed his eyes shut, a few tears ran down the sides of his face onto his hospital gown.

Bethany dialed the number, trying to keep her excitement battened down.

"*Bueno*," a woman's voice said.

"Oh, I'm sorry, *no hablo español*. Do you speak English?" Bethany asked. She let her hopes rise.

"*Un momento*," the woman said.

Bethany heard her put her hand over the receiver and call someone to the phone.

"*Vanessa!*"

A few minutes later, a young girl came on the line, her voice a little wary.

"Hello?" she said. "Can I help you?"

Bethany let out an excited breath, "I hope so," she said. "My name is Bethany. I'm an ICU nurse at the Tillamook hospital . . . We have a patient here, a man, who was in an accident." She provided a brief description and explained he had been in a coma, so was unable to communicate until recently.

She hurried to add, "He is okay, but we'd really like to find his family. Do you know this man?"

For a second, there was stunned silence, then the girl shouted, "Yes! Yes!" followed by the sound of pounding footsteps and "Mamá! Mamá!"

49

After much excited shouting and crying and holding the phone up to her patient's ear so he could hear his family's voices, Bethany was able to calm everyone down enough to learn her patient's name.

Mr. Mateo Pérez. Beautiful! The two very happy women on the other end of the phone were his wife, Gabriela, and his teenage daughter, Vanessa.

Bethany explained to Vanessa—who in turn translated for her mother—why her father could not yet speak on his own. His vocal cords would heal soon, she reassured them.

She did not share the extent of his other injuries, but knew there would be time for that later. Right now, she just wanted to let them enjoy this initial flood of relief and happiness that he was alive.

She relayed the name of the hospital and the phone number. Right now, he was in the ICU, she explained, but would be transferred to an intermediate-care floor in a regular hospital room later today. Yes, she would call and give them that room number as soon as she had it. She also gave them directions to the hospital.

The family, it was discovered, did not own a car, but the daughter, Vanessa, said she had someone she could call and ask for a ride. After holding her phone up to Mr. Pérez's ear so he could hear his wife and daughter's voices one last time, Bethany disconnected and gave her patient a broad smile and two triumphant thumbs up!

Ever the diligent nurse, she made notes on his chart first, then went to share the good news.

*****

Vanessa and Gabriela piled excitedly into Logan's car. There was road construction near Hebo, but they made the ninety-minute trip in just over an hour, getting them there as soon as Logan's lead foot and rear mirror monitoring would allow. She couldn't wait to meet the infamous Mr. Pérez and see the joy on Vanessa's and her mom's faces when the family was reunited.

Even more, she wanted to know how Mr. Pérez wound up badly injured in a hospital in Tillamook, miles away from Newport. What kind of job had he taken that took him that far north? And why had no one reported him missing?

When the phone rang earlier this morning, Logan had been sitting on the back deck, enjoying her coffee, listening to her owls—she thought of the pair as hers because they came back every winter to set up house in the forest just behind their house. Barred owls, she learned, nested early because their young needed a longer time than most birds to become independent.

When Vanessa told her that her father was alive and they could go see him, a flood of relief swept through Logan. When Mateo's DNA wasn't a match, she had all but given up hope that they would ever find him—especially if he were alive and didn't want to be found—so this was great news.

Her initial relief was immediately followed by a waterfall of questions about what happened to him and why he hadn't been in touch before now. She also worried that this turn of events would alert ICE to Mateo and Gabriela's presence in the country without documentation, but she kept those worries to herself for now.

Logan was happy to give them a ride up to Tillamook. On the drive down to Newport to pick them up, Logan called Sam hands free from the car. Morning sunbeams danced across the denim blue sea, and everything looked a little brighter. After the depressing report from Witcomb about Doyle, Logan didn't realize how much they all needed some positive news.

With the birth of Sam and Tim's daughter, a new life had entered the world, and now, a beloved father and husband whose life had been assumed lost had been found. That was a good day in Logan's book.

Sam, the new mom, was enjoying another day of rest with Magnolia in their luxury birthing suite at Good Samaritan, but Sam, the reporter, was bummed she couldn't be there with Logan to get the whole story from Mateo and his doctors and nurses about what happened. She immediately began peppering Logan with questions she didn't have answers to yet.

"Whoa, woman!" Logan said, laughing. "I promise to call you as soon as the visit is over and tell you all about it."

Not trusting Logan to ask the right questions, Sam said she was texting her a list right now, and she was to get the answers to each and every one of those questions before leaving the hospital.

"Talk to the nurses," she said, "They always know what's going on. Doctors won't tell you anything. And see if you can track down whoever brought him in."

✳✳✳✳✳

After passing through the guardians at registration and checking in at the nurse's station, Logan, Vanessa, and Gabriela were directed to the second floor, Room 219, where a Latino man with stitches along his eyebrow lay pale against the pillows, his right arm in a blue cast. But when he saw his family, his whole face came alive! The two women rushed in and for a few minutes, there was a lot of hugging and kissing and flurries of happy Spanish.

Logan smiled and waved but stayed back to give the trio some privacy. There were only two visitors' chairs in the room, so she went to hunt down another one. One of the nurses said she could grab one from an adjacent room, which was unoccupied at the moment.

On her way back with the chair, a nurse with sandy hair pulled back in a ponytail stepped out of the elevator and headed for Mr. Peréz's room. Logan flagged her down.

She introduced herself as Bethany, the ICU nurse who had cared for Mateo the last few weeks. She had a short break and had come down to see how he was doing. Not wanting to interrupt the joyful family reunion going on in the room, she waited outside with Logan, who took the opportunity to get started on Sam's long list of questions.

One of Sam's questions was how the nurse had figured out her patient's phone number when he couldn't yet talk or hold a pen to write. Although Bethany downplayed it, Logan thought her whiteboard trick was very ingenious and told her so.

After answering a few more questions, Bethany said she'd be back later when she got a longer break to talk with the family. His medical team had already done rounds, but she would be happy to give the mom and daughter a full report when she came back.

Logan walked her back to the elevator and asked about his injuries.

"Right now, other than the orbital fracture and the broken arm, which will simply take time to heal, Mr. Pérez is in very good shape. He could possibly be left with blurred or double vision in his eye, even after the fracture heals, but that's a small price to pay for being alive."

She pressed 'up' and when the doors opened, got in.

Holding the doors open with one arm, she added, "Oh, and if you're staying through lunch, steer clear of the chicken cutlet. The vegetarian lasagna is much better!"

Logan made a note and went back to join the party in Room 219.

50

It was a good thing Ben remembered holidays, because most of them blew right by Logan unless she marked them on the calendar.

So Valentine's Day was not on her radar a couple of days ago when she accepted an invitation from her friend, Will, to join him and his band, *Woodlander*, for one of their gigs at the Oregon Garden Resort in Silverton.

For the last thirty years, *Woodlander* performed original Americana music all over the state. They'd even been inducted into the Oregon Music Hall of Fame. When they played at the Oregon Garden Resort, they often invited Logan to join them if she was available. She brought Bella and contributed backup fiddle. They always had a blast.

The Resort's rooms were reasonable, especially their winter rates, so Logan had decided to stay over and check out Silver Falls State Park this morning before driving home. Her friend, Rita, had been raving about it ever since she moved to Oregon.

Due to the weather and time constraints, Logan only had time to hike down to the main attraction, South Falls, a gorgeous 177-foot waterfall you could walk behind, but she quickly made mental plans to return with Ben for the full Trail of Ten Falls this summer.

Ben stayed home this trip—said he needed to finish his water catchment project. Logan had been independent for so long, she didn't mind traveling alone, but was surprised that even one day away from Ben made her miss him. Marriage had taken some getting used to, but she liked it.

Driving home, her stomach started rumbling. She wondered what Ben was making for dinner.

Ben had not forgotten it was Valentine's Day, but he didn't greet her at the door with roses. He knew the way to his woman's heart was through her stomach.

Dinner was beautifully prepared butterflied pork chops, Brussel sprouts topped with crispy bacon and french fried onions, a triple-threat dish of cheesy scalloped potatoes layered with sour cream, a huge tossed green salad, crusty French rolls, real butter, and a decadent flourless chocolate cake served with a dollop of homemade whipped cream.

Oh. My. God. *So* good!

But that wasn't the best surprise. After they'd enjoyed a finger of fine bourbon by the fire, they decided to turn in early and finish their Valentine's Day evening in bed. Later, when she went to take a shower, she saw the project Ben had *really* been working on while she was gone.

A gleaming, sexy-looking, smooth, soft-white, curved slipper tub glowed from the lights of multiple candles Ben had arranged along the windowsill and on two tall pillar candles he'd placed on a teak shelf.

All Logan could do was stare with her mouth hanging open.

"How did you . . . ? When did you?" she stuttered. "How did you do this in only two days!"

"Clay helped," Ben said, with obvious pleasure in her reaction. "Just ignore the back wall and that part of the floor. The tile guy is coming tomorrow, but this baby is fully plumbed and ready to go. Wanna take her for a spin?"

He waggled his eyebrows up and down.

She did. They did. There was room for two.

Even the owls hooted their approval.

51

It was late, but no one was sleeping.

Four men hunched around a small, square table bolted to the floor of the cabin. Two had claimed spots on the more comfortable L-shaped bench seat, the other two were on chairs. Black rubber bumpers around the edge of the tabletop kept the cards and chips from sliding onto the floor in rough seas, but tonight was calm and they only felt a gentle rocking as the *Sea Gypsy* motored south.

Søren looked at his hand, then at the piles of chips in front of the others. Slater, one of the full-time crew members, boasted the largest pile, Turnbull was next. Søren made sure he kept his pile respectable, but not bigger than the other two. The newbie's chip pile was pitiful.

The captain paid well and in cash, but none of them would get paid until they docked, so Turnbull kept a running balance of wins and losses. They'd settle up when they got back.

This was the Guatemalan's first run. He wasn't getting as big a cut as the more experienced crew, and unless his luck changed, he wouldn't be getting anything at all. As long as the idiot stayed out of the red, he'd survive the night. This wasn't a crew you wanted to owe.

The other newbie, the Mexican, was smarter than his compatriot. He had gone up on deck, as far away from the rest of them as he could get. Søren respected him for that, but still, he didn't like it. He should be down here with his buddy, celebrating.

Maybe he was saving his money for his wife and kid. Søren knew he had a family because that's how they'd convinced him to come tonight. The unspoken threat to his wife and daughter, if he refused to cooperate, had been very clear.

But was it enough to keep him quiet once they returned to Newport? The captain always selected illegals to do the actual exchange, giving himself some distance from the actual crime should anything go wrong.

Everything had gone smoothly tonight. The two illegals picked up the product just off Garibaldi and were back on board within the hour. It wasn't a big boat, and the captain was smart. He never did big runs, so as not to attract attention from the Coast Guard. Once on board, packages were attached to the hull with magnets or suction cups, so even if they were boarded, the coasties wouldn't find anything.

Søren refocused his attention on his cards. Worrying about the Mexican was not his job. Any decisions regarding the illegals were above his pay grade. The captain was up there. He'd know if there was anything to worry about. They still had several hours to go.

In the close quarters, Søren could smell the sour, moldy canvas cushions on the bench seats and the four men's collective stink. These runs were profitable, but he was glad he didn't have to eat, sleep, and shit next to these guys all the time. He tried to avoid using the head after Turnbull.

An hour later, the skinny Guatemalan was out of chips and sniffling in his bunk. He not only lost all of the money he didn't have yet but would now have to do another run to pay Stater back. Turnbull started to deal him in, but Søren bowed out.

He patted his pockets and pulled out a crumpled pack of squares. Pushing his stool back from the table, he grabbed his jacket and started up the stairs.

Up on deck, the cold air made his eyes water momentarily. The Mexican was on his left, standing at the railing, looking out to sea. Søren headed starboard, to the other side of the wheelhouse, intending to enjoy his cigarette alone. But the captain saw him and waved him in.

They chatted.

A few minutes later, Søren exited the wheelhouse and went below, cigarette forgotten.

He lay in his bunk until he heard Turnbull's buzzsaw snores and Stater's even breathing, then leaned over and poked the Guatemalan. Putting his fingers to his lips in the universal *shhh* signal, he mimed putting on his boots and whispered a few words in the man's ear.

If either of the other crew members had been awake, they would have heard Søren give the Guatemalan a way to pay his debt. In full. Plus some.

All he had to do was go topside and get rid of his competition. Simple. Søren was back-up to make sure he went through with it. The captain thought of everything.

He had also noted the Mexican's restlessness and knew he couldn't be trusted not to turn them all in. Although it wasn't Søren's idea—it seemed a little drastic at first—he had to admit it was a brilliant solution.

Middle of winter, middle of the night, miles away from shore. Even if the guy was an Olympic swimmer, his chances of surviving a midnight swim were next to zero. Especially in the shape he was going to be in before he hit the water.

3:21 A.M.

The air felt different, somehow. Electric.

When he opened the hatch, cold air rushed in and ragged clouds cruised across the face of the moon, allowing nothing more than a dim light to illuminate the deck, silhouetting the captain briefly in the pilothouse, before passing on.

Nudging the Guatemalan slowly forward, Søren stayed in the shadows, every muscle tense.

The Mexican was still at the railing, his back to them, arms folded, feet firmly planted on the deck, looking out to sea. He wore a jacket, but no life vest. The night was calm and the sea smooth.

Søren held his breath. His heart started to pound. He hadn't noticed it before, but the Guatemalan was much scrawnier than his target. He hadn't realized how broad-shouldered the Mexican was. A gentle rumbling of the engine muffled the sound of the Guatemalan's footsteps. Mateo never heard him coming.

Without a weapon of any kind, the Guatemalan had thrown himself onto the Mexican's back, trying to push him overboard, but had only succeeded in spinning him around. Then it was all swinging, kicking, and wrestling, one man trying desperately to gain the advantage, the Guatemalan trying to push the Mexican overboard, the Mexican fending off blows with his forearms, only trying to defend himself. Frozen to the spot, Søren could do nothing but watch. If he jumped in to help, he was afraid he'd be the one taking an involuntary swim.

LOST AND FOUND

After what seemed like forever, but was in reality only seconds, it was over. Unfortunately, the wrong man was left standing.

Bleeding badly from a cut above one eye, the Mexican stood over the crumpled body of the man who just tried to kill him, wavering slightly as if his legs were about to give out.

Knowing it was up to him, now, before the Mexican could regain his balance, Søren roared out of hiding and shoved him as hard as he could up and over the railing. There was a sickening thud as the man hit something on the way down, but soon it was silent.

Shaking slightly, Søren followed the directions he had been given, hoisting the second body over the railing and into the sea, then went below. A few minutes later, lying on his bunk, he started to feel better. He had just tripled his pay.

The captain never left the wheelhouse.

52

Søren sat at the light, pressing on the gas every now and then to keep the engine from dying. He really needed a new truck. As soon as Roxy had her money. He'd found his sugar mama and they would be out of here by the end of the month. Roxy was just waiting to sell the boat and get the life insurance money. Then it was on to Vegas! Hot, dry, fun Las Vegas. Roxy thought they were getting married, but he had other plans. Run through her money, then dump the bitch. Roxy was fun, but she could be bossy. And he'd had enough bosses.

In the meantime, he'd taken another temporary job with a crab boat. They'd be on the water for a few days, so the captain sent him into town to pick up some groceries at Freddie's.

Something about the first car in the opposite lane caught his attention. He squinted to see better. The long-haired woman driver was a looker, but it was the man in the passenger seat that made him stare. Søren took a good, long look before the light turned green and as the SUV passed him, going south.

It *couldn't* be! But it was. It was *him*!

Søren could scarcely breathe. This was not good news. He knew he should call the captain of the *Sea Gypsy*. But, no, he would handle this himself. Quickly, he nosed his truck into the left lane, made a U-turn, and followed the SUV. Freddie's would have to wait. If the Mexican had talked with anyone, being late with the groceries would be the least of Søren's worries.

Having no exact idea what he was going to do when he got there, Søren continued to tail the SUV through town. He changed lanes occasionally but didn't let more than two cars get between him and the other car. He didn't have to work very hard to conceal the fact he was following them. They weren't expecting anyone to be on their tail.

Sure enough, the copper-haired woman drove them right to the building in Newport he'd seen when they scouted out where this guy lived so they could scare him into accepting the job.

Søren cruised past the duplex and parked in front of the paint store. From here, he could see their driveway. He needed to think.

He watched as they helped the man into the house. The Mexican could walk, but just barely. He looked pretty weak, had stitches or something over his eye, and one arm was in a cast.

Søren settled in to wait, turning options over in his brain.

Thirty minutes later, he still hadn't come up with a plan. He wanted to go have a quality talk with the Mexican, but not with an audience. He waited another ten minutes.

Finally, the two Mexican women—the wife and daughter—hustled out. They parted at the end of the driveway. The girl with a backpack on her shoulder turned right toward the high school, and the mom with a tote bag walked toward the bus stop. Work and school, he assumed.

Good, they'd be gone a while. But the white woman was still in there. Who was she and what was the Mexican telling her? He needed to know how she fit into the picture.

LOST AND FOUND

When he spotted the SUV near Freddie's, they were coming from the north. The guy must have made it to shore somehow. His family didn't have a car, so the white woman must be some do-gooder who gave them a ride. But from where? Where had the Mexican been for the last month? Who had he talked to and why was he just now coming home?

He had seen the article in the paper about a dead body washing up in the rocks in Depoe Bay. Given the timing, he thought it might be either the Guatemalan or the Mexican. With winter currents, it was possible it could have drifted this far south, but when nobody had been reported missing and no one had claimed the body, he figured they were safe. Until now.

Maybe he didn't need to worry. If the Mexican had talked with anyone, the police would have come asking questions, but no cops had been around. The *Sea Gypsy* was still operational as far as he knew. Maybe the captain's wisdom in only selecting illegals for the jobs had paid off. Maybe the Mexican hadn't talked.

But he couldn't be sure. And he needed to be.

53

The weather was clear and there wasn't a lot of traffic on the 101, so Logan and company made good time. Mateo dozed off and on in the passenger seat while Logan caught up with Vanessa and her mom.

When they got home, they helped Mateo out of the car and into the house. They started to put him to bed, but he said he'd rather sit. Said he'd had all the bed rest he needed in the weeks he lay in a coma in the hospital.

Besides, the nurse told him he needed to rebuild his muscles and stamina. She sent him home with a set of exercises he was to do three times a day and instructions to buy a walker until he was steadier on his feet.

So they settled him on the couch and Gabriela went into the kitchen and made everyone some strong coffee. Vanessa put her father's bag of medicine and eye drops next to him and went to get a box of tissues and a glass of water.

When they were all seated in the living room, enjoying Gabriela's strong brew, Mateo, in a rusty voice, thanked everyone, including Logan for the ride, but said he didn't need fussing over. He insisted his wife and daughter not miss another day of work or school because of him. He was fine, he'd said.

It wasn't until Logan said she would check on him after she finished her errands in town that Vanessa and Gabriela finally allowed themselves to gather their things and be shooed out the front door. Hoisting her backpack onto her shoulder, Vanessa gave her dad a kiss on the forehead and told him she'd be back in time to start dinner.

Mateo waited until he saw his wife and daughter part ways at the end of the driveway before turning to Logan, who had just returned from using the bathroom—for real this time—and asked her to stay for a minute.

"Of course," she said, "what can I get you? Would you like another glass of water before I leave? More coffee? I'm not much of a cook, but I can run get you something to eat."

"No," Mateo said, pointing to the chair she had just vacated. She sat.

"You have already helped so much, and I would not normally ask you for another favor, but I need someone who speaks English and I do not want to involve my daughter or put her in danger. She should be focusing on her school, not on my problems."

He paused for breath, then continued, "I need to tell you a story and to warn you about a man named Søren. He is very dangerous."

Logan put her bag on the floor.

How did Mateo know about Søren? Gabriela had seen him and Roxy at the motel where she worked, but that just meant he was a sleaze. Why did Mateo think he was dangerous?

Just before Sam went into labor, Logan had realized Søren was the only other crew member besides Doyle on the deck of the *Freya* when Craig went overboard and given his affair with

Roxy, that gave him the motive to get rid of the husband, but how would Mateo know that?

Mateo wasn't on the *Freya* the night Craig was killed, and as far as she knew, had never crewed on her, either. He worked at a restaurant on the Bayfront. How did he even know Søren?

Mateo started to speak, but grimaced and reached for his water glass, but it was empty.

Logan went into the kitchen and refilled it, adding ice. Maybe that would soothe his throat. When she returned, he was unwrapping a lozenge he'd taken from the paper sack Vanessa left for him.

"These help," he said.

Logan sat back down and decided the direct approach was best.

"How do you know Søren?" she said. "And how do you know he is dangerous?"

"Until six weeks ago, I'd never met him," Mateo said. "Wait, let me tell you the whole story, then I have a favor to ask of you."

For the next few minutes, Mateo haltingly told her about the two men showing up one night outside the restaurant where he worked, offering him a job, but not telling him what it was. When they said how much he would make for one night's work, Mateo turned them down. He knew that much money could not be made legally. But he soon realized it wasn't really a suggestion, very much like the cartels back in Mexico he'd run from. When they not-too-subtly threatened his family, showing him a picture they'd taken of Vanessa at her school and Gabriela walking to the bus, he'd reluctantly agreed.

"I am so sorry, Mateo," Logan said. She understood protecting your family. If anyone ever threatened Amy or Ian, she'd move heaven and earth to keep them safe.

Mateo continued.

"They told me to meet them at Dock Three and they would walk us back. Another man was there, too. I didn't know him.

For the next few minutes, Mateo proceeded to tell Logan what he remembered of what happened on that awful night on the *Sea Gypsy*.

She sat, stunned. Horrified at what this man had been through.

"It's a miracle you're alive," she said. "Do you know what happened to the other man? The Guatemalan?"

"No," Mateo shook his head. "When he came at me, I didn't understand why. It didn't make any sense. I fought back, but I tried not to hurt him. I don't think he wanted to attack me. I just wanted him to stop. He hit me very hard, and I almost passed out, but I fought back. I had to! I must have hit him harder than I meant to. He fell and then he wasn't moving. I felt very bad. I don't know what happened to him."

Logan had a pretty good idea. She'd have to check with Jean, but maybe she would be able to identify the deceased man who washed up on the rocks in Depoe Bay. The timing matched. She didn't share these thoughts with Mateo. He felt bad enough already. Besides, if he had been thrown into the ocean, Mateo hadn't done it. Someone else did and Logan was betting it was Søren or someone on the *Sea Gypsy* cleaning up loose ends.

"Why didn't the captain come out to help?" Logan asked. "He was right there in the wheelhouse. You said it wasn't a large boat. He must have seen what was going on, right?"

"Yes, he saw," Mateo said. "He looked straight at me. He did nothing to stop it. He must have wanted it to happen."

Logan's head was spinning. "How many crew members were there? Who else was on board?"

"There were six of us all together. The captain, three regular crew members, Jairo—the man from Guatemala—and me. After the pickup, everyone but the captain went below to play poker. I wanted to be alone, so I came up on deck."

"Which man attacked you?" Logan asked, "Who pushed you over the railing?"

54

"Søren," Mateo said.

Okay. The last piece clicked into place in Logan's mind.

"Søren's was the last face I saw before I went into the water," Mateo said. "That's how I know he is a very bad man. I don't remember anything after that until I woke up in the hospital."

Logan's mind started whirring. She had to make sure this was the same Søren. It was an unusual name, but she thought it was Scandinavian and there were a lot of Swedes, Danes, and Norwegians in the area.

"What does this Søren look like?" she asked.

"Light-colored, stringy hair, a little long in back, blue eyes," Mateo said. "He isn't a big man, but he's strong."

Yep, that was him.

"In a real fight, I could have defended myself," Mateo said, "but it all happened so fast. I was confused about why Jairo had just tried to kill me—and then I was afraid I had accidentally killed *him* while trying to stop him."

Logan had only seen Søren from a distance when he took the *Freya* out with Liv to help search for Craig, but the description fit. And that's how Gabriela and Vanessa had described Roxy's lover, who they'd seen at the motel in Yachats.

From what she remembered from Sam's article, Søren was hired at the last minute the morning the *Freya* left on her second trip out. Liv had been sick, so Craig hired him temporarily until Liv could return to work.

Søren was the one who made the emergency call and brought the *Freya* back in after the storm. Søren had helped pull Doyle into the wheelhouse, and Søren was the only other person on deck besides Doyle when Craig Peterson was killed and pushed overboard, never to be recovered.

But was Søren a killer? The *Freya* didn't smuggle drugs. It had to be something Roxy and Søren cooked up between the two of them. Get the husband out of the way so they could be together. From what Sam had said, Roxy didn't care for fishing and Craig was never going to leave Newport or his family. Murder may have seemed the only way out.

Roxy liked money. Her shop didn't make any money. Unless Craig had a very large life insurance policy, the only way she benefitted from her husband's death was to sell the *Freya* with its lucrative crab fishing permit—Liv said Craig didn't own the *Freya*, his mom did.

It's possible Craig hadn't told Roxy that. Maybe he was embarrassed that as the man of the family, he didn't have title to the boat he captained, that his mom did. Yeah, that made sense. If Roxy didn't know she wouldn't get the *Freya*, she'd have motive to get rid of Craig, take it all and get out of Dodge.

It all fit, but how could she prove it? She was just guessing and who would trust Mateo's memory when he'd been in a coma for a month after a serious head injury? He was undocumented and if he told his story, would have to admit he was on the *Sea Gypsy* to help smuggle drugs. No one would believe he'd been forced to do so.

What a mess.

And Doyle's murder trial was still on the calendar. In fact, Witcomb said he had a meeting with the judge in his chambers tomorrow. Against his attorney's repeated advice, Doyle was insisting on his right to a speedy trial and wanted to move the date up. She needed to get this information to Witcomb before he met with the judge, but first, she needed hard evidence. Right now, all she had were loosely connected facts and wild guesses.

With Mateo's first-hand testimony that Søren had pushed him overboard, they might at least have him for attempted murder on the *Sea Gypsy*, but without concrete evidence that Søren had murdered Craig at sea and that he and Roxy had planned it and somehow conspired to plant evidence pointing the police toward Doyle, Doyle was still going to be convicted and sent to prison for the rest of his life.

Logan pulled her mind back to Mateo. She really wanted to help this man and his family but didn't see what she could do.

He clarified his problem. "If I go to the *policia*, Mrs. McKenna, they will call ICE and Gabriela and I will be deported. They can say I did this work, this drug smuggling, willingly and was part of their operation."

Logan had forgotten about that wrinkle. Like most citizens, she took for granted her ability to call the police for help without worrying about being deported as a result.

He took a drink of his water and swallowed painfully.

"And even if they question Søren or any of the crew on the *Sea Gypsy*, they might say I killed Jairo to keep his share of the money. If that happened, they would never let me back into this country. I would have a criminal record," he said. "I would never see Vanessa graduate from high school, and definitely not from college."

His eyes filled with tears.

Logan truly felt for him but had no idea how she could help. And somehow, she needed to figure out how to help Doyle, too.

Mateo's voice was giving out. He struggled to his feet and hobbled into the bedroom, returning with a business card and a few bills in his good hand. He dropped back onto the couch and handed the money and the card to Logan. Two twenties and a ten. The card said "Patricia Haggerman, Attorney at Law."

Several months ago, he told Logan, he had gone to see this woman. She helped immigrants. Because he and Gabriela had entered the country illegally, she told him straight out that there was almost no chance of her being able to help them. At least she had been honest about it.

The first person he had gone to several years ago for help had not been. A co-worker at the restaurant said his brother worked for immigration and could speed up the process and get them a temporary visa, but it was expensive. Mateo and Gabriela scraped together the money and gave it to him, but it turned out he had no such connection and left town after taking money from several other families in the area, too. He knew they would not report him.

At least this woman had told him the truth.

Haggerman said there was a chance she could apply for a waiver for them in a few years when Vanessa turned twenty-one. Until then, their application was on hold.

Mateo told Logan that this woman was the only person he could think of who understood the system and may know if there was anything he could do to bring the bad men to justice, without endangering Gabriela and Vanessa.

He gestured to the money he'd given her. "It's not very much, but please tell her I will pay her more as soon as I can get back to work."

Mateo was barely whispering now, his voice almost gone. He could also barely walk. It was obvious he would not be able to come with her to see this attorney.

Logan tucked the money into her bag and pulled out her car keys. She doubted thirty dollars would buy very much of any attorney's time, but giving Haggerman a call was the least she could do for Mateo, a man who had already survived against such overwhelming odds.

LOST AND FOUND

The card indicated the woman's law office was not far from Witcomb's. She'd call him on the way to share what she'd learned about Søren. If she hurried, she'd be able to see both of them before they left for the night.

She gave Mateo a careful hug and told him to get some rest. She'd let him know if the attorney had any advice.

Once in the car, she texted Ben to let him know she might be late for dinner. Again.

55

Arriving a few minutes early, Logan checked the address and parked. Entering the two-story professional building she ran her finger down the directory until she found the name she was looking for.

Patricia Haggerman
Attorney at Law
203B

Logan started toward the elevator, but when the door shuddered open and spit out the last occupant, she changed her mind and took the stairs. Haggerman shared the floor with a tax accountant, a psychologist, and Simon Litgeist Consulting. Logan wondered what kind of consulting Simon did.

The door to 203B was open.

A sixty-something woman with a cap of wispy, white hair half-stood and waved her in. She reached across a large, messy desk to shake Logan's hand, before sitting back down, indicating Logan should do the same in one of the two ladder chairs available.

The rest of the tiny room was lined with bookshelves. In the middle of one of them sat an old-school printer and fax machine. Framed on the wall behind Haggerman hung a brightly-colored child's drawing—a painting of a happy, stick-figure family. A massive, striped tabby napped on top of a four-drawer filing cabinet by the door. He barely registered Logan's arrival with a twitch of his tail.

"Thanks for agreeing to meet with me, Ms. Haggerman," Logan said.

"Please, call me Pat," said Haggerman, leaning back. Pulling a Diet Pepsi out of mini refrigerator under her desk, she offered one to Logan, who declined. She took a long drink herself, then pulled out a yellow legal pad. Pen poised above it, she gave Logan her full attention.

"Mr. Pérez just called," she said. "He was losing his voice, so wasn't able to explain to me exactly what he needed, so I don't know if I can help, but he did give me permission to speak with you, so let's start at the beginning. How do you know the Pérez family?"

Logan summarized how Vanessa was one of the students she tutored at the high school and how she had shared that her father, Mateo, was missing, up until the nurse's phone call several weeks later from Adventist Health Hospital ICU, telling them he'd been in a medically induced coma, and then offering to drive Mateo home earlier today.

She ended with the story he had just shared with her this morning in confidence after Vanessa and Gabriela left for school, about how he was coerced into helping the *Sea Gypsy* on a drug smuggling run, which ended with Søren throwing him into the sea and probably Jairo, the Guatemalan as well.

"Wow," Haggerman said, sitting back in her chair, tapping her pen on the yellow pad, the first page now filled with her notes, which were neat and angular, almost like calligraphy.

"Yes," said Logan. "It's a lot to take in, but that's where he's at."

At this point, Logan dutifully placed the money Mateo had given her to pay for the attorney's time on the desk. Without comment, Haggerman respectfully took it and placed it in her desk's top, right drawer.

"Tell Mr. Pérez thank you, that will cover our conversation today."

"So," she continued. "Mr. Pérez has not yet contacted the police or even told his wife and daughter about this . . . this . . ." She referred to her notes . . . "Søren, or the *Sea Gypsy*, correct?"

"That's correct," Logan said. "He is afraid of ICE. He doesn't want him or his wife to be deported and leave Vanessa alone. That's why neither Vanessa nor her mother called for help when Mateo went missing originally. She only confided in me because she broke down during one of our tutoring sessions."

"And they were right," Haggerman said. "That's almost definitely what would have happened."

More scribbling on the legal pad.

"Hmmm . . . give me the exact dates, again," she said. "When did this happen?"

"January thirteenth—he said they had him meet them down at the docks that night, then they motored up to Girabaldi to do the pickup. They were on their way back when the first man attacked him."

"Name?"

"Mateo only knew his first name, Jairo. He said he was from Guatemala," Logan said.

"Did Søren throw this man overboard, also?" she asked, not looking up as she continued to take notes.

"Mateo says he didn't see that," Logan said. "When Søren rushed out of the shadows and lifted him over the railing, he said the Guatemalan was still knocked out—or dead—he wasn't sure, crumpled on the deck at his feet. But I am pretty sure he must have thrown him over next. I think I know what happened to him."

Haggerman paused her scribbling and looked up.

Logan then proceeded to tell her about the dead body that washed up on the rocks in Depoe Bay on January 17. Middle-aged Latino male but, as of yet, no one had come forward looking for anyone of that description, so he remained unidentified.

Haggerman nodded and went quiet, her face set in fierce concentration.

Logan waited, not wanting to interrupt.

Finally, Haggerman turned to her right and flipped open a laptop computer Logan hadn't noticed was there and started tapping.

While she was doing that, Logan took the opportunity to ask a question she had had ever since Vanessa first told her about her parents running from the drug cartels eighteen years ago.

"Why can't Mateo and Gabriela get accepted as asylum seekers?" she asked. "I mean, can't people come here if they're running away—if their lives are in danger? Mateo said the cartel threatened to kill his family if he didn't work for them. That sounds like a situation that would qualify them for asylum, right?"

"Unfortunately," Haggerman said. "No."

She explained. "The definition of asylum is a bit narrower in immigration policy. An asylum seeker has to belong to a specific group that is being persecuted—they need to be members of a religion or political group or a forbidden sexual orientation— the Rohingya in Burma, for example, or being a homosexual man in Saudi Arabia, or being a family member of dissidents."

"Oh," Logan said. "I didn't know that."

"Neither did Mateo and Gabriela," Haggerman said. "When they arrived at the border, that's what they attempted to do. They thought they were safe. They had no idea they'd be turned away. They'd spent all of their money getting that far, but when that happened, all they could do was try to find work there in the border town in Mexico, but there wasn't any. It was very crowded already. With other people in similar situations.

"Mateo and Gabriela were camping out in the desert with another family who had paid coyotes to smuggle them across the border several miles away, when a couple members of the family got food poisoning or something—they never found out what it was, could have been meningitis or anything else.

"Anyway, the mother and one of the older boys died, so the father offered Mateo and Gabriela their places in the truck if Gabriela would take care of the baby and keep it quiet during the crossing."

"Mateo never told me any of this," Logan said. She couldn't imagine being in that kind of a life-and-death situation.

"Well, as bad as it was, Mateo and Gabriela were lucky. Many coyote stories are worse," Haggerman said. "Just last year, in San Antonio, fifty-three migrants were discovered in a tractor-trailer abandoned on the side of the road . . . dead."

"That's awful!" Logan said.

"Yes, it is," said Haggerman. "They were locked in."

She let that sink in. "Just coming from a violent area is not enough to grant an immigrant asylum."

"So where does that leave Mateo and his family?" Logan asked, feeling very discouraged at this point. Then she started getting pissed. Sorrow was sometimes a useless emotion. Anger was much more productive.

"What can I tell him? Not even counting all that he went through to get here, he and Gabriela have worked hard, and have raised a good daughter who's doing well in school. All of them work hard and stay out of trouble. All he wants is to continue doing that without having to look over his shoulder the rest of his life."

Haggerman started to say something, but Logan was on a roll. Injustice had always infuriated her.

"And now, someone tried to kill him! First, they force Mateo to do the drug run—just like the cartel tried to do by threatening him back in Mexico—then he's attacked by one man, and when he survives *that* attack, he's thrown overboard by Søren! It's winter and that water was freezing. He'd be dead if another fishing boat hadn't come along and spotted him and got him to a hospital in time."

Logan sat back in her chair in a huff and folded her arms.

"I just can't go back and tell them there's nothing we can do," she said. "There must be *something*. *Some* way to help these people."

Haggerman took another look at her computer screen, scrolled down a bit, then turned back to Logan.

"This is a long shot," she said. "A very long shot," she warned, "but hear me out."

"When Mateo came to see me, I told him straight out how impossible his situation was. The only hope he and Gabriela had to legally stay here was to apply for a waiver when Vanessa turned twenty-one."

"How would that help?" Logan asked.

"Vanessa is a U.S. Citizen. According to immigration law, she can apply to sponsor her own parents when she turns twenty-one."

"Well, that sounds hopeful, but Vanessa's still in high school. She's only seventeen."

"Exactly, that's why I told them to come back in a few years," Haggerman said. "Even then, I told them our chances of getting a waiver for them was almost zero. They were living here illegally for more than a year—that's the time frame."

"Oh," Logan said, discouraged again.

"But," Haggerman said, holding up her index finger in the universal 'wait' signal. "With the information you've given me, there may be a workaround."

Logan's hopes rose slightly.

"Tell Mateo to sit tight for now," Haggerman said. "It's a long shot, and I'm not promising anything, but there is one thing I can try . . . I'll call as soon as I know anything."

LOST AND FOUND

Reaching for her cell phone, Haggerman thanked Logan for coming—efficiently ending the meeting at the same time.

An idea was more than Logan had when she came in, so she left the woman to her work and trotted down the stairs to the parking lot.

She phoned Matco from the car and filled him in. Not much in the way of news, but at least now he had a thread of hope and knew everything that could be done was being done. Before she hung up, Logan reminded him to lock all his windows and doors in case Søren realized he was home and came back to finish the job he'd started on the *Sea Gypsy*.

56

Søren cranked the engine a few times before it started. One of the first things he was going to do with Roxy's money was buy a new ride. He rolled out of the paint store's narrow parking lot toward 2nd Street.

The light was red when he got to the 101. He nosed his way into the right lane and turned north. Might as well pick up Freddie's order. They were waiting for him at the boat. If he didn't show, that would raise a red flag. Making the delivery, even if late, would buy him some time until he figured out what he was going to do about the Mateo situation.

Getting the groceries and dropping them off at the dock only took about an hour. Yesterday, he had signed on for a short trip with the *Blue Water*, a small fishing vessel out of California. They were scheduled to leave at five tomorrow morning. Søren nodded and said he'd see them then.

Now he had that long to figure out what he was going to do. He certainly wasn't going out on the boat, only to have the cops possibly waiting for him when he returned.

Not knowing if Mateo, or his family, or the woman who drove him home had called the police about what happened on the *Sea Gypsy*, he didn't go back to his place. Instead, he did a drive-thru at McDonald's, then parked behind the dollar store to eat his Big Mac with fries and a Coke. The health food Nazis had taken the supersized option off the menu, but it was still available if you asked for it.

He couldn't go home. He couldn't go to work. What he really needed to do was get out of town. He already had plans for Vegas with Roxy, but she'd been stalling, saying they needed to lay low a little longer. Said Craig had a life insurance policy that was worth waiting for. Said it would be here soon.

Making sure no one was looking, Søren pulled his seat forward, then reached around behind it and unlocked the small, metal box he had bolted to the floor and lifted the lid.

He pushed around the money with his finger. Yep, looked like it was all there. His most recent take from the *Sea Gypsy*—which included Mateo and the Guatemalan's cut—minus what he'd spent on food and gas the last few weeks. Only a few thousand left. Closing and locking the lid, Søren turned back in his seat. Not enough. He wouldn't get far on that.

But he knew where he could get a little more.

He was pretty sure the *Sea Gypsy* had just made another overnight run up to Girabaldi. He'd seen her docked three boats down when he dropped off the groceries for the *Blue Water*. She was back in port with no one on board that he could see and no one getting ready for a fishing trip.

Probably all home sleeping in. The captain kept some extra cash, hidden inside a zippered pouch in his captain's chair. Which explained why he rarely left the wheelhouse.

Søren didn't know how much was in there, but one night he'd seen him pull out what looked like five or ten thousand, to pay off a fisherman who'd stumbled across their operation. When the captain handed him the money, the man just tucked it into his jeans and motored away. Søren hoped the captain hadn't changed hiding places.

It was worth a look, anyway.

And if anyone was on board, he'd just say he was there to see if they needed any help on the next run, to keep him in mind.

He pointed his truck south again, turned left when he got to Hurbert and headed down the hill toward the Bayfront. Even though it was almost two o'clock, the sky was still a dull, gunmetal grey and it was colder than a witch's tit in a brass bra, an expression he'd picked up from his father, a man he hadn't thought of in years.

This had been the coldest, wettest winter. He hadn't been warm since last August. Vegas couldn't come too soon! He couldn't wait for the bright lights and hot sunshine. He was going to lay by the pool and soak up the sun, watch hot babes in skimpy suits rubbing suntan lotion all over each other.

He felt better already.

Hurbert Street ended at Bay Blvd, which ran along the marina. Søren turned left. Not much happening in town, but something was going down at the docks. He saw a patrol car and several other official-looking vehicles, noses all pointing toward Dock 5, blocking all through traffic.

A crowd of looky-loos had gathered on this end of the boardwalk, in front of the barriers, phones out, taking pictures and shooting video, but he couldn't see what of.

Søren slowed the truck to a crawl. Foot on the brake, he leaned over and called out the passenger window to a man and woman closest to the street.

"Hey, what's all the excitement for?" he said. "Do you know what's going on?"

The woman kept filming, so the man answered over his shoulder.

"Big drug bust!" he said, sounding excited.

Søren felt the blood in his veins turn to ice.

Inching forward past the crowd, he rolled by, cutting his eyes to the right as he followed a patrol officer's directions to all incoming traffic to turn around.

One boat in the harbor was crawling with cops. It was the *Sea Gypsy*.

He tried not to panic, but why would the cops take any interest in one small smuggling boat?

It's not like Newport was a cartel hub or anything. The captain only did occasional small runs, whenever his cousin, who did work with the cartel, could shave off a little from large deliveries and send them his way. He didn't sell the product himself but pushed it on down the line to a long-distance trucker based in Medford, Oregon, where meth was king.

He doubted the captain kept any drugs on board, but Søren was glad he hadn't gone with the *Gypsy* this time, and that he hadn't gone home. The cops would be rounding everybody up who ever worked on her.

As he followed the officer's directions, he rounded the cones that had been set up for this purpose. He nodded at the officer and kept a slow speed as he cleared the cones and drove back the way he had come.

He wanted to get as far away from here as fast as he could. He knew the moral fortitude of the captain and crew. If they hadn't turned on him yet, they would soon. He bet they'd each be ratting out the other ones to see who could work a better deal with the DEA.

Part of him wondered how they got caught—whether it was Mateo who'd called in a tip or someone else, but he didn't allow himself to dwell on that. At this point, it didn't matter. He had learned to compartmentalize. What he needed to focus on now was how to get out of town as soon as possible, without losing his meal ticket.

Twenty minutes later, he was past Waldport and still hadn't seen any police. He breathed a little easier, but knew it was just a matter of time, now, before they tracked him down. The cash behind his seat made him feel marginally better, but he needed more to get set up in Vegas.

His head hurt and it was freezing. He'd gassed up the truck yesterday, so he allowed himself the luxury of letting the heater run while he pulled over to the side of the highway and made a call.

57

Roxy sat on a stool behind the counter in her empty store, scrolling through her phone, trying to decide between Bel Air and the Hollywood Hills as her target neighborhood. She'd already decided her stage name would be Sunny Jet. Easy to remember. Sounded rich and fast. She wasn't sure about the tattoo. Maybe something discreet, like a butterfly on her ankle, but maybe it would be hard to get roles with a tattoo—she'd have to ask her agent once she got one.

It was so quiet she almost dropped her phone when it rang. She looked at caller ID and frowned.

She answered in a furious whisper, "What are you doing calling me on this number? We're supposed to lay low, remember?"

Søren's voice came back in a low, sexy purr, "I know, baby, but I need to see you."

"Well, you can't see me now," Roxy said. "We need to stick to the plan. Better to play it safe."

He started to say more, but she asked him to hold on and put the phone on mute. She needed to think.

It was flattering to have Søren miss her, but she had been avoiding seeing him until she figured out how she was going to tell him she couldn't find the title to the *Freya*. She'd been putting him off, telling him she was waiting for just the right buyer.

They'd been counting on that money to get them out of town and set them up someplace sunny and warm. She was worried Søren wouldn't be so keen on being with her if she wasn't bankrolling the trip, or that she'd decided against Vegas.

Roxy looked down at her phone. Søren was still waiting.

Tapping one of her nails on the counter, she quickly ran through her options.

The life insurance was coming in a couple of weeks, but it was only $50,000. It wouldn't go very far for two, but for one person . . . it could get her as far as LA and help pay for the clothes she'd need and a few months' living expenses until she landed her first role.

Once she got there, all she had to do was get a couple of movies and she'd be fine. She glanced at herself in her phone's reflection and pulled on her bangs, pushing strands of hair here and there until she had the sexy, messy bedhead look she liked. Yes, she still had it.

But she needed cash to get through the next few weeks. She had a few thousand dollars in what was her and Craig's joint checking account, but that was all. She still didn't have access to the business account.

Hmmm . . .

She could dump Søren now, but a little extra cash for the road wouldn't hurt and he had been hinting he'd made a chunk of money recently. She knew Søren didn't trust banks and kept his cash in a lockbox in the truck, so he'd have it with him if she met him at the motel.

She didn't have to actually leave town, just pretend to . . .

She tapped off the mute button and said she was thinking about it, she really wanted to see him, too, but she wasn't sure it was a good idea. What if someone saw them and started asking questions? Made the connection between them being lovers and Søren being on board the *Freya* when Craig was murdered and then lost at sea.

"Come on, Roxy," he pleaded, "one night."

Roxy pretended she was almost convinced. "But I can't just drop everything, Søren. I'm working, I can't leave until four."

"You can close a little early. It's Wednesday and freezing outside, no one's out shopping now, right? No one will think anything about it if you close early."

Then in a low, husky voice, Søren proceeded to elaborate how he planned to make it worth her while.

Delighted at this sudden change in attitude from her lover, Roxy smiled. She had him in the palm of her hand.

Her mind jumped ahead. This might change everything. Søren was right. Why should she wait? She could clear out her checking account, have the life insurance check sent to a PO Box in some podunk town on Highway 5 and pick it up on her way to LA. What was to stop her?

All she had to do was beef up her traveling money. After the incentive she planned on giving Søren tonight, it would be in her pocket tomorrow. She would think out the details on the drive down.

Right now, she had a store to close.

She promised Søren she'd meet him in a couple of hours. She *might* be able to stay the night. Disconnecting the call, Roxy looked around the shop and out of the window toward the town. She suddenly wondered why any of it—owning the shop, marrying into the Peterson family, keeping up appearances—why any of that had ever been important to her.

Shrugging into her jacket, she looked around for anything she wanted from the store and then headed to the bank to get her cash, then home to pack. She wasn't taking much, but there was no way she was going to LA without her new stiletto boots.

By the time she left the bank, she had a pretty solid plan. She'd let Søren give her a great going-away romp in the hay, totally wear him out, then while he was sleeping, find the key to his lockbox. As soon as she had the cash, she'd ditch him and head south. No muss, no fuss. He didn't need to know she was almost broke. Søren would be fine.

Besides, she wouldn't take it all. She'd leave him enough for gas and food. She wasn't a bitch.

58

Witcomb wasn't in, but Logan left him a voicemail, said it was important—to call her back before he left for court. She had to reach him before he put a plea bargain on the table or ask the judge to move up the trial date. She didn't know if it would do any good, but she was going to do her best to convince Witcomb his client was innocent.

Even if she didn't have any evidence yet to prove Doyle had been set up by Roxy and Søren, she wanted to share Mateo's story with him. Combined with what Gabriela and Vanessa told her about them meeting secretly at the motel in Yachats, proving they were lovers, she hoped it was enough.

She couldn't imagine what Doyle must be going through right now, sitting in jail, knowing he was innocent, but without hope of proving it.

Logan sent Ben a text and asked if he still needed her to pick up potting soil or if he'd rather she come straight home. He said he hadn't put the pork chops in yet, so she had time to finish her errands.

Before she made it to Walmart, Logan's phone rang. She glanced at the number, which she didn't recognize. Disappointed it wasn't Witcomb, she almost didn't answer, but tapped it open on the third ring.

"Hello?" Logan said, expecting a robocall.

"Ms. McKenna?"

It was Vanessa. Logan was glad she picked up.

"Hi Vanessa," she said. "Is everything okay? How's your dad?"

The light turned red, so she rolled to a stop behind a green Mustang and let the engine idle.

"Dad's fine," she said. "I finally got him to go to bed. He's sleeping."

Then Vanessa lowered her voice to a stage whisper, "But before he went to sleep, he told us to be sure and let him know if we saw that man, Søren, around here. He said he couldn't tell us everything, but said he is a bad man and he wanted to make sure we understood we had to be careful. That he couldn't protect us when he was asleep."

"Is he there?" Logan said. "Did you see him?"

"No, but Mom just called from the Hideaway and said they're there. Roxy checked in and went straight to her room—the one they usually get, 105."

"Søren's there?" Logan asked.

"Yes, Mom said he got there right after Roxy did—and Mom said she saw a suitcase and some shoes and things in the back of Roxy's car."

Not good. If Søren and Roxy left town, the police might not ever find them. They could use cash and reinvent themselves somewhere else.

Vanessa broke into her thoughts, "I need to get down there and protect my mom! Can you give me a ride?"

Logan's maternal instincts kicked in. "No!" she said. "I don't want you to get involved, Vanessa. Hold on."

Søren needed to be stopped and probably Roxy, too. Whether Roxy was an accomplice or just got mixed up with the wrong man, Søren was definitely a killer.

LOST AND FOUND

"Look, I have an idea," Logan said. "You sit tight and take care of your dad. Call your mother back for me and tell her not to go near that room until I get there. I'm on my way."

Logan wasn't sure what she was going to do when she got there. Maybe she could take a picture of Roxy and Søren together and of the suitcase in the backseat of her car. If nothing else, she could give Gabriela a ride home so she wouldn't have to take the bus. She knew she would want to be home with Mateo as soon as possible.

Making a U-turn at Walmart, Logan headed south toward the Hideaway Inn in Yachats. Next, she texted Ben that she forgot she told Sam she would stop in for a short visit and to drop off a gift for her new baby. She wouldn't stay long. Ben sent a thumbs-up.

Lying to Ben wasn't her usual modus operandi, but Logan didn't want him to worry about her when she didn't know yet what she was going to do. Besides, she hadn't really lied exactly—she *did* want to visit Sam and drop off a baby gift, she just wasn't going to do it tonight.

Her little white lie to Ben gave her an idea.

She called Sam. Magnolia was down for the night and Tim had gone back out on the water, so she was all ears. Having been an investigative reporter for a big paper before moving to Newport, Sam had a few tips on information gathering.

"What's the name of the hotel?"

"Hideaway Inn."

"One-level motel, right? Not a two or three-story hotel?" she asked.

"I assume so, but don't know," Logan admitted.

Sam Googled the Hideaway Inn. "One story," she said. "Got it . . . Satellite view only shows the front of the motel, but it looks like there's an alley or parking area in back as well as the parking spaces in front of each room."

Logan waited while Sam thought of the best approach.

"Here's what we're going to do . . ." she said. "How fast can you get here?"

Logan was just around the corner by then, so pulled into Sam's driveway just as she hustled out.

Holding her coat closed with one hand, Sam reached through the open window on the driver's side and handed Logan a slim, black rectangle with earbuds and a cord. Pointing out the on and off buttons and showing her the best way to position it, she stepped back.

"Remember, the red light needs to be on. I'm not sure if it's charged, so plug it in on the way," Sam said, hugging herself against the cold. She'd thrown a North Face jacket on over her pajamas but was only wearing slippers.

She told Logan to be careful, but her eyes glittered with excitement. "Just like the good old days!" she said, pointing to the electronic listening device. "This little baby brought down a federal judge."

As Logan rolled up the window and backed out of the driveway, Sam called out, "And don't forget, I get the scoop!"

Logan laughed and plugged the device into the charger as instructed.

She buzzed with anticipation. Finally! She had something productive to do. Waiting for someone else to take action was not in Logan's nature.

Her first thought had been to position herself outside Roxy and Søren's motel room window and record anything incriminating they might say with her phone, but quickly realized this was the middle of winter and the window was unlikely to be open. Besides, she couldn't count on Roxy and Søren discussing how they murdered Craig—suspects only conveniently confessed to murder in the movies. But they might talk about where they were going or information about the *Sea Gypsy*—she'd record it all and hope at least some of it would

272

help Witcomb in Doyle's defense and later, help the police track Roxy and Søren down.

Sam's little gadget not only recorded sound but amplified and cleaned it up so Logan would be able to hear conversations clearly through walls and windows. She just had to hope the curtains were shut and nobody was taking their dog for a poop walk behind the motel while she crouched beneath the window, pressing the device against the glass.

She could only hope Roxy and Søren's pillow talk proved informative. It was a long shot, but worth taking to keep an innocent man from prison and maybe even bring down a killer. If they didn't say anything incriminating, all Logan would risk was getting a leg cramp and being late for dinner.

Sam had emphasized that even if she got a good recording, it wouldn't be admissible in court, but with Mateo's firsthand account of Søren's actions on the *Sea Gypsy*, it would hopefully be enough to get Witcomb to dig for evidence that was admissible.

59

It was close to six-thirty before Logan passed the "Welcome to Yachats, Gem of the Oregon Coast," sign. Following her GPS, she located the Hideaway Inn and pulled into a gas station across the street.

Sunset was at five, but it wasn't quite completely dark yet. Hopefully, Roxy and Søren were staying the night and not just here for an afternoon hookup, but there was only one way in or out of the motel, so she'd spot them if they left. She would recognize Roxy's car from when she sped down Bayfront that day and sprayed her and Sam with muddy water.

She popped the gas tank cover open and was halfway out of the car before she remembered that Oregon didn't let you pump your own gas. She met the attendant halfway, handed him her card and asked him to fill it up with regular, she'd be right back.

Dinner was a far cry from Ben's pork chops. She'd have those for dessert. In the meantime, she grabbed a couple of containers of yogurt and a hot pretzel from the mini-mart.

Next, she gave Vanessa a call and asked when her mom got off work. She was going to offer to give her a ride home, but Vanessa said she already left in order to catch the last bus back to Newport. She should be home in a couple of hours.

Logan hoped she would be, too.

She decided against telling Vanessa where she was or what she was doing, telling her instead to focus on taking care of her dad and keeping up with her homework. She reminded her they still had a tutoring appointment next week. Kids shouldn't have to worry about grownup problems.

Going to work on the second yogurt container, Logan already felt foolish for thinking this idea would work. She wasn't an experienced investigative journalist or a spy, but she was determined. Once she committed to a plan of action, Logan always followed through. This wouldn't take long.

While she waited, she studied the Hideaway Inn across the street. It was typical of the motels she and Rick had stayed at on the few vacations their dad had taken them on after their mom left. Ten or so bright colored doors all in a row, facing the street. Metal and concrete staircases on either end of the structure, leading up to the second floor if there was one.

They did have those unattractive, flickering fluorescent lights and she was pretty sure there would be a vending machine with stale peanut butter and cheese crackers, nuts, and candy bars, next to a soda machine that said it had six selections, but only had three and usually kicked back your dollar bill fifteen times before it finally took it and sent you a Mountain Dew instead of the Coke you wanted.

Logan smiled at the memories. Those were the good old days. She made a mental note to call her brother, Rick. Tomorrow was his day off. He and his wife, Paula, lived down in Jasper, and were supposed to come up for Memorial Day. She hoped they could make it; she hadn't talked with him nearly often enough since she'd moved up to Oregon.

Logan tilted her head out of the car window and looked up at the sky. It was almost dark enough. She refocused on her mission.

LOST AND FOUND

Gabriela had given Vanessa Roxy's room number before she left. Room 105 was the third room to the right of the pass-through that led to the ice machines and the alley out back.

Feeling like an idiot, Logan pulled her hair back into a scrunchie and jammed a baseball cap on her head. Grabbing Sam's little black box, she tucked it into her pocket and got out of the car.

Traffic had died down on the 101, so she was able to jog across fairly easily. In Oregon, pedestrians had the right of way, so the one south-bound driver who did get close braked and allowed her to get across safely.

Once on the other side of the highway, she edged around behind the office, but ran into a mass of blackberry brambles that prevented access to the back alley area. Lowering the brim of her baseball cap as much as she could, she walked quietly past the office and the ice machine toward the back, which she was hugely relieved to see was not well-lit. It took a massive amount of self-control to pass up the Butterfinger and Reese's Peanut Butter cups in the vending machine.

January was not a big month for tourists, so there was only a beat up Toyota truck in the back, probably belonging to the manager. She heard TV sounds emanating from a small window behind the office as she slipped past.

Until she got out of the lighted pass through and into the shadows behind the rooms, she didn't realize how nervous she was. She took a few deep breaths until her heartbeat returned to something resembling normal, then took stock of her surroundings.

A few bulky, square, metal cubes with louvers hummed quietly outside many of the windows. Heaters, she assumed, but her heart sank. The windows were tiny and too high up to reach. Bathroom windows. Of course, she hadn't thought this through. Unless Roxy and Søren were having a conversation with one on the toilet and one in the shower, she wasn't going to be able to hear anything. The only other windows were out in front.

Damn.

Logan thought through her options. Walking back toward the office, she snuck a sideways glance to see if there was any place to hide between the cars and the rooms.

A narrow sidewalk separated the asphalt parking lot from the rooms. A low, thick hedge, intermittently broken by short paths leading up to each door, bordered the inside edge. Each room had a large, picture window.

Security lights did not penetrate the hedge, so the area between it and the picture window was in the shadows. But it would only shield her from the view of people in the parking lot. If either Roxy or Søren looked out the window or came out the door, her ass was grass.

Logan squared her shoulders and started walking along the sidewalk. She wished she had thought to ask Sam for a roller bag or something to make her look like she belonged.

Strolling nonchalantly past Room 105, she quickly checked her surroundings, then ducked behind the hedge and lowered herself into a crouching position. Her knees protested, but the location was great. She could not be seen from the parking lot or the office. *This might go okay after all.*

She quieted her breathing and carefully pulled the listening device from her pocket and made sure it was on. She could hear voices coming from inside the room. Carefully pressing the black box against the lower, right-hand corner of the window, she made sure it was on, then put in the earbuds and listened.

60

7:00 P.M.

At first, Logan could hear nothing but muffled voices, then she moved the device around and fiddled with the volume buttons—at least she thought that's what they were—she hadn't listened very carefully when Sam was giving her instructions.

She must have done something right, because suddenly, a woman's voice—Roxy's, she assumed—came in loud and clear.

"What's the rush?" she said. "Why can't we leave in the morning? I hate driving at night."

Then came a long zipping sound and a dull thud, followed by the same sound a minute later. Roxy must be taking off a pair of tall boots.

"We could, but why wait?" Søren said. "The longer we stay here, the longer it will be before I get to see you stretched out by a hotel pool in Vegas. You're gonna look great in one of those thong suits. We'll get you one in every color. If we leave now, we can be there tomorrow, in time for lunch. Where do you want to stay? Caesar's?"

Søren's soft, smooth voice sent a chill down Logan's spine.

Roxy seemed to think about it for a minute before answering.

"Tell you what," she said. "I'm beat. Let's get a few hours' sleep, then leave around midnight. That would get us into Vegas by three or four. They won't let you check in until then, anyway."

Søren grudgingly agreed, "Okay, but midnight we're on the road."

This scintillating conversation was followed by bed noises, a feminine shriek, and a slap on someone's butt, presumably Roxy's. A bathroom door shut, and Logan thought she could hear the sound of a shower running. Then Søren turned on the TV and started flipping through channels—local news show, weather report, an old movie where people overacted and spoke in earnest voices, an ad for dog food.

Logan doubted she'd get any more conversation out of them before they went to sleep but decided to give it a few more minutes. See if there was anything of interest after Roxy got out of the shower. Shifting her weight onto her left leg, she attempted to massage out a cramp on her lower, right calf.

This had been a colossal waste of time. She'd tell Ben all about it when she got home. She hoped he'd see the humor in her playing Nancy Drew.

Just then, the door to 105 yanked opened and Søren, keys in hand, stepped out toward his truck. Silhouetted in the doorway against the bright light in the room, she couldn't see much of his face, just his eyes, but he seemed as stunned as she was to see her crouching there beneath the window.

Never breaking eye contact, in two long strides, he'd covered the short distance between them. Before Logan could get to her feet and run, Søren got his fist to her face. After a blinding stab of pain, the world went dark.

LOST AND FOUND

TEN MINUTES LATER

Roxy emerged from the bathroom in a cloud of steam, wrapped in one towel, drying her face and hair with another. When she opened her eyes, she abruptly stopped, staring straight ahead in disbelief.

"Oh my *god!*" she said in a panicky whisper. "Søren! What is going on? Who is this?! What's she doing here?"

Without looking up, Søren said, "Get some clothes on."

"What are you doing?" she asked, tucking the corner of her towel tighter into the top edge.

What Søren was doing was finishing a wrap job on a woman with long, auburn hair who was slumped into one of the motel chairs, being secured to its arms and legs with duct tape.

"Where did you get tape?" Roxy asked, as if that were the most important question.

"My truck, where else?" Søren said. Then, in answer to her next question, he nodded at the woman, who was just coming to. "She was out."

Blood was streaming out of the woman's nose creating a bright-red, river delta pattern on the silver tape covering her mouth. The front of her black jacket was splattered and some kind of black electronic device about the size of a phone lay on the cheap, motel table next to her.

Roxy made it to the bed and sat down, staring at the woman, who was just coming to.

"I can't get dressed," Roxy said. "My clothes are in the car, in my suitcase. I was going to have you get it for me."

"Put what you were wearing back on," Søren said. "We're leaving."

His voice was no longer in the sweet-talking range.

Roxy did as she was told.

When she got in the bathroom, she shut the door and finished drying off, taking her time to carefully hang the bath towels over

"

the shower stall. She then retrieved her clothes from the floor where she'd thrown them and began putting them back on.

Turning the water on in the sink, she leaned forward on the heels of her hands and looked at herself in the mirror. Hard.

Well, girl, what do we do now?

This was not the scenario Roxy had planned for.

Until she could take these new circumstances into account, the only thing she could do right now was play along. Obviously, Søren was not who she thought he was. Yes, she knew he'd killed Craig, pushed him overboard, and then planted evidence to blame it all on Doyle.

But until now, that had all seemed like a game. A game to get her what she wanted. Get rid of a boring husband and drive off into the sunset. She should have known it wouldn't be that easy. Nothing ever was for her.

She stared into her own eyes in the mirror and watched as they turned a dark, steely blue.

She could still do this. LA was not off the table. She hadn't touched the woman in the chair, whoever she was. And she'd be very careful not to. All she had to do was get away from here, from whatever Søren had done. Then leave Søren. Very carefully.

Pinching her cheeks and scrubbing her damp hair into a cute shape, she opened the bathroom door and swept back into the room.

61

One look at the woman taped to the chair wiped out the majority of Roxy's false bravado.

Still bleeding slightly, the woman was fully awake now, glaring at Søren with glittering, emerald-green eyes. Even in her vulnerable position, she radiated fury. What were they going to do with her? Leave her here?

Roxy tried for a tough tone.

"So who is this bitch and what's the plan?" she asked.

Søren ignored her. Instead, he grabbed the black device off the table, threw it on the floor, and smashed it thoroughly with a wrench.

"Nice try," he said, looking at the woman in the chair.

Roxy immediately thought of the bloody hammer that Søren used to kill Craig and her blood ran cold. He must have gone out to his truck and gotten the wrench when he got the duct tape.

"Who are you?" Søren said to the woman, before thrusting his hand into her jacket pocket and pulling out a set of keys, which included an electronic key fob. "That's the real question."

"Watch her," he said to Roxy, "I'll be right back. She's gotta be parked around here somewhere." He exited the room pointing the key fob in different directions, repeatedly pressing the unlock button, listening for a beep.

Roxy sat on the bed, fidgeting. Finally, avoiding looking at the woman in the chair, she pulled on her boots and zipped them up.

A few minutes later, Søren came back in, carrying a wallet. Closing the door behind him with his foot, he opened the wallet and fished out a driver's license.

"Well, well. Our mystery woman has a name. Logan McKenna," he said. "Let's see what you have to say for yourself, Logan."

He picked up the wrench and started toward her, his eyes on her knees.

Roxy jumped up off the bed and grabbed his arm, "No!" she said, "Søren! No!"

"Look," Søren said, turning back to Roxy, lowering his arm, but not letting go of the wrench. "She was outside the window, spying, recording us," He kicked the remains of the device he'd smashed. "We need to know why. We need to know what she knows and who she's been talking to."

"She couldn't possibly know anything, Søren," Roxy said. "I don't know why she was there, but let's just think about this for a minute."

Roxy pulled him back toward the bed. "Look, I agree we can't stay here tonight, not now, but there's no reason to do anything to this woman. Whoever she is and whatever she knows doesn't matter."

She lowered her voice to an urgent whisper, but hoped it was still loud enough for Logan to hear. "Even if she knows you killed Craig, it won't matter once we're gone."

Then in a normal tone, she added, "You wanted to leave tonight, anyway, right?"

LOST AND FOUND

For a minute, Roxy was afraid she'd gone too far. Søren wasn't completely stupid. Had he figured out she was trying to blame Craig's murder all on him?

He didn't say anything right away. Roxy sensed he knew more about this Logan McKenna than he was telling her, but at this point it didn't matter. Her only goal now was to convince him to leave without breaking the woman's kneecaps—or worse, violence *she* would be held accountable for just by being there with him.

Right now, all the police would know was that Søren killed Craig. Sure, they would find out she and Søren were having an affair, but that just made her guilty of adultery, not murder.

With the evidence she had Søren plant, it would look like Søren was infatuated with her like Doyle was, which would give him a motive for murder. Roxy didn't care which of them went down for the crime, as long as it wasn't her.

Yes, this would work, but she had to get away from here, first. Then she could figure out a way to ditch Søren and hit the road to LA.

She grabbed her phone off the nightstand, quickly pulling up Google maps. When she found what she wanted, she showed it to Søren.

"It will take hours for someone to find her. The longer we stay here, the more chance there is we'll get caught. If we leave now, we can be halfway to Vegas by the time housekeeping checks this room. Even if she talks, no cops are going to be looking for us until tomorrow."

Roxy made sure to mention Vegas loud enough for Logan to hear because she was planning to continue driving south to LA, not east to Vegas. When this Logan McKenna talked to the cops, she'd point them in the wrong direction—toward Søren, not her.

"We can sell my car, it's practically brand new. It's worth at least thirty grand, even selling it to a dealer. We'll ask for cash, buy another car somewhere else and we're gone! Invisible! If we use cash along the way, there won't be any paper trail—no way they can find us!"

Søren seemed to consider this option. Roxy knew the mention of money always got his attention.

"Get your stuff," he said, getting up off the bed.

As he walked past Logan, he stroked her thigh with the head of the wrench. "Looks like it's your lucky day, sweetcakes," he smiled.

Roxy gathered her things and waited by the door while Søren tested Logan's bindings, paying particular attention to the tape wrapped around her mouth. Satisfied, he turned out the light and shut the door, leaving Logan in the dark.

62

After several tries, Logan heard an engine rumbling roughly to life, followed by the smooth start of another, newer car, then the sound of both vehicles driving away. She'd seen both an old truck and Roxy's green Range Rover with the FASHN4 vanity plates parked out in front, noses pointed toward the room, like horses on a hitching post. The truck must be Søren's. She hadn't noticed the license plate number.

Fine spy she turned out to be.

She started to scooch her chair a few inches toward the door, thinking she could fall against it and get someone's attention, but after the first awkward try, pain shot across her face, and she could already feel her nose swelling. It hurt like hell.

She'd never been so angry in her entire life.

While she sat here, trapped in this chair, two killers were getting away. She hadn't bought the hints Roxy dropped, blaming Craig's murder on Søren. Even if Roxy hadn't directly pushed Craig overboard, she was deeply involved. And there was no doubt Søren killed the Guatemalan man and thought he killed Mateo.

There had to be something she could do!

Looking around the room for ideas, she realized her door plan wasn't a good one, anyway. If she did manage to get someone's attention by forcing herself to fall against the door, her body and the chair would block their way in.

And there were two other problems with that plan. It was mid-week in the middle of January, not a lot of tourists around. She'd only seen one other car in the parking lot, and it was on the far end of the row of rooms. At this hour of the night, they might not hear her even if she could fall over and make some noise. With her nose swelling and her mouth taped, she almost couldn't breathe. She didn't want to risk falling in some way that would make her situation worse.

Willing her nostrils to open slightly, even though it caused more pain, she took a life-saving sip of air, then sat very still. As her eyes adjusted to the dark, she saw the illuminated numbers on the digital alarm clock/radio by the bed said 8:21.

Ben was going to be so pissed. He didn't like it when his pork chops got dry. And Sam. Logan didn't know how expensive that listening device was, but she'd replace it, of course.

Then those two thoughts cheered her up. Of course! Ben would call Sam eventually, when she didn't show up for dinner, and Sam would worry when she didn't call to check in. All she had to do was hang on for another hour or so and someone would come to get her! She wished she hadn't trained Ben so well to not panic when she was a little late. Tonight she hoped he reverted to his old, over-protective self.

Until then, she would just have to sit here very quietly and breathe. She hoped the swelling wouldn't completely close off her nostrils before her rescuers arrived . . . or she had to pee.

*****

LOST AND FOUND

It was almost one o'clock in the morning before Logan heard Ben's truck pull up out front. Besides Amy's first cry when entering the world, it was the sweetest sound she had ever heard.

Later, she learned Ben had resisted calling Sam to see if she knew where Logan was. Besides not wanting to sound like a worry wart or jealous husband, he was afraid of disturbing Sam or her newborn baby's sleep unless it was a real emergency.

When hours passed and Logan still wasn't home, he finally gave in and called. Sam was deep asleep, so it took several rings for her to answer and a few more minutes for her to fully wake up.

When she did, she quickly gave Ben the name and address of the Hideaway Inn to plug into his GPS. She told him what Logan was up to and made him promise to call her as soon as he knew anything, no matter what time it was.

When he spotted Logan's car at the gas station across the street from the Hideaway, he rousted the manager out of bed to let him into Room 105.

When Logan heard the manger's key in the lock and heard Ben's voice telling him to hurry up, her face broke into a smile, or tried to—it was tough to do with her mouth taped shut.

The manager came in first. He took one look at her and went to get some ice while Ben dialed 911 and started working on the duct tape with his pocketknife. Tears leaked out of the corners of Logan eyes in relief—and pain—as Ben carefully peeled the first piece slowly off her mouth.

Logan took in a big gulp of air through her mouth and burbled, "Thank you, Ben Halvard, you are a god!"

It took several more minutes to free her from the chair and for her to use the bathroom—she really did need to pee—then another hour to get checked out by the EMTs and give a brief statement to the police, including a description of Roxy's car and Søren's truck and that they were heading to Vegas after selling her car somewhere along the way and buying a new one with cash.

Still trying to protect Mateo and his family, she did not mention what he had told her about Søren. She didn't have to. Assault and battery and attempted kidnapping were enough for the police to go after him and Roxy for now.

The EMTs wanted to take Logan to the hospital, but she insisted on letting Ben drive her to the ER in Newport. The ersatz ice pack the manager had created with a Ziploc baggie and a hand towel had helped. She knew she needed to get her nose treated but wanted to go home as soon as possible.

Wherever Roxy and Søren were, she hoped they would soon be caught and both of them would be cooling their heels in adjoining jail cells within twenty-four hours.

It would be gravy if Søren's nose got smashed all to pieces in the process.

<h1 style="text-align:center">63</h1>

Although the highway was pretty empty this late at night, Roxy jumped every time she saw headlights coming up behind her. Logically, she knew there was no way the police were looking for them, yet, but a lot of things she had been sure of were turning to shit, so she wasn't counting on it.

Since both cars had full tanks of gas, Søren insisted they travel caravan style, with his truck in the lead. No stopping until they got to Medford. She let him think he was the boss, and it was his decision, but she was very happy to put as many miles between her and Yachats as fast as possible. She needed to part ways with Søren before he turned east toward Vegas, and she continued on the 5 all the way to LA. But she was starting to fade. She didn't think she could drive straight through to Vegas or LA.

In the last four hours, Roxy had come to two clear decisions. One, she needed to ditch Søren as soon as possible, and two, she needed to get whatever cash he kept in that safe bolted to the floor of his truck behind the passenger seat. She had a few bucks, but without the sale of the *Freya* or access to the business account, Roxy needed that money to get herself started in LA.

And that *was* going to happen. When Roxy made her mind up, she always got what she wanted.

The elevation had been climbing, but she was still surprised to see snow on the sides of the highway as they approached Medford. The road had been cleared, but she was glad the Range Rover had all-wheel drive. Craig had insisted she get a model that had that feature and not just the four-wheel drive that came standard. He'd explained the difference, but she couldn't remember what it was. He'd just said it was better. He wanted her to be safe when she drove back and forth to Portland. Some of those passes get icy, he'd said.

Thinking of Craig made her sad. He really had been a good guy. Her eyes watered and she allowed herself a few minutes of self-pity before blinking her eyes to focus on following Søren's taillights.

He had just put on his blinker and taken the next exit, circling back on a frontage road to a small motel. Pulling his truck past the office, he let the engine idle and waited for her to go in and get them a room.

Grudgingly, since she had no other choice, Roxy grabbed her wallet and went in. She had to ding the bell a few times before a woman came out in a faded nightgown and ratty bathrobe to take her cash and hand her a key card. She signed in as Brenda Smith. She could have scribbled Kim Kardashian and the woman wouldn't have noticed or cared. She shuffled back to bed without saying good night. She did not tell them when the continental breakfast would be served or mention a Wi-Fi password. This place was even more no-frills than the Hideaway.

Søren removed one of his license plates and smeared some mud on the other before parking his truck in front of the room. He did the same to the Range Rover before coming in.

Roxy wasn't sure how long they were staying but brought in her rolling carry-on bag. There was no way she was going to go to bed without brushing her teeth at least.

LOST AND FOUND

Søren made no attempt at small talk. He used the bathroom, leaving the toilet seat up. Roxy got out her toiletries bag and did a much-shortened version of her nighttime routine, then came back into the room. She suddenly felt shy about taking off her clothes to get into bed.

Søren was sitting on the bed, looking at his phone. Her eyes were drawn like a magnet to the small sprinkling of dried blood splatters on his t-shirt. Luckily, when he put his coat on, it covered that part.

"Okay," Søren said, breaking the silence. "Medford's good. Over 88,000 people. Big enough for what we need. First thing tomorrow we'll head into town and find a used car dealer who'll give us cash for our cars and sell us another one. Then we'll grab some breakfast and hit the road."

Roxy noticed he had the titles and registrations to both their cars on the bed next to him. In preparation for the trip to LA this afternoon, she had put hers in the glove compartment. The fact that Søren had helped himself to hers infuriated her, but for now, she let it go.

"Once we have the cash," he continued, "we'll pick up another car—again with cash, and then we're home free," he said.

That wasn't a bad idea. She didn't want the cops knowing where she was whether she was with Søren or not. She sat next to him on the bed.

"But won't there be a record of all that?" she asked sweetly. "Even if we pay cash, there will be the title transfer and all that, right?"

Søren smiled. "Not where we're going. You just have to know what to look for, baby." He took off his shoes, pulled off his jeans, and got into bed. Folding his hands behind his head, he stared at the ceiling.

Roxy took this opportunity to slip off her own clothes and slide in next to him. He reached over and turned off the lamp on the nightstand.

His voice took a faraway tone in the dark.

"When I was in juvie, I learned a few things. Picked up a few useful tips. There's another whole world out there, Roxy. It just operates in the shadows. But I can spot them—people like us, people who operate in that world. We'll have a new set of wheels under us by noon tomorrow. I guarantee it."

He said nothing more. Eventually, he rolled over and his breathing settled into a deep, even rhythm. Surprisingly, he didn't snore. Roxy thought all men did. She and Søren had never spent the night together. How could she have gotten in this deep with a man she barely knew?

She couldn't have slept if she'd wanted to, so lay there, making and discarding plans until she came up with one that would work. Finally, she settled on the quickest, simplest solution. She focused on her two main objectives. Get the money and get rid of Søren.

K.I.S.S. Always the best answer.

Making sure Søren was still sleeping soundly before she made her move, Roxy carefully lifted the covers and slid out of bed. Lifting her roller bag so it wouldn't make any noise, she helped herself to Søren's keys on the dresser and let herself outside.

It was freezing, but she didn't care. She'd soon be warm enough. When she got on the road, she'd turn the heater in the Range Rover up full blast. Since the cops would soon be looking for her car as well as Søren's truck, she would have to sell it in the next biggest town she came to in Northern California, then take a Greyhound bus or Uber or something somewhere else and pay cash for a car later. She wasn't sure how that all worked, but she'd figure that out later. She was going to change her name anyway. There were probably places you could get all that done in LA. If Søren could find shadow people, she could, too!

Putting her roller bag in the Land Rover, Roxy turned her attention to Søren's truck. She hoped he hadn't moved his safe or decided to keep his cash somewhere else. She needed this money—and after all he'd just put her through, she deserved it!

Luckily, Søren's truck was old, so didn't have an electronic key fob that would make noise. Once she was in, she lifted the driver's seat forward and leaned in. Good. The safe was still there.

Cupping one hand over the other to muffle the sound, she inserted the key and heard the satisfying click. Yes! She was in!

There were only six or seven stacks of bills, but they were twenties, so would be easy to spend. It didn't look like a ton of money, but it would have to do. She would count it later. Stuffing her coat pockets with the cash, she started to back out.

Before her head cleared the car door opening and she could straighten up, Søren clamped his hand over her mouth. Keeping her immobile, he swiftly shut the truck door with his elbow and pushed her toward the room.

Roxy struggled desperately to wriggle out of his grasp, but Søren easily maintained control, shoving her into the room in front of him.

Terrified, she knew it was a room from which she would never leave.

64

Logan hadn't been able to reach Witcomb until early this morning. Speaking through swollen lips and a splinted nose was difficult, but she had been able to make herself understood well enough to fill him in about Søren and Roxy. She caught him in his office just before he left for the courthouse.

To his credit, Witcomb listened to the whole story without interrupting. He said he was very sorry she had been attacked, then got right to the cogent point.

"Did you hear either Søren or Roxy confess to killing or arranging the killing of Craig Peterson?" he asked.

Logan wished she was a better liar.

"No, Roxy never used Craig's name, just said 'him,' but I'm sure that's who she was talking about."

Witcomb thanked her again and asked her to let him know if anything changed, but without even a shred of hard evidence, he couldn't use any of the information she'd just given him.

"Can't you ask for a continuance or something?" Logan asked.

"That's only during a trial," Witcomb explained. "Even so, it would simply piss off this judge; he hates unnecessary delays."

Whether they liked it or not, he said, in a few months, the murder trial of Doyle Jefferson would begin. He assured her he would do everything in his power to free Doyle, including discrediting witnesses and trying to throw out evidence. He told her it was good to know his client was innocent, but that he would have worked hard for him either way. That was his job.

But in many ways, Logan thought, knowing Doyle was not guilty made his situation all the more horrific. Unless she could find something admissible in court to substantiate Mateo's story, an innocent man was probably going to prison for the rest of his life.

When they got off the phone, Logan made up her mind. If it was the last thing she did, on the first day of Doyle's murder trial, she would make sure he saw supportive, friendly faces on his side of the courtroom. She, Ben, and Sam would be front and center. Hopefully, by then they'd have something more to lend the defense team other than moral support.

Later that afternoon, Sam brought her up to date on the search for Roxy and Søren. According to the police scanner, which Sam kept on even while she was nursing, the police had put out an APB on both, but neither had yet been apprehended.

65

Slipping into a booth where he could keep an eye on the car, Søren ordered a double grand slam and a Bloody Mary. Damn, he was hungry! Amazing what a turnaround in fortune did for a man's appetite.

Two days ago, his world had turned to shit. First, he discovered Mateo, the man he thought he'd killed, was still alive, and then watched as the *Sea Gypsy* was being raided and the captain and crew hauled away by the cops—DEA, Coast Guard, state or local police, he didn't know. He hadn't stuck around to look at their uniforms that closely. He had almost no money and was a heartbeat away from being picked up by the cops himself. He knew one or all of them would rat him out.

Then that Logan woman tracked him to the Hideaway. How she'd found him, he had no idea, but lucky for him he'd wanted a smoke. He'd caught her red-handed and stopped her. He would have done more than that if Roxy hadn't been there.

She, for sure, had been discovered by now and spilled her guts to the nearest cop.

But forty-eight hours later, here he was. Not arrested. Not in jail! Sitting pretty in Denny's, free as a bird! The waitress plunked his plate in front of him, then returned with the caddy of syrups. He chose maple.

That first bite of maple syrup-drenched pancakes went down nice!

Removing his celery from his drink—he had no idea why they put that in there—he looked over the rim of the glass at the almost new Range Rover in the parking lot and smiled. After discovering Roxy red-handed, breaking into his truck, stealing his money, he'd made a slight change in plans.

Early this morning, before dawn, he drove his truck a few blocks away, ditched it behind a liquor store, removed the other license plate and all the paperwork, and walked back to the room, staying in the deepest shadows. Couldn't drive two cars and this one was newer.

He still planned on selling the Range Rover, but not in Medford. Even if he found a shady dealer who would buy a stolen car, he didn't think they'd take it with a dead body in the trunk.

He needed to dump her first. He'd done some searching on his phone. Yreka looked like a good area. The Siskiyou National Forest. Acres of remote land and remote camping sites. He wouldn't even have to bury the bitch, just dump her off and let the critters do the rest. No one was going camping back in there until spring. He'd be long gone by then, enjoying his new life in Vegas. With his newly-discovered skill set, he could probably make a lot of money.

Before she died, Roxy had finally convinced him she didn't have any other money besides the couple thousand in her wallet. She said Craig's life insurance money was coming, but it was in her name, and he wasn't planning on keeping her alive long enough for her to pick it up and cash it.

The biggest blow was discovering she hadn't sold the *Freya*. She *couldn't* sell it because she didn't have the title! And never would! She'd lied to him about that, too. He had to hand it to Craig, though; he wouldn't have trusted Roxy with the title if she'd been his wife.

When she finally confessed to being broke, Søren really got the urge to do some damage to that face of hers, but he learned his lesson from busting Logan's nose yesterday. This time he wouldn't leave any blood behind.

It turned out to be easy, though. All he had to do was let Roxy think sex would change his mind and he'd let her live. Once she was on the bed, he simply pushed her face into the pillow and keep it there until she stopped kicking and squirming. It took a little longer than he thought, but eventually, her body went slack, like a rag doll.

When she finally stopped moving, he rolled her over and looked down at her. She wasn't so pretty, now.

Not being a serial killer, Søren didn't have a roll of plastic or a blue tarp in the back of his truck, so he'd had to improvise. Stripping the bed, he rolled her up in a blanket, carried her out to the Range Rover and put her in the back. She didn't have one of those cargo cover things that would prevent people from looking in, so he tossed the bedspread in for good measure. Without it, you could clearly see the outlines of her body wrapped up in the blanket.

With the bedspread thrown carelessly on top, all bunched up, if he got stopped and the cops asked him any questions, he'd just tell them those were his dirty clothes in the back. He might even ask them directions to the nearest laundromat. That'd be rich!

He wasn't sure how long it took a body to start smelling, but he assumed he'd be okay for a few more hours. To be on the safe side, he turned off the heater as he drove through Medford heading south.

Siskiyou National Forest was only an hour away.

66

Driving always put Søren in a contemplative mood.

Roxy was his third kill. Craig had been his third, but Mateo had survived, it turned out, so really, Craig was only his second. Still, Søren didn't think of himself as a killer. It's not like he was some sick psycho or anything. He didn't kill for kicks. He just did what he needed to do.

The two illegals weren't even his idea.

He passed a semi and thought back to how that had all gone down.

He'd gone with the *Sea Gypsy* for one of their short, non-fishing runs up the coast. The captain could be trusted. One night. Easy money. Very organized, very safe. Limited crew. Never been caught.

The captain had never been caught because he had a system. He hired two or three men he could trust to crew the boat, then used illegals for the actual pickup. He either tempted them with money or threatened them or their families if they didn't go along, or both.

Either way, he was covered. Illegals never went to the cops and as an extra layer of security, they were kept in the dark until the night of the run. Neither man was given the name of the

Sea Gypsy before they left. They were just told to meet at Dock Three after dark, then were walked in.

Foolproof.

They'd left the dock around nine. Thin clouds, but no weather. Anchored off Garibaldi around one o'clock in the morning. Put the Mexicans in a small boat and sent them in. Søren had wondered if they knew how to handle a boat. The one guy was clueless, but the older man knew what he was doing.

That night, when the two men returned to the *Sea Gypsy*, unloaded the product, and climbed back on board, the captain congratulated them all on a job well done and said to go down below and relax, drink, play cards, whatever. They'd earned it.

So when Roxy kept blathering on about her husband, the solution seemed simple. Still, he'd thought it through before dropping Roxy the hint. Looked at it from every angle. Fishermen were lost at sea every year. No one even questioned it when the ocean took a life, particularly during a fierce, winter storm. It was all pretty easy.

It's funny how trusting people are, he thought. They leave themselves wide open. He remembered looking at the back of Craig's boring, trusting head, knowing in the next second it was going to be split like a melon. With the Mexicans, he'd just pushed them in. This time, he'd wanted to make sure his victim was dead before hoisting him over the railing. They wouldn't be far from Newport where the Coast Guard was stationed. He wanted no chance of Craig being rescued.

He'd waited until Craig was leaning out to catch the pulley, which Søren had just made sure was broken. He'd come out of the wheelhouse to help Søren repair it. The hammer connected with Craig's head with a solid crack, and poof, he was in the water.

The hammer blow vibrated up his arm. It was thrilling! The man went down like a rock. There was some blood, but he wasn't too worried about it. The sea was building. The storm was almost there. The rain would take care of it.

If Craig wasn't dead when he went in, he soon would be. He'd made sure he stripped him of his life jacket before he threw him over the railing. He'd secured the hammer and life jacket in his gear bag, which he'd stowed in the wheelhouse, before dealing with Doyle.

Doyle had been a little more complicated.

It wasn't essential to their plan, but ideally, he and Roxy had needed Doyle to be alive. Doyle was insurance.

The plan had been to wait until Doyle came up to relieve him, then knock him out, but not so hard as to kill him. He'd decided on a lighter-weight tool, a wrench instead of the hammer. Besides, he didn't want Doyle's blood to be on the hammer, just Craig's. So many things could go wrong. The devil was in the details.

The storm had also complicated things. He didn't want their patsy being washed overboard. Twisting a line around Doyle's legs with that rope had anchored him long enough for Søren to 'save' him and drag him into the wheelhouse. *Søren to the rescue!* Ha!

He'd actually been surprised Roxy had so readily agreed to the idea. He'd thrown it out there in such a way that he could claim he was just joking, but he needn't have worried. Turns out, she was as ruthless as he was, and more devious. Good girl. Good partner.

Well, at least until yesterday!

67

11:17 A.M.

Wauleka and Bud were in amazing shape. At seventy-three and seventy-one, other than one knee replacement and having to keep a lifetime supply of Alleve on hand, neither of them had any complaints. As long as they could continue to fish with the grandkids in the summer and cross-country ski in the winter, they were—pardon the pun—happy campers.

Their kids worried about them being out in the wilderness with no cell phone reception, but they always carried their Baofengs with them, which, for small emergency radios, worked pretty well. They couldn't check their email, but that wasn't a feature they missed while enjoying the great outdoors. Unlike their children and grandchildren, they were not tethered to their phones. As long as they stayed within the twenty-five mile range, they'd be able to call for help in case of a bear attack or zombie apocalypse.

January had been a great month for snow. The last few days had laid down a carpet of thick, fluffy, flakes. Perfect conditions for their favorite activity—cross-country skiing. They hesitated to call it a sport, as neither of them was very competitive. Unlike downhill skiers, they did not wear anything neon or spandex that made them look like race car drivers complete with helmets with lightning bolts on the side.

No, Wauleka and Bud kept their excursions to day trips, their main objectives being to enjoy the clean air and the beauty of nature, taking frequent breaks for the hot toddies and sandwiches Wauleka put in their packs before they set out.

They'd been at it for a couple of hours already, shuffling and gliding over the virgin snow, reveling in the stillness, while keeping the road in view on their left. Bud started looking for a good place to sit and take their lunch break.

Spotting the end of what looked like a large, downed pine up ahead, just before a sharp bend in the road, he signaled to Wauleka and started poling in that direction. The part of the log he could see looked big enough to sit on comfortably. He hoped it was also dry. Even though it was close to the road, it faced into the forest, so would do for their lunch break.

Wauleka cut in front of him and playfully raced ahead. Watching her taking the turn with ease, Bud thanked his lucky stars again that he'd met and married this amazing woman all those years ago.

Then he heard her scream.

*****

Sheriff's Deputy Arturo Manuelo was late. He'd promised his mother he would be at her house in time to help set up for his nephew's birthday party in the morning. He was the only one of his four siblings who was single—a fact of which she never failed to remind him—so his mother had him on speed dial.

But, he teased her this morning on the phone, if he were married, who would she get to fetch the bags of ice, pick up the piñata, hang it in the garage, and ride herd on his sister's kids while she helped their mom in the kitchen? Her oldest boy was into video games. His nephew's current favorite was Rocket League. Manuelo always let him win, or at least that's what he told himself.

Even though he was in a hurry to get to his mom's, Arturo slowed his new F-150 to a safe speed. They didn't have enough money to hire another deputy, but at least they'd gotten the department a new vehicle.

They'd had an unusually heavy snowfall this month, which was good for the water table and made the skiers happy but made his job difficult when unprepared motorists tried to drive in it.

Which is what had happened today and was the reason he was running late. A family of five in a minivan not suited for the weather had decided to 'take the kids to the snow' but had quickly gotten lost. Eventually, they ran out of gas. The father had been able to pull off the road, but he'd gotten stuck in a snowdrift, and it had taken Deputy Manuelo longer than expected to pull them out.

He gave the kids some bottled water he kept in the back of his truck and sent the family back into town with a new map and stern admonitions to get chains before they got on the road again. He should have given the father a ticket but let them off this time with a warning. The toddler in the back seat had looked at him with big, puppy-dog eyes.

Other than the family in the mini-van, his shift had been uneventful. He loved patrolling this area in the winter. The campgrounds and trails were closed from October to May, so other than the occasional cross-country skiers or intrepid winter campers, he had the place to himself. Miles of tall, stately trees interspersed with shallow running streams, and a few craggy rocks, all stark against a pristine backdrop of sparkling white snow.

A few minutes ago, big fat flakes started drifting down, sticking to his windshield. So far the wipers had been able to keep up, but the road in front of him was quickly being obscured.

He wasn't too worried. Even with the snow, as long as nothing else happened, he'd make it to Mama's in time for some of her *posole* and homemade tortillas. His stomach growled just thinking of the welcoming aromas that would surround him the minute he opened the front door.

Keeping his speed under thirty-five miles an hour and his headlights on, he was just starting to congratulate himself for making good time when a dark green Range Rover came roaring up from behind, swerving around him as he sped by. If there had been any oncoming traffic, the driver of the Rover would for sure be dead.

The look on the driver's face as he barreled past, gripping the steering wheel, was one of grim determination or panic—it was hard to tell which. Deputy Manuelo sighed. If that guy made it more than a mile down the road, he'd eat his hat.

Damn. He was gonna be late for Mama's *posole* after all.

68

Arturo hated being right. Sure enough, the Range Rover had hit a patch of ice and slid off the road. The driver was still inside but seemed okay. The snow covered the front almost up to the windshield. Really? These idiots should really stay home if they don't know how to drive in the snow.

He started to run the plate but couldn't clearly read it. Most of the plate had been smeared with mud, obscuring all but the first letter, F.

The small hairs on the back of his neck started to prickle. There wasn't much mud around here, and it looked like it had been smeared across the license plate thickly, by hand. Guy probably hadn't paid his registration and wanted to hide the old tag.

Well, he was going to now, plus a big, fat fine.

Manuelo turned on his brights and thought about the best way to handle this. Something was off, but he didn't know what, and until he did, he needed to avoid escalating the situation. Other than domestic disturbance callouts, traffic stops were the most dangerous.

Normally he'd call for backup, but the other deputy was out sick, so dispatch would call in the state police and he'd have to wait for them, which would make him even later for dinner. And they'd be pissed if they got called out on a wild goose chase. No, he'd take care of this himself.

Checking his duty belt, he got out of the truck. Keeping his driver's door between himself and the Range Rover, he used his electronic bullhorn so he could be heard.

"Driver, shut off your engine. Do you need assistance? Are you injured?"

He waited. No response.

"Driver! Let me see your hands."

Still no response. The driver didn't move, other than to lift one of his hands to his face, but he was still just sitting there, not turning around.

He noted the details he could see from his position. Wool cap pulled over light colored hair, curling at the bottom. Male. Dark jacket. Alone. But there could be someone hiding down on the floorboards on the passenger side.

Now he was pissed.

"Driver! Put your hands behind your head and get out of the car!"

Was this guy deaf? It was possible. But even so, his vehicle was stuck. There was no way he didn't see the bright lights behind him. Why wasn't he coming out for help?

What happened next took only a few seconds but felt like hours to Deputy Manuelo. In one smooth movement, the driver dropped his left shoulder, pushed open his door and launched himself out of the car, rolling to a crouch.

Well, the driver had finally gotten out of the car and showed his hands, but unfortunately, his hands held a gun, and it was pointed straight at him. Manuelo froze, all of his senses going on alert, taking everything in. He assumed if the man was going to shoot him, he'd have done so by now. He studied his opponent, waiting for an opportunity to act.

LOST AND FOUND

Except for a cut over his left eye, which was bleeding, the driver appeared uninjured. He kept wiping away the blood with the back of his left hand so he could see, keeping his gun trained on Manuelo.

Crab walking to his right, the driver waved the barrel of the gun at Manuelo, and said, "Come out from behind there where I can see you. Throw your gun over there." He waved in the general direction of the forest.

Keeping eye contact, Manuelo slowly came out from behind his door, then lowered one hand and carefully lifted his gun out of its holster. The man was now only a few feet away. His whole demeanor screamed desperation. He looked like a trapped weasel.

The cut above his eye was bleeding so much he must have had trouble seeing out of that one eye. Finally, the man dragged his wool beanie off his head with his left hand and pressed it against the cut to staunch the flow of blood.

In that split second, Manuelo charged, catching the assailant off guard, knocking the gun out of his hand and the man flat onto his back. Quickly flipping him over, he had him cuffed and secured in a seated position in the snow while he stalked back to his truck and called the incident in.

Then he retrieved his first aid kit and patched up the cut over the man's eye. This guy's actions made no sense. Could be a 5150. Ever since he'd been cuffed, he'd refused to speak. Manuelo checked the Range Rover but saw no skis or other winter sports or camping equipment in the vehicle.

What had he been doing up here?

The man had nothing to say when asked what he was doing in the forest—or why he was driving a vehicle at breakneck speeds down the road, or why that vehicle was registered to a Roxy Peterson. Had he stolen the vehicle?

Other than not talking, once he had been cuffed, the man was surprisingly subdued—cooperative even. He almost seemed in a hurry to be taken to jail. He kept looking back up the road from where he'd come as if Sasquatch was after him. Maybe he was crazy.

Giving up on trying to figure it out here, Manuelo hauled the man up by his upper arm and marched him back to the truck. F-150s weren't designed for prisoner transport, so the department had the new vehicle fitted with the Single Cell Lite Prisoner Transport System. He had thought it a waste of money, as they rarely had to arrest anyone, but he was sure glad he had it now. At least he wouldn't have to worry about this guy if he started getting worked up again. He looked like a spitter.

Once he had his prisoner secured in the back, he flipped open the man's wallet to see who he had. Søren Vestergaard. Not Peterson.

Well, Søren, let's see if you escaped from a mental hospital and stole yourself a Range Rover for a getaway car.

Just then, a couple of elderly cross-country skiers came poling down the road.

"You got him!" the woman cried.

"Oh, I'm so glad!" she said. "We just called it in on the radio. How did you get here so fast? We just called!" She slid to a stop and bent over to rest her hands on her knees and catch her breath.

"She's back there," she added, pointing behind her with one of her poles, "back about three miles." She turned to the man that was with her. "Wouldn't you say, Bud? About three miles?"

Seeing the confused look on Deputy Manuelo's face, the man poled over, keeping an eye on the prisoner in the police vehicle.

"I'm Bud and this is Wauleka," he said. "We're the ones who called it in."

"I'm sorry, but called what in?" Manuelo asked, thoroughly confused. "And who's back there? Is someone in need of help?"

"The *woman*! She's dead. Didn't they tell you?" she said, "We surprised him, this man—she pointed at his prisoner, slouched in the back of the truck—caught him in the act of dumping a woman's body in the forest. Just threw her out like a bag of trash! It was horrible!"

"Okay," Manuelo said. "I'm listening. Start from the beginning."

"Our skis are quiet," she explained, "He didn't see me, and I didn't see him until I came around that bend. We were racing, you see, Bud and I, to get to the log. It was time for our lunch break. This man was on the other side of it. I'm afraid I screamed, it was such a shock, and then he just dropped this woman's body and ran to his car and drove off!"

Just then Officer Manuelo's radio crackled to life.

69

A life-size cartoon mermaid with a blue, sequined tail welcomed everyone at the door. A banner across her chest read "Miriam Magnolia Pullman, One Month Old Today!"

Inside, as the aquarium staff put out sandwiches, cake and coffee, Logan dutifully walked along the edge of the long table on the left, stubby pencil and index card in hand, studying the numbered entries.

#1 Butterfinger?

#2 Snickers? Mr. Goodbar?

Which candy bars had peanuts in them?

This game was a lot harder than it looked.

When everyone else had filed past and made their guesses as to which candy bar had been melted inside which disposable diaper, Taunette quickly tallied the results.

Surprisingly, Jean, their resident health-food queen, got the most right, with Logan a close second. No one was surprised that Logan knew every candy bar known to man, but Sam teased her sister-in-law that she must have a secret junk food habit. Jean gave a Cheshire cat grin and tucked the prize, a giant one-pound Snickers bar, into her purse.

No one was tempted by the melted candy bars in the diapers. Those were quietly disposed of.

An hour later, baby gifts opened and most of the refreshments polished off, Sam sat down to nurse Magnolia while Logan helped Jean bag the wrapping paper and load up the gifts into totes that Taunette had helpfully provided. As president of the Newport Fisherman's Wives, she had hosted the party. About thirty women had turned out to support the new parents.

The new father had also been invited, but Tim made his excuses early and was out on the water, fishing. Not a big baby shower person.

Neither was Logan, but she was surprised at how much she had enjoyed herself. And she got an aquarium pass out of the deal, which she planned on using when the kids came up for a visit this summer.

When everyone else had left to tour the aquarium or go home, Logan, Jean, and Taunette sat down with Sam, who was putting Magnolia back in her carrier.

"I want to thank you again, Taunette," Sam said. "I can't believe all this! I've only been here a few years. You guys didn't have to do all this for me, but I appreciate it."

"Nonsense," Taunette said. "You're one of us, now. We're just happy Tim found a good wife. He could have wound up with . . ."

LOST AND FOUND

She stopped before finishing her sentence. Everyone mentally filled in the blank.

Roxy.

From what Logan had learned in the last month, Roxy had not been anyone's favorite person, but there were different levels of evil. If it hadn't been for her talking Søren out of rearranging her kneecaps with a pipe wrench and into driving to Medford that night, Logan knew Søren would have killed her. She had seen it in his eyes. So she had Roxy to thank for that.

Yes, Roxy was bad, but she'd more than paid for her sins. Only in the movies were people 100 percent good or evil. Real life was a lot messier than that. Between genetics and circumstances, none of us knew how we would have turned out if born to different parents or had different life experiences.

"Well," Taunette said briskly, "speaking of husbands and kids, I need to get home to mine."

She bent down and gave Sam a quick hug and made goo-goo eyes at Magnolia. "You need any help hauling this stuff to your car?" she asked.

"No, I'm good," Sam said, smiling up at her, pushing her glasses back up on her nose. "Again, thanks so much for the party. It was awesome!"

Jean flagged down one of the servers for a final cup of coffee and asked if anyone else wanted one. Logan did and Sam said she'd take a bottle of water if they had one.

While they waited, Sam asked Logan how Vanessa was doing.

"Great," Logan said, "Passing all her classes with honors. Thanks for helping her with her essays. She's going to be way ahead of the pack when it comes time to submit her applications for colleges."

"Is her mom still working at the Hideaway?"

"Yes," Logan said, "but now she doesn't have to take the bus. Someone donated a used car to the family. We think it was Emma Peterson, Liv's mom, but it was an anonymous gift."

One of the servers returned with their beverages. Sam unscrewed the cap off her water bottle and took a long drink. Now that she was nursing, she was eternally thirsty.

Jean asked, "Anyone heard any more about what's happening with Mateo and his wife?"

70

"I don't know all the details," Logan said, "but Mateo's immigration attorney knew someone at the DEA or ICE, I'm not sure which.

"They formally interviewed him and because he was able to provide information leading to the takedown of the *Sea Gypsy* drug smuggling operation, plus testify against Søren for murder and attempted murder, they decided not to pursue deportation. Both Mateo and Gabriela are back at work and no longer have to fear being kicked out of the country."

"And it gets better!" said Sam.

Even though Sam wasn't officially back at work yet, she'd been working on this story for the last couple of weeks, fact-checking, doing interviews on the phone, making all the connections.

"The captain of the *Sea Gypsy* was just a small-time operator," she explained. "Turns out he was getting his drugs from a cousin, who was skimming a few packages here and there from his bosses. After the pickups, the captain then passed them along to a long-distance trucker who sold the drugs in Southern Oregon and California. His hands only touched the package once, so he never got caught.

"His cousin, on the other hand, was part of a larger crime organization. Drug smuggling was only one of their many businesses. Human trafficking, prostitution—you name it, they had their fingers in it.

"It's actually a fascinating system. They bring drugs in from China on huge container ships. They have tracking numbers and everything—ship the stuff right under everyone's noses after it's brought to shore and offloaded. A lot of drugs come through Mexico, now, but they still get some from Asia."

She took another drink of her water.

"To shave off a few years of his sentence, the captain of the *Sea Gypsy* helped DEA set up his cousin. The next time a container ship came in, boom! Big bust! *Much* bigger score than the little, piddly *Sea Gypsy*!"

Sam was rocking Magnolia's carrier with one hand while she talked. As her enthusiasm ramped up, so did her rocking. Logan grabbed the end to slow it down before her goddaughter got flipped onto the table.

"And that's not all!" Sam said, oblivious to Magnolia's rescue. "The captain also ratted out Søren, as did the rest of the *Sea Gypsy* crew. In his version of the story, Søren was responsible for everything that went down that night. Said everything was his idea.

"Whoever's idea it was, we know from Mateo that Søren tried to kill him and probably did kill the Guatemalan and threw him overboard. But the captain is far from innocent; Mateo said he watched the whole thing from the wheelhouse and did nothing to stop it," Logan said.

"Even if they can't get him for everything, combined with attacking and kidnapping Logan, killing Roxy, then dumping her body in the Siskiyou National Forest, Søren's going away for a very long time," Sam said.

"Which brings me to *my* news," Jean said. "The DA is charging Søren with the murder of Craig Peterson as well as

Roxy. They went back through Doyle's apartment and found one of Søren's fingerprints on the baseboard in the back of the closet. They were so focused on Doyle, no one had looked for anyone else's prints. And Roxy bought the burner phones with a credit card. Not the sharpest tool in the shed."

Logan shook her head. That was putting it mildly.

"The DA sure did a quick turnaround. He was hell-bent on convicting Doyle," Jean said.

"He only changed his mind in the face of overwhelming evidence," Sam argued. "He's still hell-bent on convicting somebody for Craig's murder, I just don't think he cares who it is as long as it all happens before Election Day."

"I'm just glad Doyle was cleared," Logan said.

"Yes," Sam said. "Tim and I picked him up and took him out for a steak dinner when he got released. I have never seen a happier man!"

"Is he back working on the *Sara Lynn*, again?" Jean asked. "Or the *Freya*?"

"Nope," Sam said. "He decided to set up a small tax and bookkeeping business in town. He didn't think he could afford it, but he got a great deal on office space, so decided to take the plunge."

"I just saw his office the other day when I stopped by to visit with Patricia Haggerman, Mateo's attorney. They were putting up the signage," Logan said. "Turns out Haggerman owns that whole building and when she heard Doyle's story, let him have it for a fraction of what she usually gets."

"And guess who was there helping him move in?" Logan asked, eyebrows raised. She was enjoying this. It was rare she got to scoop Sam.

No one knew.

"Liv!" she smiled smugly.

"Awesome!" Sam said. "Tim and I always thought they liked each other, but Doyle was probably too shy to do anything about it when they worked together on the *Freya*.

"Now there ain't nothin' standin' in the way of true love!" she added. Closing her eyes, she hugged herself and made kissy noises at the ceiling.

Logan laughed and Jean rolled her eyes.

"So, getting back to Mateo and Gabriela," Jean said, "they won't be deported, but where does that leave them? Will they ever be able to apply for temporary work visas without leaving the country first?"

"Oh!" Sam said, "I forgot to tell you! Given all they've been through and because of Mateo's help in bringing down two drug operations and a murderer, ICE said they would be able to apply not just for temporary work visas, but for *green cards*!"

"Good!" said Jean. "We need more people like the Pérez family in this country."

71

While Ben was giving Tim a tour of his water catchment system, Logan lifted the lid of one of the bubbling pots on the stove and peeked inside.

"Smells great," Sam said, relaxing at the table, sipping her wine. Tim had taken Magnolia out with him to give Sam a break.

"Short rib vegetable soup," Logan said, wafting the aroma toward her with one hand before replacing the lid. She could eat bowls of the stuff. She'd once caught Ben putting parsnips and turnips in there, but he swore it was just the once. She didn't tell Sam, but she suspected Ben always put them in, just chopped them very fine so they either dissolved or he could pass them off as diced potatoes.

Refilling her own glass, Logan joined her friend at the table. She'd already made the salad and the sourdough bread was in the oven warming. It was a tight fit for six, but it was just a casual dinner, so they decided to eat at the kitchen table. They'd eat as soon as Clay and his wife got here.

Clay had helped Ben with the finishing work in the bathroom. They'd gone with his recommendations of black river rock, tilework, and pale, sage green paint. The calming color scheme showcased the piece de resistance, her luxurious slipper tub.

"We still on for Cormorant Coffee Crew this Wednesday?" Logan asked. "I missed last week. Anything new with Jean?"

"Not with Jean, but she said they finally decided what to do with that floater that washed up in Depoe Bay."

"When no one could ID him, they stored him up in the morgue in Portland, right?" Logan said.

"Did they ever find out who he was?" Ben asked as he checked on the soup. He and Tim had just walked back in. "I thought Jean did a DNA test and it wasn't a match for Mateo. Who'd they match it to?"

"No," Sam said. "No one has reported anyone missing who fits that description. In cases like this, after a certain amount of time, the county just disposes of the body."

That sounded very sad to Logan. She remembered Mateo saying that the man had recently arrived in the U.S. and hadn't mentioned a wife or children. But everyone came from somewhere. He probably had a family somewhere.

"Well," Sam said. "Jean said when Cyndi Birdwell, the ME up in Portland, heard the whole story, she quietly picked up the tab for a proper burial. That way, if he does have a family and they ever come forward, they'll at least have a grave to visit. She got a nice headstone and put his first name, Jairo, then had them leave room for his last name, just in case they ever find out what it is."

"That woman is a class act," said Sam.

Logan nodded. It was the countless small acts of kindness like this that gave her hope for humanity.

When Clay and Betty arrived and they were all seated, Logan caught up on what everyone had been doing.

LOST AND FOUND

Betty had been gardening.

"Summer took its sweet time getting here this year," she said. "No hope for the tomatoes, but I put in some more lettuce and spinach starts and the snow peas are still producing. I'll bring you some fresh broccoli when it's ready."

Tim was operating the *Sara Lynn* with just a two-man crew, but they were doing okay. Francis had healed up well enough to come back full time. They were out for black cod, also called sablefish, now.

Magnolia was a happy, healthy baby, hitting all her benchmarks—she was about fifteen pounds now, and was sleeping through the night.

"Usually . . . ," Tim said.

Sam was back at work full-time.

"No rest for the wicked!" she vamped. Daycare had been a challenge, but recently, they'd worked out an arrangement with a neighbor, a woman with three grown children who missed having a baby around the house. Sam credited her with getting Magnolia on a regular sleeping and eating schedule. "The woman's a miracle worker!" she said.

As everyone continued eating and talking, Logan looked around the table. A feeling of deep contentment washed over her. Yes, the world had problems and people weren't perfect, but right here, right now, she was so grateful for all she had. Life, in all its messy glory, was good.

Just then, her phone rang. She'd left it in the living room.

Giving Ben's arm a quick squeeze as she passed his chair, she picked it up on the fourth ring. It was a 541 number, but she didn't recognize it.

"Hello?"

"Ms. McKenna?" it was a young woman's voice.

"Yes," Logan said. "How can I help you?"

There was a moment of silence. If this was a robocall, she was going to hang up.

"Oh, good!" said a breathless voice. "I was hoping I still had the right number."

"I'm sorry," Logan said, "but we're in the middle of dinner right now . . ." She was quickly losing patience with this caller.

"Oh! Don't hang up! This is Kaylee! Please don't hang up! I wanted to see if you're still looking for a dog to adopt?"

Logan remembered her heart being ripped out when they visited the animal shelter a couple of months ago and a dog she had unexpectedly fallen for had been snatched away at the last minute because of a mix-up. Someone else had already adopted the dog.

She'd told Ben about the whole situation, and they had looked a couple of times since, but all the shelter ever had were tiny, yappy dogs or pit bull mixes who "didn't get along well with other dogs or children." *Yikes.* It had been heartrending. They hadn't looked in a while.

She needed to cut this conversation off quickly.

"I'm sorry, but we're no longer looking for . . ."

"But, but . . . *Dixon* is back!"

Without waiting for Logan to answer, she rushed ahead, "The woman who adopted him had some health issues and had to move back to Colorado to be near family and she can't keep him, so she dropped him off. I'm looking at him right now!"

Logan looked back over her shoulder at Ben, who had resumed his conversation with Tim, and smiled.

ACKNOWLEDGMENTS

As always, I have many people to thank for helping me bring you the book you hold in your hands today. Commercial crab fishing was definitely foreign territory for me and I thank everyone who not only answered my interminable questions but who also didn't kick me off their boat when I showed up at the docks or called or emailed out of the blue. Here are just a few of the wonderful people, listed in no particular order, who were so generous with their time.

Michele Longo Eder, local attorney, legend, and author of *Salt In Our Blood: Memoir of a Fisherman's Wife,* is a woman I was lucky enough to meet several years ago. We shared a delicious lunch at Ove Northwest, a restaurant in Newport, and were still talking hours after we cleaned our plates.

She recently passed away and is missed by all who knew her. Many of the nitty-gritty details of a commercial fisherman's family, from the dangers inherent in the job to the packing of meals for the boat, came from our conversations and her poignant memoir. We also shared the unfortunate life-altering event of having lost one of our adult sons. She lost hers while he was doing this dangerous job. It is for this reason it took me so long to write this book featuring commercial crab fishing families. Hopefully she will be happy with the story and the way I represented this generous community.

Cari Lee Brandburg and Cody Chase, owner of several fishing vessels as well as the Chelsea Rose, and local fisherman, Rex Young, also helped me on my research journey.

Matthew Roque, Coast Guard Station, North Bend, Oregon, explained how search and rescue operations are run, and Troy Buell, ODFW Marine Resources Program, Newport, Oregon, explained the nuances of season openings and fishing zones.

Liz Martin, scion of a local fishing family and active community member, always answers my questions, or finds someone who can, and is also a good friend.

Mitchel Kiyotakitsune, NOAA special agent in Newport, Oregon, taught me a lot about local fisheries and permits and how they are regulated. I now know more than any landlubber needs to know about tiers, slinky pots, and fish tickets! A big thank you to Stuart Cory, retired NOAA special agent, who introduced us.

Al Boersma, Captain, U.S. Coast Guard (Retired), gave me a leg up in understanding currents, water temperatures, and all sorts of details about dead bodies floating, not floating, and even decapitated bodies. And in addition to lending me his expertise, he keeps me on my toes with his dry quips. If you blink, you'll miss one, so it's worth listening to every word he says or reading his emails two or three times. There's always a tongue-in-cheek bit in there that makes me laugh.

Taunette Dixon, former president of Newport Fishermen's Wives and owner, with her husband, Kevin, of the f/v Tauny Ann, was incredibly helpful and patient with all of my follow-up emails and efforts to find an image suitable for the cover.

Speaking of the cover, we have Yale Fogarty of Finer Image Photography in Newport, Oregon for donating the perfect image of a working, commercial fishing boat going out to sea.

Mark J. Miranda, Chief of Police, Newport Police Department (retired), provided an insider's view of jurisdictions and local law enforcement procedures, and Joseph M. Yoo, an Immigration Attorney, helped me create a plausible workaround for Mateo's immigration woes.

Fellow author, Kevin Chapman, my favorite attorney at law, gently reminded me that murder trials do *not* start in two months . . . it takes at least a year to a year and a half to prepare for a murder trial. He also served as my alpha reader on this book. After plowing his way through the first draft, he sent back twelve pages of notes! The man is a gem.

Once I did the initial revisions, I sent it off to my intrepid beta readers: Maurice Davisson, Kell Caldron, Mickey Boersma, and Ronda Hipshman. Each of them helped shape the story before it went to my editor. Any remaining errors are mine.

And my biggest thanks, as always, goes to my husband, John, for understanding when I start a new book, don my noise-cancelling headphones, and tell him 'the Logan light is on!'"

Enjoyed the Book?

If you enjoyed *Lost and Found*, please consider leaving a review on Amazon, Goodreads, or BookBub. And be sure to check out the rest of the Logan McKenna series.

Novels
Shattered (Book 1)
Forest Park (Book 2)
Devil's Claw (Book 3)
Vanishing Day (Book 4)
Safe Harbor (Book 5)
Lies That Bind (Book 6)
Whisper Creek (Book 7)
In Plain Sight (Book 8)

Logan McKenna Prequel Novellas
Bella: An Appalachian Love Story
Jagged Dawn: Logan's Beginning

Want to know more about Valerie Davisson or her next book? Make sure to visit valeriedavisson.com and sign up for her newsletter.

ABOUT THE AUTHOR

A self-admitted book addict, Valerie Davisson was the kid with the flashlight under her pillow, reading long after lights out. After a life of travel, she now lives on the Oregon coast with her husband, John, and their new puppy, Finn. When not working on her latest book, she's probably in the kitchen, cooking up a storm for family and friends.